SYNOPSIS

Ethan Winter's world is rocked after a tragedy leaves him an empty husk of who he once was. He lives his days focusing solely on his patients and not much else. He used to have it all and now found himself empty handed. There was nothing that could make him feel any better.

Crow Kensworth is ready for the time of his life. He just recently came out of the closet and is preparing for his first national tour, his music career taking off. Things couldn't get any better.

When Ethan's world crashes into Crow's everything gets thrown off course. Suddenly, Ethan is reminded of how good it feels to hold someone. At the same time, Crow is learning how good it feels to be held.

The two men start believing things actually could get better.

Then the letters begin, and Crow's world is threatened by a stalker who seems to have their eyes fixed on the swoon-worthy singer. Both Ethan and Crow will need to find strength in each other as the stalker becomes more and more desperate for Crow's heart, going to lengths that neither of them imagined possible.

Code silver- Wraeofm

Code red - Wraeofm

(w gaeofm will yet
at elid
of mouth

Start tonight
6 or 7PM

1 CROW KENSWORTH

(finished)

The beach-side bar was packed with people, all standing shoulder to shoulder, beers in plastic cups threatening to spill while they bobbed left and right with the music that filled the space. The beat pounded through everyone, making the front row closest to the stage start jumping. They were the lucky ones. They had enough room to jump.

But, even for those stuck at the very back by the bathrooms, one thing was for sure: they were all having a *fucking blast*. Another thing they had in common? They were all there to see one person:

Crow Kensworth.

He sat on a stool in the middle of the stage as a white beam of light rose from behind him, casting its bright glow out onto the crowd, cutting out his shadow as it slowly crawled over Crow. He had timed this moment during rehearsals. He followed the line of light as it rose, letting his voice rise with it, singing louder and louder into the microphone as his song picked up the tempo. Drums kicked in. The guitar hit. Once the beam of light cleared Crow and was aimed at the ceiling, it flashed and started changing colors like a wild kaleidoscope. It was then that Crow jumped from his stool and smashed the chorus, practically lifting the roof off of the Santa Monica bar with his voice alone, helped by the cheering crowd.

Crow smiled from ear to ear as he looked out into the crowd, jumping on the stage to the beat as he sang his heart away. It was one of his favorites, a song about fragile young love turning into something as solid as scripture. He had written it during a particularly lonely night where his thoughts had seemed consumed with securing a perfect future that felt just out of his reach.

On stage, with the music vibrating in his bones, the last thing Crow felt was lonely. He lived for this. He looked to the front row and immediately spotted a dancing Red, his hand in the air, holding Caleb's tight as they pumped their fists together and danced to the beat.

"Thank you! You guys are *fucking crazy* and I love you for it!" Crow shouted into the crowd as his song ended. There was only one song left before his performance was over. He wanted to make sure to end it on a high note. This performance meant more than usual. It was the official opening night of his American tour, the first tour he had ever headlined. It was nerve-wracking. Although he had a big YouTube following, he was still scared of showing up to empty venues or disappointing fans that were excited to see him live for the first time. He had confidence in himself, but it wasn't unwavering. He still carried scars from a rocky road to adulthood, and that scar tissue was hard to ignore.

"What do you all say about me bringing up a special guest?" Crow said, laughing as the crowd sounded out a resounding 'yes!'. He put a hand over his brows and looked out into the bar. He already knew who he was bringing up on stage, but he liked to put on a show. His eyes glided over eager faces, jumping and waving hands as much as they could without hitting their neighbors in the face. He was about to look back toward Red when someone caught his eyes and completely disarmed him. A man he had never seen before, but felt like he had known since the beginning. A face etched in his dreams and forged from his fantasies. He was sitting by the bar, his elbow leaning casually on the edge, a drink held loosely in his hands. People were packed in around him, but it seemed as though everyone else was disappearing. Even with the dim lighting on the crowd, Crow could still make out the man's features as though the spotlight had been turned to him for the entire performance. He had a lethal combination of light sky blue eyes and sleek dark black hair with a strong set face and lips that immediately transfixed Crow and had his jeans feeling a size too tight. He thanked god the stylist had insisted he wear a pair of dark black jeans.

What the...

This had never happened to him. He had never been so taken by someone in the crowd. He heard the thump of his drummer behind him, reminding him that he wasn't supposed to be standing there, frozen in place. He jerked out of his fixation and snapped his eyes back to the front row, where he locked his gaze with Red Miller.

"Alright, come on up here," he said, reaching a hand down from the stage and closing his grip around Red's. His best friend was smiling as Crow pulled him up from the crowd. Immediately, the bar erupted into cheers. Everyone knew who Red Miller was, they just hadn't known he was partying with them until he was up on stage.

"Wow," Crow said as the crowd calmed down. "That was almost a better reception than I got!"

The two men laughed as Franklin, the drummer, punctuated the comment behind them with a slap on the cymbal.

"Now, I'm not sure if you guys know, but Red doesn't *only* know how to act for a living. This guy can match a note with the best of them."

Red waved a hand in the air, as if he wasn't going to admit it. Then, in one swift move, he grabbed the microphone from Crow's hand and sang a crooney "Hello" which had the crowd howling. Crow laughed as Red took it away. He knew he was going to be pulled up on stage, so they had prepared a song for him to sing. It was one of Crow's biggest hits and the entire bar started cheering the moment they recognized the beginning melody. Angela, Crow's tour manager, came from the side of the stage with a microphone stand, placing it in front of Crow before running off with a wave to the crowd. The stagehand looked scared that they had messed up, but Crow knew Angela just liked taking control of things. He grabbed his mic and jumped in on the song with Red as he was hitting the chorus.

"And I'm looking for something
And I'm hopin' you're something
Because, damn, from here you've got everything.
So I'll dance over with nothing, boy, hoping for something."

He started to lose himself in the melody, riding the high of the crowd with the pulse of the beat, mixing together to create an unbeatable euphoria.

And then their eyes met again and all bets were off.

Breathtaking blue in a sea of gray. Color exploded from the man's gaze, locking Crow in a trance. Thankfully, it was Red's turn to take over the vocals, jumping in and slaying the second verse, all while Crow swayed to the song with his eyes pinned on the man in the crowd.

He's smirking.

And then the man looked away, down at whatever drink he had in his hands. This had the effect of poking a bee's nest —no, no, *fuck that*, it had the effect of slamming a beehive with a baseball bat. Crow felt a swell in him, ready to explode outward. An energy that had him ready to bring the house down with his voice. He wanted this man's attention again. The rest of the crowd faded. The only one that mattered was that square-jawed god sipping on his damn drink like there wasn't a kickass concert feet away from him.

Crow grabbed the mic off the stand and started to jump as the drums kicked in harder behind him. Red, who was loving all the attention, reached down and grabbed Caleb's hand. He pulled his husband up onto the stage to another round of applause. He did it all while keeping time with the song. Caleb wasn't exactly a show boater like Red and Crow, but he was already a few beers in and the rush of the moment seemed to have taken him to a more comfortable place. He danced around the stage, jumping up and down, lifting his hands up and asking the crowd to do the same.

Then came Crow's solo. He held onto the mic with both hands and slammed into the vocals, lifting the crowd with him, giving them exactly what they came for. He closed his eyes at first, drowning in the lyrics, letting himself feel the story he had written. The next moment, his eyes were open, his voice rising, and his body tuned in with the man who no longer looked down at his drink and instead was locked on Crow.

And then the song was over and Crow was left on the stage, hearing the blood pumping in his ears, the cheering of the crowd wanting more.

The man, he was clapping too. Not as much as the surrounding crowd, but he was clapping. A smile spread across that sexy face, wrinkling the corners of those mind-melting baby blues. Red came up to Crow's side and grabbed his wrist, raising it as they took a bow, Caleb joining in. The moment snapped Crow out of whatever spell those blue eyes were casting.

"Thank you!" Crow said, catching his breath. He ran a hand through his sweaty mess of a head, fussing up the thick brown locks in a way that only managed to make him look sexier. He was all smiles as he turned to exit the stage. He suddenly felt as though he had put on this show, this entire fucking tour, just for that one man with the blue eyes.

Damn. I need to talk to him.

"That crowd is crazy, you blew them away," Red said over the still cheering crowd as they started to walk backstage. Caleb had already waved goodbye and was waiting in the wings, his smile wide and his expression saying 'holy shit, that was crazy'.

Crow looked over his shoulder, his eyes immediately going to the spot at the bar. To his surprise (and his *surprisingly* strong disappointment) the man was no longer there.

"Yeah," Crow agreed. "I can't believe it."

"I can," Caleb chimed in as he grabbed Red's hand. They walked down a small hallway behind the stage to a separate room for performers. Crow's crew was already hanging out inside. Angela, who was clutching her favorite Simpsons beer mug, jumped up from the couch and opened her arms wide, spilling some beer onto Troy, who was sitting on the couch and flirting with Erica Stonestreet. She was Crow's opener and performed under the name Caeri, a play on her birth name. She laughed as Troy shook his head, smiling as he soaked up the beer from his white t-shirt, using the sleeve of a discarded black sweater.

"You did amazing," Angela said after ending the hug. "Sorry, Troy."

"No worries, Ang. At least it's the good stuff."

"Damn right, it's the good stuff! I don't skimp out on you guys."

Crow smiled as Angela nodded over to a small table at the back of the room. Drinks were lined up against the wall. As Crow got closer, he could see that the labels on the bottles had all been custom-made and all of them had to do with songs off his new album.

"You're crazy," he said, shaking his head as a wide smile spread across his face.

Another voice joined in. This one sing-songy. "My favorite is the 'Boom-tini' but the 'Come Get Me' is a *really* close second." It was Jordan Arey, his PR guy. He put a hand around Crow's lower back and led him to the jug of Boom-tinis. Angela busied herself by the 'First Class Gin & Tonic', striking up a conversation with Red and Caleb as Jordan tried to steal Crow away.

"Thanks, Jordan," Crow said, smiling as Jordan poured him a drink and handed him the plastic cup filled to the brim with the dark red cocktail. They cheered to a good night. Behind them, Troy got up from the couch and opened the door, answering the three knocks. The stage manager stood there, her dark brown curls a little frazzled from running around all night. She held a bouquet of big blue and yellow roses with a card attached.

"Hey, Crow," Troy called out. Crow secretly thanked him, seeing as Jordan was getting way too touchy feely. He must have been drinking since before the show started, which guaranteed Crow a few butt slaps and chest rubs.

Normally, he didn't mind it, and only because he thought he and Jordan had established that they were just friends. Lately, though, Jordan had been really pushing at that friend-line.

"These for me?" Crow asked, recognizing his two favorite colors.

"Yeah," Angela answered from the couch.

"Awesome," Crow said. He loved receiving gifts, and not so much because of the gift itself (although obviously that was great too), but also because he could never really believe people liked him enough to send random flowers and gifts. He connected with them while he was on stage and out by the bar, and he had confidence in his music to know that he was good, but he still had a hard time comprehending how people could like him *that* much.

With a huge smile on his face, his grabbed the note that was sitting shut under the bouquet. He opened it and read the first sentence, going on to the second, and the third. It was on the fourth that his mood soured and his smile faded. By the end of the note, Crow was staring down at the floor, his brows furrowed, his brain trying to piece together whatever the hell he had just read. A cold tendril of fear curled around his spine, causing him to shiver it away.

Well... fuck.

2 ETHAN WINTER

(finished)

W hat the fuck is going on here tonight?
Ethan looked around at the increasingly packed bar as he drank his whiskey. He had come from a long shift at the hospital and was ready to unwind at his favorite spot: The Spout. It was normally a quiet place during the early evening, with a casual mix of professionals and party-goers pre-gaming before they went off to a bigger club. He used to enjoy sitting at one of the farthest booths, the one with the palm tree etched onto the corner of the table, but now-a-days his spot was right at the bar, where the drinks came faster and the conversations kept his mind from racing. He wasn't expecting a swarm of well-dressed young people to storm through the doors and pack his usual haunt. He looked around as people started elbowing their way to the back of the bar, where a large stage was set up. The bartenders looked like they were having a blast as they tossed and twirled vodka bottles and bottle openers, their dark shirts tied up in the back, showing off all of their impressive midriffs. Boys and girls alike came to gawk at the bartenders.

"Are you guys giving away free drinks tonight?" Ethan asked Jessica, one of his favorite bartenders. She always had a great story to entertain him with. Last week it was the one about her new puppy waking her up in the middle of the night with what she called a 'five alarm septic disaster all over the beige carpet'.

"Some big music guy is kicking off his first tour here." She smiled as she wiped down the bar in front of Ethan before her attention was caught by a waving dollar bill. She wrapped a knuckle on the bar and went to pour more drinks. Ethan turned back toward the stage. It wasn't a huge space, but the dance floor was big enough to fit a good sized crowd. A hundred? Maybe more if Ethan had to guess. He had never seen it this crowded though. He was usually back home before the night really began.

Reminds me of college.

The good old days. When Ethan didn't constantly feel like the world was set on destroying him bit by bit. The past few years had really hammered that feeling home.

He drank another gulp of the cold whiskey.

The performance didn't take much longer to start. Ethan considered leaving but he had nothing better to do and had the next day off, so he said 'fuck it', ordered another drink and pivoted on his stool so that he could watch what the fuss was about.

The opening act was nothing special. Ethan felt like he had seen it a dozen times. A song about lollipops and kissing girls and champagne showers. The singer, Caeri, put on a good show, Ethan couldn't deny that, but her songs just weren't for him. The rest of the crowd seemed to be eating it up though, bouncing up and down along with her as she sang her heart out. The lights on the stage shined bright on her short neon blue hair, making her pop like a fairy out of a storybook.

When she was done singing four of her songs, the stage went dark and the main act was teased by Caeri. The crowd started cheering the moment a shadowy figure took his spot on the stage. The lights hadn't even come back on yet and people were already losing their minds. Ethan felt the energy of the moment rush over him. He had no idea who the hell he was about to see perform, but he was going to enjoy it regardless.

And then the lights came on and Ethan came undone.

There, standing on stage, framed by the strong white lights beaming from behind, was a man who literally took Ethan's breath away. He felt himself inhale sharply, as though he were about to be dunked headfirst into a pool.

It was in the man's stance. The strong shoulders and powerful arms. Even more so in the man's eyes. They were a soft brown in color that caught the stage lights and reflected back like endless pools of liquid amber. And that smile as he looked out onto the crowd.

Holy *fuck*, that smile.

Ethan managed to tear his eyes away long enough to take another drink. He had to soften this swell of lust that had suddenly consumed him.

That was all it was; lust. He hadn't gotten any since... well, it was going on almost two years, now.

Maybe it's about time.

That's when the man — Crow Kensworth, he said his name was — that's when *Crow* started to sing and cast an entirely different spell over Ethan. He looked up from his glass and found himself instantly transported to the world Crow sang about. It was like the words had been written specifically for Ethan, an absolutely ridiculous thought that had his pulse run a little quicker. Crow's voice had a croony aspect to it that quickly picked up and turned into a poppy sort of rap during the chorus, rising up into a harder hitting rock tone that reminded Ethan of Paramore, one of his favorite bands. He was blown away by the notes Crow was hitting, all while jumping around the stage and putting on a performance made to sell out entire stadiums. It was obvious that Crow lived to perform, and that feeling was infectious, spreading out into the crowd and creating an unmatchable energy.

He sang three more songs before their eyes met and the entirety of both their lives changed forever.

Jesus.

Crow had been looking in the crowd for someone to bring up onto the stage when he looked to Ethan. The world caught fire the instant they locked eyes. Ethan felt like he should look away, down at his glass, he felt guilty for feeling this much sudden want for a person, but he was transfixed. He wasn't too far from the stage, but he didn't have front row seats either, and yet he could make out the man's features as though they were a story he was telling for the hundredth time.

He had only felt this way once before, and that story ended in tragedy. He wasn't about to open up another one of the same books.

Ethan managed to break his gaze. He looked down at his empty glass, wondering what the hell he was doing there, surrounded by a bunch of drunk college kids, some looking younger, worshipping the Adonis with a voice. He should have just gone straight home, like he had been planning. A new season of *House of Cards* had dropped and was begging to be binged, but Ethan had decided a drink at his usual spot wouldn't hurt. He had only started coming back to this place again in the past five or so months. He found that the memories it held were easier to bear as time passed.

The crowd exploded when Crow brought up his guest. Ethan looked up and recognized that one film star everyone seemed to be drooling over lately. He had seen him on a billboard on the way here, looking like the next James Bond, jumping out of a racing Ferrari with guns in both hands, arms outstretched. He definitely *looked* like a movie star, but that wasn't enough to keep Ethan's eyes from immediately going back to Crow; the main course. He took a moment to admire the man from the white Converse, up the tight black jeans, over the button-down shirt with scrunched up sleeves that highlighted some sexy ass forearms, and right to those light brown eyes that caught the light in a magical kind of way. Crow wasn't looking at him in that moment, allowing Ethan a little more freedom to unabashedly check the singer out.

The men started to sing, then. Everyone seemed to be surprised by how well the actor was doing, but Ethan didn't really care. All he focused on was Crow, watching him sway to the music, his body working like a hypnotist's pendulum. He was mesmerized. A snake held by the sensual notes of a flute, dancing and swirling in a pattern that locked the snake in place. Soon, he found himself swaying too, moving to the music, not even listening to the lyrics but being moved by Crow's voice alone.

And those eyes. They were light brown, Ethan could see them from where he sat, lit up by the stage lights, radiating a warmth of their own. Alluring. Ethan immediately felt comfortable, even though he had absolutely no prior knowledge of who this man was or how he even acted. But something in those eyes felt so familiar. Like a friend from long, long ago, only now bumping into one another.

Then, Crow seemed to have found him in the crowd and he began to sing those crooney words directly to Ethan, and Ethan melted. He fucking melted. He didn't know what came over him, but he was sitting there with his heart racing and his palms sweating and his whole world funneling in on the man with the other-worldly voice.

"Crazy good, huh?" It was an extremely excited fan, her blonde hair streaked with a bright slab of pink. "I've been following him since he first started his YouTube channel." She was smiling proudly, as though she was wearing a badge of honor. "You a big fan?"

Ethan was still caught off guard by how affected he had been by the man on the stage. "I think I am now," he said in a moment of simple honesty. The girl broke into a fit of giggles and turned her attention back to the stage as Crow ended his set. The audience cheered and clapped for more, they didn't want the performance to end.

Ethan, on the other hand, was finding himself to be ok with it ending. He felt like if he sat there for a second longer, he would have completely lost himself. It wasn't like him. He was never taken this badly by a man he didn't even know. He just had to go home, jerk off, have another drink, and go to sleep. He'd wake up, go back to work at the hospital, and forget all about this night. That was how things were going to go. How they were supposed to go. Ethan remembered the last time he had felt like this, and he was scarred from the way that ended.

He got up from his barstool, glad that his legs decided to work, and started to try and get the bartenders attention so he could close his tab. The faster he got home, the faster he could start forgetting about Crow Kensworth.

3 CROW KENSWORTH

(finished)

Crow sat on one of the couches, sandwiched between a drunk Angela and an even drunker Jordan, whose arm was thrown across the top of the couch, his hand dangerously close to Crow's ear. He was starting to feel a little uncomfortable. Not that he didn't like attention, but he also knew how Jordan felt and the last thing he wanted to do was lead the guy on. Crow glanced at his watch, finished what was left of his drink, and slapped his thigh. He was going to get up from the couch to get another drink when they all heard knocks on the door over the music. Crow turned away from the drinks and toward the door. He had a feeling he knew who was knocking.

"Shepard!" he said as he opened the door. His twin brother was looking a little exhausted, sporting heavy dark bags under his eyes. Other than that, they looked identical. If his brother wasn't wearing a gray sweater and light jeans, the complete opposite of what Crow had on, then they would have been much harder to tell apart. Crow also occasionally sported a beard while his twin enjoyed keeping a clean face.

"Crow," he said, shaking his head as they hugged. "Sorry for missing your performance, man. There was just no way I could get out of this test. And of course it landed on my evening block, so I couldn't even finish early enough."

"Don't even stress it," Crow said. "Jordan caught it all on camera, so he'll post it online later if you really want to watch."

"Still, this is your first big opening night. Fuck. This whole medical school thing better be worth it."

Crow arched an eyebrow. "I'm sure it will be." He dropped his voice to a stage whisper. "Especially when I don't have to pay to see a doctor anymore."

"You're not getting a family discount."

"What?! I'm your twin. If I wanted, I could open up my own practice under your name."

"Yeah and then land up in a federal jail cell."

Crow shrugged. "It would make for a good documentary, at least." The twins laughed, their pitches matching as Angela came over with a cup in hand, shaking her head and admiring them both.

"You guys should have totally been a duo, *imagine*." Angela tsked. She handed a red solo cup to Shepard. "The world hasn't seen that. You'd both blow up."

"Yeah, two identically scorching hot guys with crazy good voices?" It was Jordan, he was walking past them, eyeing up Shepard like he was the last piece of steak he'd ever taste. "I'm going to the bathroom," Jordan said as he was half-out the door, looking over his shoulder pointedly at the twins.

The group cracked up. Jordan's forwardness was funny, if a little inappropriate at times. He left the room, the music from the bar outside muting as the heavy door shut.

"Our parents would have disowned both of us if they didn't get a doctor in the family." Shepard spoke with a smile, but Crow knew that there was a huge underlying pressure there. They had fallen into their established roles pretty early on: Crow, the artistic free spirit that flew around from interest to interest, finally landing on music, while Shepard always excelled in school since the time he could first pick up a pencil and write his own name. When their parents saw that Shepard was bringing home the straight As, they started steering him toward a career in medicine. Luckily, Crow knew that his twin brother genuinely loved helping people which was the M.O. of every physician, but the road was undeniably hard and Shepard was showing the wear and tear of constant study-ing, endless working, and little sleeping.

That's when the flowers caught Shepard's eyes. "You didn't tell me you were seeing someone," he said, walking over to the explosion of blue and yellow sitting next to a bowl of chips.

"I'm not." Crow was starting to feel a little loose. His limbs were taking on that jelly-like quality. Whatever was in the Boom-tini was strong.

"Oh," Shepard's brows furrowed as he read the card out loud "Dear Crow, wow, your voice is incredible and your music really speaks to me. You make my life that much better. So much brighter. I was ruined by a man, but you give me hope that not all men are the same. I love you. Like, I'm in love with you. Sorry, that might be a lot. I'm a lot. I'll be going with you on tour though, and I'm so excited. I'll be at every stop. You won't know — holy fuck" Shepard said, pausing from his reading for a second. "This is fucked up."

"Yeah," Crow said. Hearing it out loud, the words coming from his twin, it was a little too surreal.

Shepard continued where he cut himself off. "You won't know who I am, not until I'm ready to show you. I have to make sure it's the perfect moment. If not, then we might not work. I'll make sure it's perfect. Love you and kick ass on the tour."

Shepard shook his shoulders and dropped the note on the table as though it had caught fire.

"Fuck."

"Yeah." Crow shook off the weird feeling. "We talked to the police. They opened a file and took the original. That one you have is a copy. They left it, as if I wanted a souvenir or something."

"You can frame it," his brother joked. "Like a college degree."

Crow laughed at the ridiculousness of that. His twin always knew how to turn things around and ease Crow's worries. Growing up, Crow had always been the more nervous of the two, finding inspiration in Shepard's courage with the world. He was always ready to handle every challenge and he always nailed it. Crow was a little more emotional, more loose. He would never have survived through medical school, but he could shape his inner-most emotions into a song that touched people all around the world. They definitely both had their strengths and weaknesses, and most of the time, the sets complimented each other.

"The party's still bumping out there, huh?" Frankie asked, nodding toward the door.

Crow could hear the thumping of the music outside. He wanted to go back out there. He wanted to talk to his fans and get to know some of them. He wanted to dance the night away, forgetting about creepy notes and instead celebrating a killer start to his tour.

Most of all?

Most of all, he wanted to see the man with the crystal blue eyes.

There's no way he's still outside. It's almost been an hour.

It's still worth a shot. He was about to ask his brother if he wanted to go out and brave the crowd when Troy came up to them, immediately latching on to Shepard. Crow watched as Troy pulled his twin over to the couch, chatting him up about something Crow couldn't quite make out.

———

THE BAR WAS STILL PACKED, and the fans immediately lost their collective shit when they realized Crow had come out from backstage and was trying to make his way over to the bar. He was pushed around and groped and offered drinks and had the brightly colored shadows of cellphone camera flashes in his eyes by the time he reached the bar. He couldn't even make out if his target was there until he had reached it, and, sure enough, the man was no where to be found.

Great. Of course. He probably sat long enough for drinks and left before traffic got bad.

Crow felt a soft swell of sadness rise up from his chest. He couldn't quite pinpoint it. He leaned on the bar and got the bartender's attention, figuring he might as well have a drink. He could feel a group of college kids clustering up behind him, mustering up the courage to ask for selfies with him. He'd gladly pose, but first he needed the drink. He wanted to numb some of the disappointment that was growing sharper by each passing moment. Why was he feeling like this over some rando in the crowd?

A rando that blew me away with a look.

"You drink gin?"

It was a gravely voice coming from behind him, on his left. He swiveled on the barstool and felt his gut tighten and his head lighten all at once. He was looking right down the barrels of those crystal clear blue eyes. The ones that had hypnotized him from a distance. They were so much more captivating now that Crow was inches away from them.

And everything else: those slightly pouty lips, the five o'clock shadow, the close cut hair that framed a flawlessly cut jawline.

"Whiskey?"

Crow shook his head, snapping back to reality. "No, no, I hate whiskey. I'll take the gin, though."

The man's eyes searched Crow's. There was something there. He didn't look at Crow the way people had when he was getting swarmed for photos. Those people had a sort of star-struck quality to them, a brightness in their eyes that was mixed with a soft glaze of 'holy shit, it's him'. But that wasn't the way this man looked into Crow's eyes.

No, if anything, it was Crow's turn to give the star-stricken look. He knew he must have been giving off that vibe. But not Mr. Blue Eyes. He was looking at Crow like he wanted to pick him up, carry him out of the bar, take him to a bedroom (any bedroom), throw him down on the bed (any bed), and completely devour him, only to declare that they would spend the rest of their lives together, tangled together forever like the first night they met in the dimly lit Santa Monica bar.

I've fucking lost it.

"I'm more of a whiskey guy, myself, but I can respect a good gin."

"Did I say I hate whiskey?" Crow started, "I meant I, er, hate people that hate whiskey." Crow raised his eyebrows.

Ethan chuckled. "I didn't like whiskey either, at first. But then I was, I don't know, *taught* how to drink it."

"Taught, huh?" Crow nodded, pursing his lips. "Maybe I just need a good teacher then."

"Maybe."

Crow looked at his watch and then perked up on the stool. "Oh shoot, what do you know, school's in session."

That had the man cracking a smile. It was a smile *soo* fucking sexy, Crow had to look down at the bar for a few moments before he went from half-mast to full.

Except, all that glancing down at the bar did was give him a better look of the man's legs, which were currently spread open on the stool, his khaki shorts climbing up to about mid-thigh (and those were some thick thighs), which immediately had Crow's mouth watering. Then his gaze ran over the man's bulge, making Crow's blood run twenty degrees warmer. He wasn't sporting a boner, but he was definitely packing.

And... yep. Full flag pole between Crow's thighs.

"I'm Ethan. Ethan Winter." Ethan spoke loud enough to be heard over the pop music. He held a hand out, which Crow immediately took in his own.

"Crow," he said, shaking a hand that felt exactly right in his.

4 ETHAN WINTER

(finished)

Ethan shook Crow's hand and felt his world tilt off its axis. He never wanted to let go. When their hands parted, Ethan felt a burning imprint of Crow's fingers around his. Then a stab of guilt.

What the fuck am I doing?

He drank his whiskey, feeling the pressure of the growing crowd around them. It seemed like everyone was eyeing Ethan, wondering what made him so special, why the main attraction was seemingly interested in him. He could feel the eyes, the jealousy. It was weird. That, mixed with the ball of guilt growing in his gut, and he was ready to leave. This wasn't him. This life left him a long time ago, snuffed out in the blink of an eye. He wasn't the type to flirt with guys in a bar—much less flirt with a guy like Crow.

And then he looked up from the bar and found Crow's light brown eyes and everything he had been worried about disappeared. He saw something there, and it wasn't the reflection of the amber lanterns that hung above them.

"I have a reserved table over there, let's go," Crow said,

smiling with his drink in his hand. He nodded to the corner of the bar, the farthest, by the stage.

The booth with the palm tree.

"I should be heading home." The words burned on the way out.

"Come on," Crow said, batting heavy eyelashes in a puppy dog look that would have stopped a world war in its tracks. "Give me fifteen minutes. That's all. Then, if I don't like whiskey, you can leave."

"And if you do end up liking it?"

Crow's lips curled mischievously as he turned and started through the crowd. Ethan shook his head, feeling the anxiety in his chest start dissipating, being replaced by a warm rush. He got up from his seat and followed Crow through the crowd. Crow had his head down, clearly on a mission to get somewhere, so no one seemed to bother him, although Ethan noticed a sea of shocked expressions left behind in Crow's wake.

It seemed like everyone agreed: Crow looked even better up close and in person.

They made it to the table with only a few stealth selfies being shot on the way there. The reserved table had been roped off a few feet away with a thick red velvet rope, giving the two men some much needed breathing room. Crow slid into the booth first. Ethan slid in across from him, the soft black leather cushion shaping to his body.

Just don't look at it. No need.

Instead of looking to the corner of the table, he kept his eyes locked on Crow's. He was finding them to be a sort of antidote to the conflicting feelings sparring inside him. One side of him wanted to be there, getting to know the man who had sparked something in the very air that separated them. Then, there was the other side, the one that said this was wrong. He wasn't meant to be this happy over someone he had met minutes ago. He shouldn't be as entranced as he was, especially not sitting in the same booth that had changed his life all those years ago.

"So," Crow said, and looking over the alcohol menu. "What do you recommend first, professor?"

Ethan leaned over the table, looking at the menu which Crow tilted his way. He caught a whiff of Crow's oaky cologne in the air, mixed with a sensual scent of Crow underneath. He managed to push past that distraction and pointed out a few samplers they could try. With the order placed, Ethan sat back, doing his best to avoid the damn palm tree.

"Is it like this for you every night?" Ethan nodded toward the crowd of fans doing a terrible job of taking subtle pictures. Or, maybe they weren't even trying to be subtle.

"Not really, actually. Tonight's a little different. I'm kicking off my first national tour so everyone's here to see me, but normally, things are way more low-key. My old boss, Red Miller, he gets mobbed everywhere he goes so this doesn't even seem that crazy."

"You used to work for someone?" Ethan found that hard to believe. Crow looked like the kind of guy who had it made from day one.

Crow chuckled. "Yeah, of course. I got lucky in that we basically became best friends after a while, so it didn't feel too much like a job, but I was his personal assistant until a few months ago. That's when my music sort of took off."

Ethan couldn't hold back his smile, matching the one Crow took on when he spoke about music. It was clear he was passionate about his career, and that was something that Ethan found incredibly attractive. He thought passion was something to be admired, coveted.

"How about you?" Crow asked, putting his hands on the scratched up wooden table. "You work for anyone?"

"I'm a doctor," Ethan answered. "A family physician over at Sierra View."

Crow's eyebrows shot up. "Doctor? Wow, sorry, I was expecting you to say a detective or something."

"Why's that?"

"I don't know, you just seem... kind of like a badass. Like I could picture you figuring out national scandals, not delivering diagnosis results."

"I have great bedside manner, I'll have you know."

"Oh, I'm sure you do."

There it was. The flirty line that served as chum in shark infested waters. Crow was trying to draw Ethan in, and *fuck*, it was working.

"Not that I have absolutely anything against it," Crow said, "obviously, you said doctor and my basement *fucking flooded*."

Ethan snorted at that. It caught him completely off guard.

"That's amazing, though, really," Crow continued. "My twin is actually in medical school now, over at UCLA. I think he wants to do his residency at Sierra View."

Ethan smiled at that. "He'll be in good hands there."

The bartender showed up, placing the first tray of whiskey samples on the center of the table. This drew Ethan's eye to the corner. The palm tree.

Ethan felt himself tense. He momentarily zoned out, going back to this place, all those years ago. The day he etched that palm tree on the corner of the table, across from the man who he had fallen so desperately hard for.

"Ok, which one first?"

Crow's voice snapped Ethan out of it. He wasn't here to

reminisce and get lost in the past. As much of a stab as it was, he needed to move on and this was part of it. He would try to enjoy the next fifteen minutes and then go home, content with the twist the night had taken. He'd wake up and go on living his life as though nothing had changed.

An hour and a half of whiskey sampling passed by. It was also an hour and a half of incredible conversation and seriously delectable eye candy. Ethan caught himself, on multiple occasions, staring at Crow's lips as he tried each of the whiskeys. They had ordered a few different tasting flights, all coming out on fancy oak paddles, the thick whiskey glasses set in a row across the center, so Crow had plenty to choose from. Ethan enjoyed watching his expressions turn from 'what the fuck is this shit,' to 'eh it's alright' to 'oh ok, I think get it'. That happened toward the end, when they had reached the more expensive and lighter bodied whiskeys.

"You've got some expensive taste," Ethan joked as the waiter took away the last paddle. Time had completely slipped by them. Ethan glanced down at his Apple watch and saw that there were only ten minutes left until closing. Sure enough, the music cut out and the DJ announced last call.

"I think you did it. I think you taught me how to like whiskey. There's something about appreciating the 'notes'... fuck, that sounds pretentious."

Ethan laughed, matching Crow's. He wasn't completely at ease, but he was definitely without many walls, and the laughs only served to knock down a few more barriers. "Not at all. It's the right terminology." Ethan narrowed his eyes. "Now, if you start wearing a top hat and raising your pinky, I may start to worry."

"Are you saying I can't pull off a top hat?"

You can pull off anything.

"Potentially," Ethan said with a shrug.

Crow shook his head, feigning offense. "So, I never ended up telling you what happens if I win my side of the bet." The lights came on.

Ethan swallowed down the last of his whiskey. He was feeling drunker than he had been in a while, and that had his emotions in a whirlwind. There was a definite Dr. Jekyll and Mr. Hyde thing going on inside. He knew exactly where this was headed and he wanted it, but then Jekyll would tear through, making him realize that this was all a big farce. Crow was going to be an empty one-night stand and that was it. He would feel even emptier after, realizing that he would never find what he once had. That realization would hit like a train wreck, potentially pushing Ethan into a hole he wouldn't be able to dig himself out of.

"I'm sorry," Ethan said. He had to cut this off now. Things couldn't progress any further. "I have to go. You're an incredible singer, your tour is going to be incredible."

Ethan got up, his knees wobblier than he thought. He pulled his phone out, ready to order his ride home. That was when he felt two hands close around his wrists. Strong hands. Warm. He looked up from his phone. Crow was smiling. Those pearly white teeth were framed by a grin that warmed everything in Ethan's body, from his toes to his cock to his head. Everything was flooded with a warmth he couldn't explain.

And then came a kiss that blew that warmth up into a raging inferno. The entire bar melted away, the earth crumbling underneath their heat. A kiss so passionate, Ethan moaned seconds into it. He hadn't lost himself like that in years. To the point of being unable to control the sounds coming out of his own throat. Another moan. Crow's hands came up to tangle in Ethan's head, Ethan putting his phone on the table and then grabbing Crow's hips. Sparks —nah, fuck that, *lightning strikes* —were flying between and around them. Ethan was sure they had destroyed the entire world with the force of their kiss.

And then it was over. They separated, the moment loaded, their silence saying more than the chatter of the emptying bar around them.

"I..."

Want to go home with you. I want to talk to you all night, fuck you all day, and sleep next to you for the rest of the time. Wake up and do it again. I want to know you inside and out. You intrigue me on a level I haven't felt since I lost him. I want you, Crow Kensworth. I fucking want you.

"...should go. I have to be at the hospital early, tomorrow."

"Right, right." Crow looked disappointed. Ethan couldn't keep looking into his eyes. He felt himself breaking apart like a cocoon. He pulled out his phone again and ordered his cab.

He went to sleep that night. He never remembered his dreams when he woke up, but he did remember one thing about that night.

Ethan remembered Crow's voice, his song flowing through his dream like an ethereal thread.

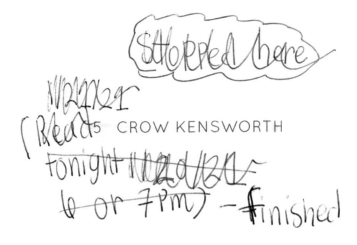
C row's head was throbbing. All that whiskey did not sit well with him overnight. He felt dehydrated and shaky, which was *exxaactly* how he wanted to feel on his first day on the road for the tour.

"Please tell me there's Advil on this bus," he groaned to Angela as he climbed up the steps and entered his tour bus. It was a pretty decked out bus, he could tell from the second he walked in. It had a nice living area at the front, with comfy looking tan leather couches and mahogany accents throughout. There was a big flat-screen TV up on the wall along with a table on the opposite side, where they could get together and play drinking games (not that Crow ever wanted to drink again)... (but, let's be real) or write new songs.

"Funny you bring that up," Angela said as she climbed up onto the bus behind him. She was looking over a clipboard, checking things off. She couldn't look more like a producer, in her dark fitted jeans, black leather kitten heels, and a casual black suit jacket that meant business. He was so grateful he had Angela around, because Crow was a mess with everything else that didn't have to do with music. He could barely produce his own breakfast, much less an entire national tour.

"What?"

"Well, I have two pieces of bad news and one good. Which do you wanna hear first?"

Crow slumped down onto the couch. He laid down across it, his arm covering his eyes from the blazingly bright sun breaking through the closed blinds. "Let's go with the bad."

"Ok. One or two?"

"Two."

"Good choice." Angela sat down at the table, still looking over her notes. "We can't leave on your tour today."

"What?" Crow shot up on the couch. The move made his head feel like it was injected with acid jello.

"Relax, relax. We're only delayed by a day at the latest, and it won't affect the dates at all. We planned some buffer time for exactly this."

"Why?"

"Doctor Cherry's wife just had her baby. There were some complications, though, and she wants to stay here to be with them."

Crow exhaled. "Fuck, is everything ok with the baby?"

"Yeah, last I heard everything was fine, she just wants to stay and be with her wife and newborn. Which means we're out a doctor, and with Troy's medical issue, we shouldn't leave without one. Just in case."

Crow sighed. "Right, of course." He let his worries go with a deep exhale. Or at least tried to. It was hard when he was feeling like shit and getting shit news all at the same time. All on top of the fact that he had to go home alone last night. He honestly didn't even care if he had gone home with Ethan and they never hooked up, all he wanted was that extra time with him. There was something about the man that was completely enrapturing. A way he only remembered feeling through reading fairytales.

"But don't worry, I think I found someone."

For a split second, Crow imagined Ethan being the doctor Angela found. That single thread of thought opened up an entire can of worms, flooding his brain with images of the two on tour together. Getting to know each other more, traveling across the country and experiencing all these different things together.

"She's one of Cherry's close friends, so we'll all be in good hands."

She.

Crow felt his moment of fantasy deflate like a popped balloon. He closed his eyes and rested his hand against the wall behind him. "What's the other bad news, no no, actually give me the good news next. I need to cleanse my pallet."

"You sure?"

"Yeah, go for it."

"You crossed a million subscribers on YouTube this morning," Angela said, excitement clear in her voice. Crow sat up straighter, the excitement pushing aside the hangover. That was a huge milestone, even though to some it may have just seemed like numbers. To Crow, it was so much more. It meant that all these people, an amount of people Crow had a hard time even comprehending, supported him and what he did.

"Yes, queen!" It was Jordan. He burst in through the entrance of the tour bus with an exuberance that immediately filled the room and sent a quake through Crow's head. He wasn't ready for that onslaught of energy. "You did it!

We have to celebrate. Here, let's do champagne." Jordan waltzed past Angela and Crow and stopped right in front of the small bar back toward the bedrooms.

"I can't do alcohol right now," Crow groaned.

"Oh, honey, you're *going* to do champagne." Jordan found what he was looking for, squealing in excitement. He waved a golden bottle of champagne in the air, pointing it toward the opposite end of the room. A loud pop followed by a fizz. The sound made Crow's stomach curl.

Then, another sound. Five rapid knocks on the bus door. Frantic giggles filtered in through the opened window.

Angela scrunched her brows together. She said something under her breath, sounding very much to Crow like 'fuckin' groupies', as she got up and walked to the door. She pushed it open, revealing a gang of six teenage girls, all bubbly and jumpy, each wearing their own handmade 'Crow Kensworth' t-shirts. Crow could see a few from where he sat, but they hadn't spotted him yet.

"Hi!" one of the girls said, the braver one of the group. He saw Angela bristle.

"How did you girls get past security?"

Jordan piped in from the back as he poured the champagne. "Security?" He scoffed. "Girl, all that's outside is an angry raccoon and a nicer parking attendant."

Angela huffed in frustration. "I'm sorry but Crow is feeling sick, he can't do any meet an—" She was cut off by a loud shriek from the girl in the back. She spotted Crow first as he walked up behind Angela, a big smile on his face. How could he not give his fans at least a few minutes of conversation? They were clearly persistent enough to spot his tour bus from the street and pull into the parking lot (which Angela apparently thought was guarded to the effect of Fort Knox). The note with the flower did pop into his mind momentarily, but he couldn't see how these teenage girls would pose any kind of threat. They were all just genuinely excited for a chance to meet him.

"Hi, everyone!" Crow said, mustering up as much energy as he could.

The girls flipped. The screaming felt like ice cold darts getting thrown at his skull, but he powered through. He was wearing a white hoodie and gray sweatpants, so he clearly wasn't looking anything spectacular, but he still posed for photos with each and every one of them. After he was through, he thanked them all for taking time to visit him.

"Are you kidding?" said the one with the dark hair and the light purple streaks. Her name was Tina if Crow remembered correctly. "I've been, like, straight up stalking twitter all day, looking through your hashtag legit twenty-four *seven*." She pushed a strand of jet black hair off her eyes. They bore into Crow, seeing him as something more than just the man Crow felt himself to be. He would never get used to that. He remembered asking Red one day if it ever stopped feeling weird to be looked at like some exotically rare animal spotted out in the wild. He answered with a shake of his head.

"The tour schedule is up there too, although I'm sure you already knew that." Crow ended it with a light laugh, his head still plagued with dull throbs.

"Hell yeah! We're going to try to make it to each stop!" It was another girl in the group that answered, her bright blonde hair drawing Crow's eyes like a lighthouse, an even brighter pink streak going down the side of her hair. "Total groupies," she admitted, causing the group to break down into a fit of giggles.

"I'm honored," Crow said playfully as he climbed the steps back up to the tour bus. "It was great meeting you all!"

Angela huffed, her shoulders visibly slumping as the door hissed shut, leaving the girls outside, scrolling through all the selfies they had just taken. "We can't have that."

"Relax, Ang, they're just star struck kids. Least I could do is take a few photos with them." Crow walked over to the mini-fridge that was set under the white marble kitchen counter. Jordan tried handing him a glass of champagne, but Crow waved it off. The overhead lighting bounced off the shiny surfaces, causing the stainless steel handles to pop. He bent down, opened the fridge, and grabbed himself a bottle of water.

"No, it *really* can't." Angela's tone changed. "This is the other piece of bad news." She was no longer in business mode, getting things done and getting them done right. She sounded... emotional? Crow looked her way as she reached into her back pocket and pulled out a crumpled note.

Crow was shocked as realization dawned on him.

"Another one?"

6 ETHAN WINTER

(finished)

The hospital intercom buzzed to life as a nurse called for a physician for one of the rooms. Ethan double checked his beeper to make sure no one was asking for him. He entered the break room, four other nurses and two fellow doctors already inside. It was a pretty large break room, seating about twenty, with two long tables down the center and comfortable seating all throughout. There was a large window on the far side of the room that gave a beautiful view of the surrounding mountains, cutting across the bright blue sky like paper mache figures, popping in contrast with the world around them. It had been uncharacteristically rainy for Los Angeles lately, which besides causing everyone to immediately forget all the rules of the road, also meant that the hillsides were bright green with lush trees and foliage that brought an entirely different feel to the city. Ethan was reminded of Hawaii when he glanced out at the emerald green, a much better alternative to the dry brown brush they had months ago.

"Ethan! Just the man I needed to see." It was Mariah Carpenter, a fellow family doctor who moonlighted at

Sierra View. Her long brunette locks bounced on the front of her white coat. Ethan always joked that if medicine didn't work out, she could easily make a living in shampoo commercials.

"Hey, Mariah, what's up?"

"She wants you to take over her prostate exams for today," said Dean Harper, an emergency doctor. He was sitting down at the closest table, the scent of his famous homemade lasagna wafting up from his paper plate.

"I definitely do not," Mariah said, her eyes wide. Ever since Dean had started dating his fiancé, his jokes were just rolling off the sleeves of his white coat. Ethan remembered noticing that shift; Dean went from a stern guy who rarely smiled to someone who couldn't hold back a joke, even if it was a little risqué.

"*Mhmm*," Dean said with a laugh. "I didn't know you were so attached to those exams."

"Anyways," Mariah said, chuckling as she turned her attention back to Ethan. "I was offered an opportunity that I unfortunately had to turn down, and I think you would, hands down, be the best person to take my place."

"Oh?"

"No offense, Dean."

Dean waved his fork in the air. "None taken."

"Ethan, I wanted to ask if you would take my place as a traveling doctor with a national music tour. It's for a guy named Crow Kensworth, not sure if you've heard of him. Apparently he's huge on the internet."

Ethan's eyebrows shot up. This had to be a joke. Somehow, Mariah was in on it and everyone in the room was gathered together to laugh at the cruel prank.

But... how would she have known about last night?

"I know, it's crazy. I have to stay here in LA, but I'll be

more than willing to split your patient load with myself and Dr. Osbourne. He already said he wouldn't mind. Cherry was originally supposed to go, but with her and their little baby Julie, well, she didn't want to be far."

Ethan's mind was storming like a category five hurricane. He couldn't believe he had woken up that morning from a dream involving the very same man he was being offered to travel around the country with. It had been so long since he had woken up with that warm sadness that accompanied the realization that an amazing dream was just that: a dream.

But this certainly wasn't a dream. This was reality, and Mariah was expecting an answer.

"Sorry," Ethan said, the only word forming in the turbulence of his mind. "I can't."

Mariah cocked her head, arms now crossed. "Ethan, I promise, everything here will be taken care of. It'll only be for three months and then you'll be home again. Didn't you always talk about how badly you wanted to take a road trip? This is your shot, Ethan."

"Yeah, plus, you'll be getting paid to do it," Dean added.

"Why do they need a doctor with them, anyway?"

"Patient confidentiality," Mariah said, "but they wouldn't ask if they didn't need one."

"Right, of course." Ethan was getting a little snappy. It happened when he grew overwhelmed, and this was one of those moments. Normally, he was fine with thinking on his feet. As a doctor, that was one of the mandatory requirements. He was often presented with cases that had him thinking outside of the box, especially with working at a hospital for the majority of his time. Weird cases always popped up. This was just one of those weird cases demanding a quick answer. An answer that could potentially alter the rest of his life.

He had to take a breath.

"Sorry, I shouldn't have just dumped this on you." Mariah sighed, her eyes filling with something else. Sadness? "I thought... well, I thought getting out of here could really help you."

Ethan took the breath. A sharp inhale. He knew what Mariah was referring to. Everyone in the damn room knew.

And, you know what?

Mariah was right. He *did* need to get out of Los Angeles. Away from it all. There were too many memories here: from palm trees to bar booths, from unforgettable date spots to streets that felt all too familiar. He had to go.

But now? And on Crow's tour? That was a recipe for disaster, he could feel it in his bones.

Or was that something else he was feeling?

"Fine," Ethan said, the feeling in his bones spreading, warming him. Adrenaline. Excitement. Nerves. He was beginning to feel it all. He had no idea what saying yes to this would bring, but there was something big on the horizon, he couldn't deny that.

"Oh, great! Thank you, thank you," Mariah said, a smile spreading across her face as he clapped her hands together. "I know it's out of the blue, but I think you'll really enjoy yourself. Plus, the singer is a total hottie. I looked him up last night and *woooow*."

Ethan was about to bring up meeting him, but he figured it was better off left unsaid. He felt like it was almost too crazy to sound real. What were the chances that the one man he was enraptured by was the same man who would be touring the country with him?

Fuckin' crazy.

7 CROW KENSWORTH

(finished)

It was the next day and Crow was feeling back to a hundred percent. His limbs no longer felt useless and his brain was functioning at full capacity. Apparently, he also looked better too, according to Jordan, who was now offering him a Bloody Mary.

"I'm ok, I promise," Crow said, moving over to the table. Troy climbed onto the bus, followed by Angela. She was looking a little more casual in a black t-shirt and light jeans with 'designer' tears along the front. Franklin, his drummer, knocked on the door, which Angela had shut behind her. She cursed an apology and pressed the button to open the door, air hissing out as it opened.

"Sorry," she said again as Franklin climbed up, his dark jeans intact but worn out at the knees. The bus could comfortably sleep seven, so they still had room for two more people. There were three bunk beds and then one king bed inside of the master bedroom, all the way at the end of the bus.

"It's alright," Franklin said, grabbing the Bloody Mary that Crow had turned away.

"So, what's this letter thing everyone's freaking out about?" It was Troy who asked. He sat down at the table across from Crow. Angela took the seat next to him, producing the note.

"You keep that with you everywhere you go?" Troy asked with a chuckle as he grabbed it and unfolded it.

"Our fingerprints are all over, so not like the cops are going to do anything with it. Hell, even if there were finger-prints, it's not really actionable." Angela shrugged as she unlocked her iPad and went straight to her emails.

Troy's eyes got wider and wider as he read the note. Franklin's interest was peeked, seeing as he shouted, "read it out loud!" from inside the bathroom.

"Dear Crow," Troy started, adopting the voice of a dreamy teenage girl. "Your tour is going to introduce you to the world, so I wanted to let you know—before anyone else got any ideas—that you're mine. All mine. I was there from the beginning, and I'll be there for the end... Sorry that sounds so creepy, but it's the truth. I won't lie to you, baby. Ever. And I know you're wondering who this is from, and you'll definitely find out, but not just yet. I have to wait for the right time, otherwise I could risk losing you. So, keep on singing your heart out, I'll be there with you every note along the way! Love, your number one fan."

"Holy shit!" Franklin yelled.

"Yeah, I know," Crow said, feeling a bad case of the chills coming on. "I mean, I've gotten weird letters and packages before—remember that one box we got a few months ago?"

"The one with only a weave inside?" Troy asked, folding the letter back up.

Crow chuckled. "Yeah, that one. People are weird...

But, that letter definitely feels a little off. More off than a lone weave."

"It'll be fine," Angela said, grabbing the letter. "I hired extra security for the trip, so no more random groupies walking up to our tour bus."

Troy's eyebrows raised. "Weren't we tight on money?"

"Yeah, but I made it work. It's not like a twenty-four seven thing, but we'll have guys watching the tour bus and some of the higher capacity venues." Angela looked down at her iPad. "I took a pay cut, it's fine."

"What?" Crow's head snapped toward Angela. "Ang, you definitely don't need to do that. Cut it from my checks, I don't care. But don't make it harder for yourself."

She shook her head, not looking up from her calendar. "No way. It wasn't that big of a cut anyway. I saved some pennies on a few other things too, so we're all good."

"Thank you," Crow said, feeling lucky that he was surrounded by such an incredible team of people. Not only were they all insanely talented and hard-working, but they were also all genuinely good people.

"Of course," she said, looking up when two knocks sounded on the door. "Oh, that must be the doctor."

For a split second, Crow's heart leaped up into his throat. It was quickly snapped back down like it was attached to a rubber band. He had no reason to be excited. There was only one doctor in this entire world that he'd be excited to see, and it definitely wasn't whoever Angela had found to tour with them. He pulled his phone out from his khaki shorts and started looking for something to entertain himself with.

"Hi!" he heard Angela say. "You must be Doctor Winter?"

Crow's eyes blazed up from the phone to the entrance.

Winter. That last name was in no way popular. Did Ethan have a sister who also happened to be a doctor? He didn't mention anything about her at the bar.

"You can call me Ethan."

Crow's mouth dried up, his pulse shot to the sky. It was Ethan. He couldn't forget that voice. The one that vibrated through his entire body. He was suddenly nervous, like a middle schooler asking his first date to the school dance. He couldn't even think about what this meant. Ethan and Crow were about to be stuck on a bus together for three months, traveling around the country, getting to know each other way deeper than Crow could have imagined.

Angela came up the steps first, moving aside so she could introduce Ethan to the crew. He climbed the last step and turned to look straight at Crow. Those baby blues were even more breathtaking in the sunlight. They glittered like they held an entire galaxy inside of them. Crow was speechless as Angela rattled off the names. Troy and the rest all went up to the front of the bus to shake hands. Jordan seemed particularly excited to say hi. Crow was last. He slid out of the booth and stood by the table, about six feet separating him and the man he thought he'd never see again.

"And this is Crow Kensworth," Angela said, outstretching a hand, showing Crow off like she was suddenly Vanna White.

"We've met," Ethan said, a smoldering smirk on his handsome face. He was wearing a simple light blue shirt and jeans, the shirt only enhancing those breathtaking eyes.

"Oh." Angela stepped back, crossing her arms. Ethan held his hand out for a shake, but Crow ignored it. Instead, he went straight for a hug. It not only felt more appropriate, but it was also a great way of feeling the solid knots of muscle that formed Ethan's back. And he smelled *sooo* fucking good, too. Like a mix between the beach and sex, two of Crow's favorite things.

"Hi again," Crow said as they separated.

"Who would have thought?" Ethan said, smiling a little wider. Crow loved his smile. It wasn't an easy one to get, but it was so damn rewarding. Especially when Ethan smiled hard enough to show off those cute dimples that made Crow's butterflies rage. They had only hung out that one night, but Crow could tell Ethan was more reserved than some other guys, so this smile felt like a damn Grammy.

"AND WE'RE OFF!" Jordan cheered from the couch as the bus driver started the engines. This was it, the official start of Crow's cross-country tour. Their first stop would be a club in Las Vegas, and so they headed east. Crow was sitting at the table, trying to keep his mind occupied by scrolling through Instagram. He couldn't keep his thoughts from swerving back to Ethan Winter, who was currently in the bedroom with Troy, giving him a physical and introducing himself. He couldn't believe how life twisted its way into the shape of a pretzel. He honestly thought he would go on the rest of his life wondering about the man that had stopped him right in his tracks.

Now that man was only a room away.

"Who wants a margarita!" Jordan slapped the table as he got up and walked over to the bar.

"Jordan, it's nine in the morning," Crow pointed out.

"Fine," Jordan said, shrugging. "Mimosas it is. There, are you happy? Is that a little more socially acceptable?"

"In that case, I'll take one," Crow said with a smile.

Angela, who was working on confirming the hotels they would stay at, hung up the phone and turned her attention to the group, "Ok, so everyone knows where they're sleeping tonight?"

"Hell yeah," Jordan sang as he popped open the champagne. "Crow, you obviously don't mind sharing the bed with me, right?"

"Very funny," Angela said, not finding it very funny. "You'll get the top bunk, Jordan. I'll get the bottom. We'll be staying at a few hotels, but obviously that costs money, which we aren't rolling in right now. We lucked out on the tour bus, though, with some decent beds and a small shower that has to be very limited use. Water isn't infinite on here. Maybe on the next tour we'll have penthouse reservations every night, but for now, we'll have to sacrifice."

"How have ticket sales been?" Crow asked. He always hated asking logistical questions because he was always scared of the answer. He had a fear of hearing abysmal numbers and realizing his music wasn't as loved as he thought it was.

"Good, Las Vegas and Phoenix are both sold out. Makes sense, they're the soonest." Angela referred to her iPad for the rest. "Then we have Albuquerque, which is almost sold out. Denver is looking good too. Kansas City, St. Louis, Chicago, and Columbus are at about sixty percent sold. The east coast is taking a little longer, but they're all proven procrastinators anyway. Don't worry, everything's going to be flawless. You've got me running this ship."

Crow had stopped paying attention toward the end, even though he was normally hyper focused on the numbers if they were ever presented to him. But not when Ethan Winter walked into the room. What were numbers? What was air? *Whastasdlahlsdf?*

That was how Crow felt. Completely haywired.

"Crow?"

"Huh?"

"Did you not listen to what I just said?" Angela was looking up from her iPad, her annoyed gaze jumping from Crow to Ethan.

"Yeah, about procrastinators."

Angela crossed her arms, clearly over it, but how could she blame him? Ethan Winter was a man that demanded complete and total attention the minute he stepped into a room. He had that kind of gravity to him. It was in the way he stood, legs apart, hands loose, jaw relaxed. And then in the way he walked, with strong, meaningful strides, even if he was just walking over to the couch. It was in those eyes.

Everything. Absolutely everything about the man was alluring.

Crow was in trouble.

8 ETHAN WINTER

Ethan sat down on the couch because that was all he could really think of doing. He had no idea what he had gotten himself into, but he knew it was big. He felt it the moment he stepped on the bus. The second his eyes went straight to Crow's. He wasn't expecting to feel the way he did when he saw him...

Relief. He felt relieved to be seeing him again. It made him realize how strongly they connected a few nights ago, and how he owed it to himself to explore some of that. This was a new start, not only for Crow's music career, but for Ethan's personal life. A way to reset things before Ethan officially lost himself to the empty sorrow that had plagued him through the past years.

And now, after examining Troy and establishing a doctor-patient relationship, he didn't know what else to do. It wasn't like Troy needed constant medical attention, thankfully. Ethan was just there in case things got bad. So after doing his job, Ethan walked over to the couch, trying not to pay attention to Crow's amber brown gaze following him as he crossed the bus.

"Don't sit so far!" Jordan called, slapping an empty seat at the table next to him. "I might need my blood pressure checked," he added suggestively.

Ethan chuckled as he got up from the couch. He went to the seat, which happened to be across from Crow. He could feel the man looking at him from where he sat. Ethan wanted to do the same. He wanted to stare at that face for hours, until he could sketch it exactly from memory. He wanted to memorize every single crease, every pore, *everything*.

What is going on with me?

"So, Ethan, as a newbie to the crew, I think we're going to need to get you properly initiated." Jordan smiled around his glass as he took a drink. "We won't go with the full on blind-fold ceremony we do, but we still have to do something."

"He's just messing with you." It was Crow. His voice was arresting. Damn, even when he wasn't singing, Crow could still take over a room with his voice alone. "We're not a frat."

"Eh, have you seen how you keep your room?" Angela added, an eyebrow arched. "It looks like you horde frat guys underneath the bed. As if they only come out at night and throw their underwea—"

"Ok, we can stop there." Crow cut her off, chuckling. Ethan glanced his way and was surprised to see a slight blush on his cheeks. It was so fucking endearing.

"Just saying." Angela went back to her iPad, eyebrow arched.

"I think I'll pass on the initiations," Ethan said. Jordan exaggerated an offended look. Troy came in from the bathroom just then, drying his hands on his jeans. He went to a cabinet and grabbed a box of cards.

"The only thing you'll need to do is play a round of Cards Against Humanity with us," Troy said, motioning for Crow to scoot down the booth so he could sit.

"Well, in that case, I'm in." Ethan was glad that the group thought to include him. They could have easily treated him like an outsider, there to do a job and that was it. Instead, Ethan was feeling more and more like this was the right decision. He had stayed up the entire night before, sick with worry that he had made a mistake. It was easier than dealing with the dreams, and so he was pretty anxious walking onto the bus.

The moment he saw Crow, that was when the anxiety was blasted away. He had to let himself ride with that, he needed to leave his fears and trepidations back in Los Angeles. This was all a new start, and he had no idea what was going on between him and Crow, but he knew it was something worth delving into a little more.

They played the card game, which involved matching random cards up with random phrases. The catch was that all the combinations usually led to something totally outrageous and sometimes offensive (hopefully funny enough to offset it). This had the group cracking up on multiple occasions with the different pairings they made. Ethan was particularly skilled, to his own surprise. He didn't think he'd be so witty, but he guessed that came with being able to think on his feet. He could also read a room pretty well and knew that the group of people playing were down for some dirty jokes. That was probably why his combination of cards that read: 'And the Academy Award for Fisting goes to Gandalf' had the entire table in tears.

It was also a great way of getting to bask in Crow's incredibly warm smile. And that laugh of his was just as warm and infectious. Even if some of the card pairings weren't all that funny, Crow would still laugh, which in turn would have the rest of the group laughing. Ethan was quickly realizing that Crow had that effect twenty-four seven. Regardless of whether they were playing a naughty card game or not, Crow had a way of making people feel happy around him. Whether it was through his endless charm or charming laughs, he managed to do it.

It was a trait Ethan admired. He was the kind of person who was shaped by the energies around him, so he was glad that Crow only exuded positivity. That, in turn, made Ethan feel happy. It was an emotion that had felt out of grasp for Ethan for a long time. So long, Ethan had begun to think he could no longer even reach for it. What had been the point? There wasn't even a use crying about it.

Not anymore, though. Happiness was no longer something he thought he had permanently lost. Ethan felt it as he sat with the group, stealing prolonged glances across the table at Crow, laughing along with the rest. His mind would wander back to that kiss they shared only a few nights ago. It was seared into his memory like a brand. He could still feel Crow's lips on his. Their warmth and wetness. And he could also feel the fear that had spiked in him. Fear of falling back into something so deep, so powerful, that he was opening himself up to a world of hurt again.

Then he looked into Crow's eyes, and an entirely different story unfolded in his head. This one had nothing to do with fear. He found himself smiling, looking back down at his hand of cards as if he was actually paying attention to the game. They kept playing for another hour or so before they broke for lunch. By that point, the bus had pulled into its first stop of the tour: a gas station that also had a Dunkin Donuts and a Burger King inside.

They all got off the bus and split off into little groups.

Without even seeming to think about it, Ethan found himself walking side by side with Crow.

"Wow, that's nice," Crow said as they walked through the sliding glass door and into the air-conditioned rest stop. The recent rain had also bought an unusual humidity, which was great for keeping lips unchapped but was fucking terrible when it came to being outside. So the blast of cool air was welcome, even though the walk from the bus to the rest stop wasn't very long at all.

Inside, they saw a row of stalls filled with all kinds of trinkets and souvenirs. From sunglasses to weird hats and funny t-shirts. The smell of cinnamon filled the air as they walked past the *Cinnabon* store, making Ethan's mouth water. He had a weakness for the sweet stuff, and a bun smothered in melted vanilla and cinnamon swirls sounded like heaven.

"That card game was hilarious. You had me cracking up."

Ethan shook his head. "You took the cake with the one about roller coasters and orgasms."

Crow laughed at that, once again drawing Ethan in with the sound. They entered the line for a burger. "That was good. But your's with Gandalf totally gave a whole new meaning to *Lord of the Rings*."

"Good one," Ethan said, the laughs bubbling up from his chest. It had been a while since he had laughed this much. "One cockring to rule them all."

Crow snorted at that. Ethan joined in. A few people behind them shuffled in line. He didn't even care if they were being loud, he just felt so full of joy again. The giddy kind of joy that lowered Ethan's walls much faster than he even realized. He felt like a kid again. He was in his mid-thirties and yet he felt like he had been thrown back to when he was a twenty-year-old.

Back to when he met Adam.

They reached the front of the line. They ordered and went to go find a table. The place was pretty packed, apparently a few school buses on a fieldtrip had stopped there minutes before they did. There were kids running around, clearly excited out of their fucking minds, all wearing the same bright yellow t-shirts with a smiling cartoon alligator on the back, wearing a bright blue shirt with the school's name on it.

It was like shirt-ception.

Luckily, an exhausted looking family finished up their onion rings and started clearing off their table the second Ethan walked by. He claimed the table and called Crow over. They looked around for the rest of the group but couldn't spot them, so they started digging into their lunches. Ethan was going to need to be extra vigilant about getting his workouts in whenever and wherever he could, because he could already tell that this tour was going to wreck his diet.

"Thanks again for jumping on the tour so last minute. You saved me from either rescheduling the tour or going on without Troy. Obviously, both of those things sucked major balls. Beside from heights, I think my other major fear is having to let down friends or fans."

"No need to thank me. I became a doctor because I love helping people, and now I get to do that while traveling through different parts of the country. It's not a bad gig."

"True, but it still must be hard to just get on and uproot yourself. You know, leaving things behind from one day to the next... did you leave anyone behind?"

Ethan could tell Crow wanted to ask that question from

the start. "No one," Ethan answered with a simple finality to it.

"Ok, good, because then I'd have to second-guess that kiss of ours, and that's the last thing I want to do."

Ethan grabbed his coke and drank, finding another situation in which his quick thinking doctor abilities were coming short. "I, uhm, —"

"Do you travel a lot?" Crow asked. He bit into an onion ring, looking so damn nonchalant even though he had brought up a kiss that had rocked Ethan's entire world. How could he do that? How did he manage to keep his cool so well?

"No," Ethan answered, realizing that he was being way too short. He was just getting too lost in his thoughts. "I've wanted to, though," he continued. Crow remained quiet, which made Ethan open up even more. "I was born in San Diego, my mom was a teacher so we didn't really have much extra money for long-distance vacations. Then I went to medical school right after undergrad and started working as a doctor eight years later, with no time off in between. So then when I finally had the money to leave LA and travel, I was too busy."

And lately, I just haven't wanted to leave.

Not until you came.

End of chapter

9 CROW KENSWORTH

(finished)

C row could have stayed in that rest stop and written an entire album in an hour, all he had to do was sit across from Ethan and listen to him speak the entire time. The man had a voice that encapsulated the essence of a muse. Even over the din of the conversation that surrounded them. Crow had never felt so inspired. He wanted to jump on the table and break out into a song about sapphires that fell from the sky and heart beats that painted a mural. Crow wanted to raise the roof off of the place, all in the name of Ethan Winter.

Instead, he remained seated and tried to bottle up all that inspiration for a later time. He focused instead on the crispy onion rings and decent burger. He had to look away from Ethan's sexy lips before he accidentally drooled all over the table. "Where's the one place you've always wanted to go?" Crow asked, wanting to dig deeper into who Ethan was as a person.

He chewed on his bottom lip, thinking of the answer and simultaneously sending a fireball straight to Crow's crotch. Ethan looked so damn sexy when he was thinking about something. Crow had noticed that during the card game. He would sometimes bite down on his lip, revealing a set of pearly whites that Crow immediately wanted to lick and then have biting on his own skin. "Hmm," Ethan said. "In America?"

"Anywhere."

"Paris."

"Nice, any special reason?"

Ethan smirked. "I'm into museums and The Louvre is one I've been wanting to go to since I could remember."

Crow recognized that glint in those sapphire blue eyes. He could tell Ethan was being genuine about liking museums, and—*somehow*—that was even sexier than the lip bite. "I love an evening spent in a museum, and the Louvre is definitely one of my dream visits," Crow said, squeezing his thighs together under the table. "But I also really love the small, weird ones. The side-show museums. Those are always a blast."

"Those are great too. Have you been to The Museum of Jurassic Technology back in LA?"

Crow chuckled, remembering a good time in that museum. "Love it. It was so weird, and half the exhibits make you wonder if they're even real, which is such a cool way to experience a museum. And the rooftop tea garden is somehow weirder than the entire place put together." He smiled, not looking away from Ethan now. The man somehow made the fluorescent rest stop lighting look like a professional setup, ready for a photo-shoot. "There aren't any museums, I think, but I'd really love to go to Santorini. I could be a huge beach bum when I have free time, so I really want to check out the black and red sand over there. Plus, I love those buildings with the bright blue roofs."

Ethan looked down at the crumbs on his tray. Crow

couldn't exactly tell, but he had a sense that Ethan was no longer smiling. Crow looked over his shoulder, wondering if maybe Ethan spotted someone he knew, someone that made him retreat from the conversation like he had.

"You ok?" Crow asked.

Ethan didn't look up, but he did nod. He grabbed his soda cup and sucked up nothing but air through the straw.

"I'm going to get a refill." He got up and reached for Crow's cup. "Need one?"

"Thank you," Crow said, watching Ethan walk to the soda machine, a crowd of kids running around him toward one of their field-trip leaders.

Was it something I said?

His phone buzzed in the pocket of his gym shorts. He pulled it out and saw it was a message from Jordan. He was about to respond when he felt someone sit back down at the table. He looked up and was surprised when he didn't see Ethan.

"Oh, Jordan," Crow said. "I was just about to text you."

"It's ok. I get it. You don't have to explain why you're ignoring me." Jordan mimed rubbing away tears. "I have enough confidence to know that no one can replace me."

"Of course not, Jordan," Crow said, clearly joking with him. Jordan knew they weren't anything romantic, he was simply having a little fun, and Crow wasn't going to refuse to play along.

"Seriously though," Jordan said, swirling his coffee cup with one hand before holding it with both. He looked put together for someone who had been on a bus all morning. Most of them were wearing casual athletic wear since it was the most comfortable, but Jordan opted for a dark gray polo and designer jeans with some serious tan leather shoes. He was definitely the PR guy out of the group, that was for sure. "You're not seeing anyone are you?"

"Why are you so interested?" Crow asked.

"Because I'm picking up on a few *cues* lately and I wanted to confirm it straight from your mouth."

"I don't know what 'cues' you're talking about, but I'm as single as can be."

"So... you don't have a secret ten-year relationship with this new doctor, like some kind of soap opera story line?"

Crow laughed at the outrageousness. "Yes, that's exactly what it is. How do you read people so well?"

"Years of watching Oprah." Jordan took a sip of his coffee. "*Years*." He emphasized.

They were both laughing when Ethan came back to the table. Jordan looked up at him but didn't move down the booth, which didn't leave him any space to sit back down.

"Here," Crow said, scooching down before Ethan turned to go back to the bus.

Ethan took the offer. He sat down, looking a little less taken aback than he was a few minutes ago. Crow still had no idea what he had said, but he definitely wasn't going to bring it up in front of Jordan. He was already acting a little weird, he didn't want to dig into Ethan's psyche while Jordan watched.

"Sorry," Jordan said, his voice taking on an odd tone. "Was I interrupting anything?"

"No, not at all," Ethan said, a little too quickly. If Crow was being a hundred percent honest, then *yes*, yes Jordan was interrupting something.

"Ok," Jordan said, not seeming to be accept the answer fully. He started looking around the room, making Crow wonder if maybe his flirty jokes were a little more serious. Was Jordan getting jealous? He had to know that it wasn't like he had dibs on Crow. Sure, they never talked about it, but Crow didn't think he had to have a discussion about it. He thought he made it clear in the multiple times Crow shut down Jordan's more forward advances in the past. He was sort of used to it. The same thing had happened with both Angela and Troy, too. Angela had made a move on Crow before she knew he was gay and Troy did the same thing, except both of them seemed to have taken no for an answer just fine. Crow thought Jordan's persistence was playful, but maybe not...

"So, doctor Winter," Jordan said, still looking around the room. "What's your story?"

"Excuse me?"

"Yeah, your story." Jordan was looking at him now. "What kind of baggage are you carrying? What's underneath those deep baby blues of yours? We're going to be traveling together for the next three months, we might as well know the best *and* the worst of each other."

"There's no need to go that deep," Crow interjected. He saw what Jordan was doing, and he didn't like it. He was trying to get Ethan to air out all his dirty laundry, probably in hopes of detracting from Crow's attraction toward him.

As if.

Ethan didn't look bothered by the question. He looked much more composed than when Crow was talking about visiting Santorini.

I wonder why?

"I wanted an adventure," Ethan said, "that's all."

Jordan cocked his head. "Eh, I'm not buying it. You seem like someone that's carrying something big on their shoulders. You're not as easy-going as you sometimes put on, I can see that. So what is it? A rough divorce? A—"

"A 'none of your business', Jordan." Crow was getting

upset now. He could feel Ethan next to him, only inches away, and he wanted to reach out and put an arm over his shoulders. Then, he'd draw him in and tell Jordan to go fuck off.

"No, that's ok," Ethan said. He could feel some of the tension growing in the air. "He's partially right. I am running from something."

Crow turned in his seat, looking at Ethan, watching his jaw tighten and flex, cutting a sharp outline on his face. He was looking across the table at Jordan, who's eyes went back to drifting around the rest stop, as if he wasn't the one who opened up this can of worms in the first place.

"See?" Jordan seemed to puff his chest up a little, as if finding pride in discovering something. "Usually it's Angela that get's all 'Miss Cleo'-like and shit. She's the one that can read auras and tell what people are hiding. Remember when she cancelled her first wedding because of one of her dreams? The night we had to bunk in the same hotel room. The one with only the queen-sized bed."

Crow took a deep breath. He was seeing what kind of game Jordan was playing, and he wanted it to end. "Yes, I remember," Crow said, hoping it would end the conversation. He did remember that night. Angela had cancelled her wedding hours before because of an intense dream she had. To her credit, the guy ended up going to jail two months later for drug trafficking and attempted murder. She never had that great of taste in men but at least her dream didn't seem to steer her wrong.

He could also see how Jordan was trying to imply that they spent that night fucking away because of cancelled plans and a tiny bed, which was the farthest thing from the truth. Crow had kept close to one edge of the bed, moving to the couch at some point during the night when he grew tired of throwing Jordan's leg off of his own.

"Oh my god!"

The yell was loud and sudden and came from the booth behind Jordan. The voice belonged to a girl, her big hazel eyes growing even larger the second she spotted Crow sitting across from her. She looked around the rest stop, which had gone deathly quiet for a second, before people realized nothing terrible had happened and they were free to go on about their day. Except for the kids close by, they all realized the same thing as the girl, and they all jumped out of their seats and rushed to Crow's booth.

That was normally what happened. He saw it all the time when he was out with Red. Once one person recognized Red, an entire group would follow, even if they weren't exactly sure who he was. Suddenly, Crow's table was surrounded by high schoolers, asking for selfies. The teachers and chaperones tried to calm the crowd and regain some sort of control over the star struck bunch. Crow, for his part, smiled in as many selfies as they could take.

Finally, the crowd dispersed, all of them happy with their souvenirs.

"Wow," Ethan said, letting out a breath. "That was crazy."

"Never happened before," Crow said, also feeling a little overwhelmed. He had been approached by one or two fans before when he was out in public, but this felt like the entire place was suddenly asking for his attention. It was weird. He enjoyed it, but also couldn't help but feel a dose of nerves during the moment. His normal level of anxiety was climbing higher and higher with each new fucked-up letter that landed on his doorstep.

"We should head back to the bus," Crow said, looking at his watch and noticing the time.

"You know what's weird?" Ethan said as they started getting up with their trays of burger wrappers. "No one asks for autographs anymore. I remember when we were kids and didn't have cameras in our pockets, an autograph would be the only thing we could take away from an encounter like that."

"I never thought about that before," Crow said. Jordan walked ahead of them, throwing out his trash and speed walking toward the bus. "I guess a selfie is going to get way more likes on their Instagram."

"I can't tell if that should make me sad or if that's just me not understanding kids."

"Probably both."

"True."

They walked past the sunglass stalls, past the racks and racks of brochures advertising a rainbow of different vacation stops. It was outside when Crow brought up what he thought was on both their minds. "Sorry about Jordan, he's normally cool. He must be having an off day."

"It's fine." Ethan said it in a way that made Crow feel like it wasn't.

"I'm here for you whenever you want to talk." Unlike Jordan, Crow was in no way going to force Ethan into digging up the skeletons in his closet. As they reached the bus, Crow couldn't stop himself from reaching out and wrapping an arm around Ethan's waist. He pulled him in for a side hug that lasted seconds, but left a warmth that lasted for days.

"Thank you," Ethan said, smiling in a way that made Crow feel like everything was going to be ok.

No, no. *Better* than ok.

ETHAN WINTER

TWO WEEKS LATER

E than looked out the window, watching the rain splatter on the glass and drip down, blurring the parking lot outside. His phone buzzed in his pocket. He took it out and saw Crow's name on the text bubble. He unlocked it and read the message:

'Turn Around'

Ethan did, looking toward the bedrooms. There, Crow was standing, wearing a black t-shirt with the sides cut out wide so that his sexy obliques were on full display, gray gym shorts that stopped an inch above his knees, and... a long top hat that tilted to the left side. He put his pinky to his lips and donned a monocle with his free hand.

Ethan burst out with a snort. "You look like you've lost your mind."

"What?!" Crow opened his arms and moved his head, modeling the hat. "Are you saying I can't pull off this top hat?"

Ethan got up and started walking toward the exit. "You pull it off just fine," he said, still laughing. "Come on, it's leg day."

"Ugh," he heard Crow groan behind him, followed by the thud of a discarded top hat.

Over the past couple of weeks, Ethan had found that Crow was an endless fountain of practical jokes and charming little stunts. He woke the gang up one day while wearing a wolf mask he had painted up with Angela's makeup (she was pissed about that for a few days). Another time, Crow had everyone thinking they had lost the tour bus, but he had just moved it around the corner (Angela was also pissed about that).

Ethan loved it. He loved the exuberant, youthful energy that radiated off Crow. It was the same energy that was amplified tenfold when Crow took to the stage, mic in hand and crowd in sight. Every single performance had been better than the last, if that were even possible. Ethan couldn't help but be blown away night after night after night.

And every morning, he would wake up feeling a little better, a little less anxious. His decision didn't feel as crazy, but more deliberate. Like this was all somehow planned. By who, Ethan had no idea, because he couldn't have even pictured this in his wildest dreams. But there was no denying that Ethan was beginning to feel like he was meant to be on Crow's tour. Maybe it was the couple of nights Ethan and Crow had spent awake, simply talking, way past the point everyone else had retreated to their bunk beds. There conversations were varied and always entertaining, sometimes getting deep but never to the core of what troubled Ethan. Or, maybe it was the cool little museums Crow kept asking to stop every time he'd spot one on the road. The rest of the crew seemed to have been getting annoyed by the fifth one, but Ethan was in heaven. They could never take too much time at the museums since they were on a schedule, but the experiences were still memorable in more ways than one.

On multiple occasions, Ethan had been struck by a deep desire to push in and close the troublesome gap between them. He wanted to feel the kiss that had rocked his core all those weeks ago, before all this was even a possibility in his mind.

But, he would always pull back at the last minute. He still wasn't sure about where this was all headed, and he knew that another kiss would only bind him tighter to Crow's fate. He wasn't sure if he was ready for that. Could he give himself to someone again? Was he even capable of it? Weeks ago, Ethan would have quickly answered with a simple 'no'.

Now, he wasn't so sure.

"Should I wear the hat to the gym?" Crow asked from behind Ethan as they climbed down the steps of the tour bus. They hurried toward the hotel with their heads bowed against the rain.

"If it'll help you squat more than me," Ethan called.

"*Ohhhh*, ok, I see how it is." Crow bumped his shoulder into Ethan as they walked into the hotel lobby. A blast of beige greeted them as they walked through, waving at the two ladies behind the front desk. They were helping two dudes that looked like they had just gotten out of prison, with dirty white tanks and baggy khaki pants. Clearly, Angela was stretching the budget with these hotel stays.

Ethan pulled out his room key and pressed it to the gym door. It buzzed open. No one else was inside the tiny gym, which only fit two treadmills and three weight machines. There were a few free weights missing and the bike machine was out of order, but, for the most part, they had everything they needed.

Ethan started them off with some stretching on the treadmill. He worked in a whole-body stretch, even if they were only working on legs. He started from the head down, having Crow mimic his every move. He admired Crow's ability to learn and his commitment to fitness. For some reason, he thought working out would be a solo endeavor on the trip, but Crow was quick to ask for personal training sessions, even though Crow already had everything down. Ethan didn't mind, he preferred working out with someone and Crow was the perfect spotter.

He also looked so damn good in workout shorts and those shirts with the sides missing. It gave Ethan an incredible view of Crow's toned oblique's and rippling abs. Ethan wasn't someone obsessed with appearances, but there was no denying that Crow was someone your eyes just didn't want to leave. Ethan had an especially hard time looking away when they started stretching their lower backs, reaching down to their toes with their legs spread apart.

Yeah. It was impossible to look away.

"It's so quiet in here," Crow commented as the stretches finished. "They don't have a sound system. Want to put on the TV?"

"Sure," Ethan said. "I don't mind either way."

"Ok, I'm turning it on. Working out in complete silence gives me serial killer vibes."

Ethan chuckled. "You could *regale* me with one of your stories," Ethan said, flourishing his sentence with a hand wave. He went to grab the forty pound weights and brought them over to Crow, who was trying to work the dusty television connected to the corner of the wall.

"Are you saying you don't like my stories?"

"Not at all, I love them" Ethan said, actually meaning it. "You're one of the few people I could actually sit down and listen to for hours without any input and be completely fine about it."

"That's actually really sweet," Crow said, turning from his channel hunting and looking at Ethan with a smile. "But please add input because, again, too much silence is too serial-killery."

"Especially if I'm just sitting there, staring at you with a vacant expression on my face the entire time."

"Yeah, don't do that," Crow said, laughing as he went back to surfing the TV guide. He landed on a show about first time house flippers just as a wooden cabinet dislodged from the wall with a loud crack and fell on one of the flippers. No one was hurt and the editing made it pretty funny, so they left it on while they went back to working out.

He turned around to find Ethan staring at him with a blank, vacant expression.

It lasted moments before they both broke into laughs.

"You're crazy," Crow said. Their gazes locked for a moment, their smiles wide and the air between them sparking. Ethan had to look away. If he looked any longer, he would fall down the rabbit hole without a doubt.

They started with the squats, which went fine. Crow and Ethan both pushed themselves, Ethan beginning to feel that pleasant burn in his thighs, both of them starting to get sweaty. It was during the lunges when things started to veer off the expected route. They were doing their lunges in place, but facing each other since that was how they could get the most room. This meant Ethan was forced to take in Crow's flushed face and perfect eyes and that lip bite he did whenever he was pushing himself to keep going past the burn.

Holy fuck, he's really hot.

The last times they had worked out together, they were always joined by Angela or Troy, who were also deep into fitness, so Ethan had other people around to keep his attention from honing in on Crow. Now, Ethan had no one to strike up a conversation with or to pretend to help with their form. Instead, he was lunging while feeling his cock growing between his thighs, held down only by the compression shorts he had on. Although if he kept getting any bigger, he wasn't sure whether the compression shorts would even be enough.

"Alright," he said, "let's do the step-ups." Those involved simply stepping up onto the bench while holding weights in both hands. It couldn't be that sexy, could it?

Of course it was. Anything Crow did was sexy. So *duh*, his muscular thighs flexing every time he stepped up onto the bench was a mouth-watering sight. Plus, it didn't help that he wasn't wearing long shorts either. No, these were *short* shorts.

Ethan had never had so many involuntarily boners before. Part of him wondered if it was because it had been so long since he was intimate with anyone, but a much larger part of him knew it was because the chemistry between him and Crow was off the charts.

His cock gave a rogue throb in his shorts. He glanced down, double-checking to make sure he wasn't sporting any visible bulges. There was definitely a lump in his shorts, but they were dark and it couldn't be discerned from a quick glance. Since there was only one bench, Ethan waited for Crow to finish before he started. They swapped back and forth for the remaining sets, Ethan making sure to keep his mind from wandering down between his legs again. He had to keep it together. He wasn't here to hook up and fall for Crow, as great as that sounded in his dreams. He still needed to work out his own shit before he could even consider going all the way with Crow.

Hell, he had never talked about what he was running from—about Adam—since he had lost him, and he could feel that weight pressing on him every day since. But, as the days on the tour went by, he could feel the story start coming unchained from his heart. He was scared to share it, but he knew it was something that had to be brought up. He knew Crow thought about it too, ever since Jordan almost dragged it out of him. He wasn't sure what came over him, but he had been really close to opening up right there in the rest stop, with the scent of onion rings and French fries filling the air. Crow hadn't brought it up since then, but Jordan wasn't the same toward him. He was never 'cool', as Crow called him, toward Ethan. There was always a cold look or a comment that felt more like a stab than a joke.

They finished up their sets and went on to the next few exercises. The burning sensation in his thighs only increased, which was making him more and more turned on. He had forgotten how much his penis seemed to like leg day. That, mixed with Crow's sweaty body feet away, and Ethan found that he had to cut the session short. He was either going to tear a hole in his shorts or spontaneously come during one of the exercises.

"Can't handle the burn?" Crow teased as he turned the TV off and checked to make sure they weren't leaving anything behind.

"I can. I just saw you looking like you were about to pass out, so I cut it short for your sake."

"Oh, please. I was intimidating you, just admit it. Too much man in one tiny room."

No such thing.

"Mhmm," Ethan said, not paying attention to the ache between his thighs as they walked back through the lobby and toward the elevators. He was going to have to go straight to the bathroom and take care of things.

F uckkkk, I need to jerk off.

Crow couldn't stop thinking about it. More specifically, he couldn't stop thinking about *Ethan's* 'it'. He wasn't sure if Ethan was aware, but the man's shorts were in no way equipped to hide the package he was smuggling between his thighs. Either Doctor Winter carried around extra stethoscopes in his crotch or, more preferably, the guy was blessed.

Crow couldn't make out any details —mainly because he was a decent human being and wasn't going to spend his workout session staring at Ethan's cock outline—but the quick glances he was able to steal had his mouth watering and his own cock twitching. The man was the epitome of everything Crow found attractive and more.

The elevator dinged up to the fifth floor. They got out, about to walk down separate directions when Crow realized he didn't want to stop hanging out with Ethan just yet. He thought quick and said "Oh! Come over and check out that weird foam roller Angela ordered for me."

Ethan smiled, his forehead glistening with beads of

sweat, his cheeks a sexy light pink under the five o'clock shadow. He nodded and started walking toward Crow's room. They headed to the end of the hallway, following the fading floral river set in the beige carpet. Crow grabbed his room key and unlocked the door, holding it open for Ethan. His scent filled Crow's senses as he walked past him and entered the room. It made Crow's dick twitch again. Maybe this massage thing wasn't the greatest idea?

What am I even thinking?

Crow couldn't deny that there was a fiery current of chemistry flowing between them, but he also felt like there was something else that was blocking Ethan from being able to explore it fully. Crow was ready from the very first night they met. He would have taken Ethan home in a heart beat that night at the bar. Even then, he could tell that Ethan Winter was a special man, so unlike the other duds he had dated since he had come out about a year ago. And over the past two weeks, that feeling was only further cemented into Crow's very core. Ethan was interesting on multiple levels, had a sense of humor that Crow couldn't get enough of, and was intelligent and driven. Never once had Crow thought it was possible to stay up all night talking with someone and still have as much—if not, *more*—fun than if they were having sex. They talked about all kinds of things; from wanting to be Jane Goodall as kids (both of them were huge animal lovers) to Crow's conservative parents finding out he and his twin were gay. They never talked much about Ethan though, and Crow was ok with that. He felt like the man would peel away the layers in time.

Right now, though, all Crow cared about was peeling away a different type of layer.

"Mind if I grab a water bottle?"

"Not at all, go for it," Crow said, kicking off his neon green and blue sneakers by the door.

"Thanks," Ethan said, ripping off the price tag and uncapping the bottle of water that was sitting next to the coffee maker. "I'll make sure to pay you back the thousand dollars it costs to drink this."

Crow chuckled, and waved. "Don't worry, this one's on me."

"So generous," Ethan said, balancing on the chipped wooden dresser while he took off his shoes.

"You can sit," Crow said, motioning toward the king sized bed in the center of the room.

"I'm just going to soak the bed in sweat."

That's fine.

"Ok," Crow said. He went to the corner of the room and grabbed the large green foam roller. It was a firm cylinder of foam that had ridges and bumps which felt like little devil hands working out your knots when it was rolled over tense muscles. It hurt *sooo* good, although Crow liked to joke that Angela had ordered him the alien dildo version.

"Look, see," he said, showing it to Ethan.

"It does taper off at the end. That's a little unnerving."

They both laughed. "Seriously, it works really well though. Here, let me try rolling out some of your knots."

Ethan drank some of the water before capping it and going to lay down on the carpeted floor.

"No, no," Crow said, "get on the bed. Who knows what's on that floor." He whacked Ethan on the side with the alien dildo-massager. Ethan playfully winced and fell back on the bed before rolling over onto his stomach on the white bed sheets.

Oh fuck. This was a terrible idea.

Crow could feel his dick swelling in his briefs. Just

seeing Ethan laying down on the bed was enough to drive his hormones into a frenzy. He looked down at Ethan's bare feet and trailed his gaze up, past the muscular calves and the peek of thighs before the shorts covered him up. They weren't able to cover up that butt though. Ethan had it going on with the junk in his trunk. Crow gave it a playful slap with the foam roller as he took a spot standing next to the bed. He leaned over and started off rolling Ethan's lower legs, applying enough pressure to get a reaction from Ethan.

"Ohhh shoot, yeah, that does work—" Crow found a particularly firm knot, "—*shit*, that works really well."

Crow continued working the foam roller over Ethan's legs. With Ethan's head in a pillow, Crow found himself admiring Ethan's strong back, his gray shirt clinging to him in spots where the fabric had gone darker. Crow noticed the back of Ethan's neck was flushing pink, a spot that now looked like a target for Crow's tongue. He was feeling his physical needs start overriding the emotional ones. He wanted to climb onto Ethan and suck at the back of his neck while he rubbed his growing cock against Ethan's firm ass.

Relax.

Crow moved the foam roller up higher, going over the shorts, rolling up to the bottom of Ethan's ass. Ethan groaned as Crow applied more pressure, using the bumps and ridges to really work out some of the tension. He started to wish he could ditch the alien dildo and just use his hands. He'd be more than happy using his fingers to knead into Ethan's meaty thighs.

Fuck it.

Crow had to ask. "Mind if I climb on you for a second, my back's killing me."

"Go for it."

Crow's back was fine, but his balls were aching. He

climbed onto the bed and threw one leg over Ethan and kept the other planted on the opposite side. He sat down on Ethan's firm butt, drawing out what sounded like an involuntary moan. It was a good thing Ethan's face was buried in the pillows because Crow did not want him to see how red his face got. He glanced at the mirror on the closet door. He was both red from the gym and from the fact that he was now straddling the man of his dreams. All Ethan had to do was lift his head up and look toward the mirror to see the massive bulge Crow was sporting in his shorts. The thin black fabric was holding back a throbbing erection that was completely obvious. He had to simmer down before he finished up the massage, because his shorts were about to tear open and he wasn't sure how Ethan would feel about that kind of massage.

"Oh *fuccckk*," Ethan groaned into the pillow, "right there."

Crow used the foam roller to go over Ethan's lower back, climbing up to his broad shoulders before rolling back down. If he moved his hips even a little lower, he was sure Ethan would feel how hard he was. He controlled himself though, unsure if Ethan was on the same level as him or not.

"Is it alright if you switch to your hands?"

Fuck no, I thought you'd never ask.

Crow contained himself, saying instead; "It'll cost extra."

"Just add it to my room bill."

"You got it," Crow said, the smile apparent in his voice. He leaned over and set the foam roller on the floor. The move inadvertently rubbed Crow's erect cock against Ethan's ass as he repositioned himself. It felt beyond-words kind of good, but it also sent a pang of nerves course through Crow. He had no idea why he was reacting so powerfully toward Ethan, and he also had no idea if the connection was reciprocated. He wanted more, so much more, and that required opening himself up to the possibility of rejection. Ethan could want nothing more than a friend, and maybe this was all incredibly out of bounds. Maybe Crow shouldn't be running his hands slow and hard over Ethan's lower back. Maybe his hands shouldn't slide under Ethan's shirt, rubbing over the soft, moist skin, feeling the hard knots and tangles of muscle. Maybe his hands shouldn't climb higher, reaching Ethan's shoulders, slowly, softly, applying more pressure.

Fuck the maybes. This was meant to be.

Crow could feel it deep down, this moment was supposed to happen and it was supposed to be with Ethan. He couldn't tell why or how this had even come to pass, but he was ready to explore it and he needed to know if Ethan was too.

"Ethan," Crow said, his voice soft.

"Let me turn over."

His request was surprising, but completely welcome. Crow climbed off Ethan. Ethan rolled onto his side and pulled his shirt off, revealing a picturesque sight of a rippling back, turning over fully to show off his sexy as sin chest, covered in a light dusting of dark hair that immediately had Crow's mouth watering.

And then Crow's eyes drifted lower, past the happy trail, and almost fell out of his skull in surprise. Ethan was rock hard, his cock throbbing against his shorts, creating a visible tent that had Crow going weak in the knees. He almost forgot what they had been doing in the first place. His mind went blank, honing in on the slab of man meat that had been laid out before him. Nothing else was processing. Luckily, he found himself seconds before his frozen-self became awkward. He licked his lips, subconsciously, and started massaging Ethan's forearm, trying hard not to drool on the man.

"Mhmm," Ethan groaned, his eyes shut as his body became jello in Crow's hands. He moved from one arm to the other, moving to the chest, squeezing and kneading and working harder and harder, encouraged by the groans of pleasure. All the while, both of them harder than steel. Crow was ready to tear his shorts off, the pressure almost becoming too intense to bear.

All he could see was lust. Crow stopped massaging Ethan and climbed onto the bed again. He moved so that he could straddle Ethan who still kept his eyes shut as Crow tightened his thighs around him. Crow lowered himself, angling his hips so that both of their hard dicks rubbed over the other through the thin gym shorts, their heat rolling off each other in waves. He leaned down lower, lower. Their faces inches apart. Crow moved in, their lips meeting once again, and once again, their connection exploding a hundred fold. He could physically feel something stir inside him. Crow had never had a kiss like the one he shared with Ethan, and it wasn't just one kiss either. The kiss at the bar felt the same way. Two for two.

Ethan's hands came up to grip Crow's hips as he pushed his upward, rubbing his cock harder against Crow's. Crow moaned into Ethan's mouth as their tongues displayed their unbridled passion. Crow could feel Ethan's stubble on his face, and he fucking loved it. Just as much as he loved feeling Ethan's fingers dig into his sides, making him gyrate harder down onto him.

Crow was ready to go all the way. He knew he'd never be able to explain it, but there was something in that moment that told him Ethan Winter was a man who he wasn't supposed to let get away.

Ethan's hands moved from Crow's hips, sliding under the waistband of his shorts, and then squeezing on Crow's ass, pulling him down even harder, their kiss becoming all the more consuming, the heat in the small hotel room ready to set fire to the thin white curtains. Crow groaned in pleasure as Ethan slipped a finger between his cheeks, feeling himself pulse harder in his shorts. He had to take them off. He needed to feel skin on skin. Cock on cock.

Crow reached down and tugged at his shorts. Ethan continued squeezing his ass, smiling as he looked up into Crow's eyes. That was it. The moment the both of them understood that this went far beyond a simple hook-up in a crummy hotel room. Way past a three-month cross country tour. This was something that neither of them could fully comprehend but both of them could fully respect. In that moment, they knew they were tied together for a very, very long time.

That was also when two loud knocks froze them both in their horned up tracks.

(End of Chapter)

(who is knocking at Ethan and Crow's hotel room door?) —The story continues

(finished)

12 ETHAN WINTER

"Crow?" Angela's voice came from the other side of the locked door. She sounded stressed, although Ethan had come to learn that 'stressed' was her normal operating emotion. Some people seemed like they strived under stress, although Ethan found that to be rare. Stress was never good on the body.

What *was* good on the body, though? An incredibly handsome, charming, sweet, and half-naked man. Crow looked down at him, his light brown eyes glittering like a mischievous teen. He put a finger to Ethan's lips as his curled into a smile.

"Crow, come on. I know you're in there," she persisted. "Jordan told me he saw you coming this way."

She knocked three more times, each one harder than the last.

"It sounds important," Ethan whispered past the finger.

Crow gave an adorably sexy roll of his eyes as he got off of Ethan. The weight of Crow's body on his was immediately missed. It made Ethan realize how good things had been and how good things seemed to be about to get. Crow was able to transport him with a kiss alone. Throw in fondling and erections, and Ethan was ready to knock down all the walls.

The knocks had thrown him back to reality, though. Crow stood up, adjusting himself so that his excitement wasn't on full display. Ethan grabbed his shirt and tugged it on, moving to sit at the edge of the bed. He pulled out his phone and tried to act as if he wasn't just about to be sucked off by Crow.

"Jesus," Ethan could hear her say. "Crow, I can't have you playing hide-and-seek right now."

"Is everything ok?" Crow's voice was immediately tense. Ethan perked up. They had talked about the weird notes and had laughed it off as a harmless teen or an immature troll. Crow had admitted that the messages had spooked him, but he had said having Ethan around was a sort of comfort he wasn't expecting to have. He said it was "cuz you feel so much like home. I'm not saying I think you're my bodyguard or anything. You just make me feel... comfortable. Safe."

Ethan had gone to sleep that night feeling the happiest he'd been in a while. He had forgotten how much pleasure he got from making others feel safe.

"Mind if I come in?" Angela

"Of course," Crow said, stepping aside. Ethan looked to the side, toward the entrance. Angela gave a mini-jump on recognizing that there was someone else in the room. She gave a curt smile and then a glance toward Crow.

"Sorry," Ethan said, instantly feeling like he was out of place. Angela must have had something she wanted to talk to Crow in private about.

"No, that's ok," Angela said, seeming to course-correct herself. She shook her shoulders and gave a little exhale.

The exhaustion of managing a tour was starting to show in the darkening bags under her eyes, and they weren't even to the half-way point yet. She was still killing it in the fashion department though, wearing a navy romper with a few artfully placed floral prints. He had to give it to her. Ethan was reminded of his medical school days, when time was short and his lack of fucks given towards his appearance were plentiful. He would go a few weeks without shaving and had a pair of lucky jeans that were rarely put to rest. He spent most of his time in scrubs anyway, so it didn't matter too much, but he definitely admired someone who was still able to keep it together when the pressure was on.

"I have an appointment with Troy in a few minutes, anyway. I should get going."

That was a lie. He didn't have to see Troy for another couple of hours, but he felt like going to his own room was the best option at that point. Angela was clearly still resisting sharing whatever she had come over to talk about, and the moment between him and Crow was gone. He got up and started toward the door. Crow stood by, tossing the water bottle in the air.

"I changed my mind. You do owe me, now," he said, clearly talking about more than the water bottle.

"We'll have to work something out. A payment plan."

Ethan grabbed the water bottle out of the air and walked by Crow with a wide smile. He had to stop himself from forgetting about the water and just grabbing Crow's face right there and then for a goodbye kiss. That would have *definitely* complicated things way past what either of them needed right then. Angela seemed to have some kind of news that was going to affect Crow, and so Ethan was just going to leave and make things as simple as possible.

He started down the hallway, looking at the generic

dark black frames hanging with generic flower photos taken by someone in their second year of photography school. He tried to distract himself, but it wasn't working. His mind was reeling, except it wasn't all about Crow. He felt like he was walking on a cloud, and, in one quick second, that feeling completely disappeared and was replaced by a resounding sadness. One left behind by a loss so deep, Ethan was still coping with it.

Adam. He felt guilty for being that happy. The therapist had said it was important to allow himself to feel those things, to not harbor the guilt, but it was useless. Whatever the doctor told him would go in one ear and out the hole left in his chest. How could he be allowed to be happy when every moment was a thought of 'oh, Adam would have loved this,' or 'me and Adam would be laughing about this for days,' or, 'Adam and I are never going to forget this day'.

Except Adam was gone. And it was all because of Ethan.

"Umpf."

Ethan hadn't even realized someone opened their room door. He didn't notice until he was walking right into the guy, who also was apparently in a world of his own and striding out of his room like nothing was going to stop him.

"Shit. Sorry, Jordan."

Ethan wasn't in the mood to make pleasantries. He had quickly soured from the moment he left Crow's to the second he bumped into Jordan. Two entirely different moods, and the one he was currently in was considerably more antagonistic. He went to keep on walking, but Jordan seemed to have different plans. He reached out and grabbed Ethan by the forearm. It wasn't a hard grab, but it was definitely obtrusive. Ethan pulled back and stopped.

"So, you and Crow, huh?" Jordan's expression was

suggestive. "I've noticed you two over the past couple of weeks. You guys really connect."

Ethan's brows furrowed. "I'm not in the mood right now, Jordan." It was true, Ethan didn't want to stand in a badly-lit hallway with Jordan's whiskey breath wafting in his direction.

"I just want to help," Jordan said, his expression morphing. He curled a corner of his mouth, narrowing his eyes. "I'm just saying, it's no secret I've had a crush on the guy for a while, but I think I'm over it, now. I think playing matchmaker between you two will really help nail that coffin shut."

"I don't need a matchmaker," Ethan said, feeling unreasonably testy. From the sounds of it, Jordan wanted to help, but Ethan wasn't having it.

"I get it. It's weird hearing this from me, but I'm serious, I just want to help. I see the way he looks at you on the bus, the way he sings his songs toward you when he's performing. The kid's fucking *smitten*. And you're not far behind, except... I do feel something holding you back. That's why I was so forward at that rest stop, I wanted you to just let it all out."

Ethan wasn't sure if he could entirely believe what Jordan was saying. At the time, it had felt like Jordan was poking and prodding at Ethan so that he could crack in front of Crow. He remembered the look Jordan had given him from across the table. It was the look of a dog getting nervous that something bigger, more intimidating, was moving in on its territory. "I'm just ready to get back to my room and shower," Ethan said, hoping he could end this.

"Wow, you and Crow must have gotten busy in that room."

"Huh?"

"You two, I saw the both of you scurrying off to his room out of the elevator."

Ethan nodded, wondering how rude it would be if he said goodbye and just turned and started walking. Thankfully, he didn't have to find out because Jordan cut things off for the both of them.

"Ok," he said, clapping his hands. He looked like he was going outside to spend time by the pool. "Well, if you reconsider, I'm here for some advice. I know he really likes the color blue and he has a weird thing for teacup pigs."

That last bit actually got a chuckle from Ethan. It was one of those things that made you think 'Of course Crow likes tiny pigs'.

"Thanks, Jordan," he said, turning to walk the few more feet toward his room.

He really likes the color blue...

HE TURNED THE SHOWER ON, setting the temperature knob to the farthest it would go. He waited naked outside the shower until steam started to fog up the glass door. He reached in and lowered the setting, making the water a little cooler. He stepped in and let the hot water fall down on his back, feeling a good kind of sore from the massage. He washed his hair, feeling the warmth engulf from, letting the steam coat him. He felt good, safe.

He started to cry.

Ethan rarely cried. He felt as though he could count the times he had cried on two hands. These weren't the kind of tears that came from a sad movie or a minor disappointment. These tears meant serious business. They were evacuating the emptiness that had formed inside him, consuming him over the past years. He kept picturing Adam smiling, beaming. His face lit like the sun during the midday afternoon. So bright and happy, and why wouldn't he be? It was their wedding day. They were set to spend the rest of their lives together, for better, for worse, for richer, for poorer, in sickness and in health.

Until death do they part.

13 CROW KENSWORTH

THREE DAYS LATER

(finished)

The tour bus was parked in an almost empty theatre parking lot. Crow looked out at the window, watching the security guards Angela hired turn away a few disappointed looking fans. He wished he could run out and gave them a surprise appearance, but Angela had them currently meeting for something she said was 'incredibly important'. She had texted the entire crew about fifteen minutes ago, asking for them all to gather at the table. Crow stayed on the couch until he saw Ethan come out from the bathroom and take a seat at the table. That was Crow's cue. He got up and grabbed the empty seat next to Ethan.

It had been an excruciatingly long three days, prior. Every waking second, Crow felt like he spent thinking about Ethan's body under his. He couldn't get the thought of them together out of his head. He walked around with a permanent chub between his legs, which had to be taken care of multiple times a day, triggered by rampant fantasies of the two men rolling around naked with each other. Crow would have considered trying something again, but they had checked out of the hotel that same day and were on the road a few hours later, making it harder to find alone time together. Crow felt awkward asking Ethan to his room while everyone sat around on the bus, knowing exactly what was going on. If something was more established between them, he wouldn't have really given a fuck, but since this still was all really new and vulnerable, Crow held off on the bedroom invites.

"Alright, is everyone here?" Angela said, looking around. Ethan was sitting by the window, Crow across from him at the table. Troy was sitting cross-legged on the couch nearby, Caeri playfully resting on his chest, her legs crossed up on the couch. She wasn't opening for Crow at every location since she couldn't travel with them, but she was able to make it to a few and Denver was one of those. Her and Troy having an open relationship seemed to have helped them with their time apart.

"Pretty much," Frankie said, leaning on the marble counter, biting into a bright green apple.

"So what's going on?" Crow asked, getting impatient. Angela never called group meetings like this. The afternoon sun was shining in from between the half-closed window blinds, causing Crow to squint in Angela's direction.

"We have to cancel tonight's show."

An immediate uproar from the group. No one understood where this was suddenly coming from.

"What do you mean we have to cancel the show tonight?" Crow was angry. He could already see the faces of all his disappointed fans, finding out that the show they were all looking forward to was cancelled at the last minute. And they were supposed to leave the next day to make their next stop, so it wasn't like they could rain check the performance. Once it was cancelled, it was done. People were going to be sad and pissed and they were going to blame Crow.

"I'm sorry, Crow, but it's for your own safety." Angela spoke in a tone that told Crow there was no room for negotiations. This was serious. "It was the venue. They called me and told me they had received a threat. Multiple threats."

Crow felt a cold chill crawl down his neck. He shivered it off. "What kind of threats?"

Angela chewed her lips, clearly debating whether it was worth sharing or not. "I don't want to freak you out, Crow. The police are already looking into it, that's what's important."

"Why didn't anyone ask me?" Crow shook his head. "This is my show. My fans. They're going to be crushed. Tonight was sold out. A thousand tickets, all of them worthless."

Angela ran a hand through her shoulder-length brown hair. "I wish there was another option. I really do. But it's out of our hands now."

"The threats. What were they?"

Angela looked out the window. "The venue said they received two calls. The first was to verify you were playing tonight, and the second was to say that no one else except you and them were walking out of there alive."

"Shit," Frankie said, chomping into the crisp green skin.

A FEW HOURS had passed since the bad news broke, and the toxic mood still hung in the air, making the tour bus feel more like a swampy prison than the lux travel home it was, the smog of fear and disappointment dimming the overhead lights and stainless steel accents. Crow was bummed, and he was scared, and he was pissed. He felt like so many people were robbed of a good time all because of one unhinged loon. He understood that it was for the safety of everyone else around, but it still sucked and it made Crow feel *real* shitty.

He was laying down on the couch in his gray sweats and an old college t-shirt, the back of his arm thrown over his eyes, when he felt the other end of the couch sink. He moved his arm and looked to see Ethan sitting there, smiling.

"You're beaming," Crow said, a little sarcastically. In truth, Ethan's wide smile was contagious. It helped put a smile on Crow's face, who moved to sit up on the couch so that Ethan had more room. Ethan was looking much more put together, in a navy shirt and white shorts.

"I am," he said, "and now you are too."

"It's hard not to match that smile of yours." Crow felt his cheeks grow warm. There weren't many people who had the power to make him blush, even if he was in a crummy mood. "What's going on?" Crow asked.

"Well, I know how shitty things have been so I hopped on the internet and found something cool I wanted to do with you today."

Crow arched a playful eyebrow. "The *internet?*" he asked.

Ethan gave him a look and ignored his comment, continuing to talk with that devastating smile of his. "So I need you to get ready. You've got five minutes."

"Five minutes?" Crow got up from the couch, looking down at what he was wearing.

"Fine, I'll give you ten."

"Where are we going?"

"It's a surprise."

"Give me a hint!" Crow called as he ran to the bedroom for some jeans.

"I think you'll like it."

"That's not a hint."

Ethan laughed from the other room. "It's all you're getting."

Crow tossed off his sweats and hopped into a pair of light jeans. He kept his orange and blue university shirt and grabbed a blue LA Dodgers cap that was hanging off a hook on the wall. As he was exiting the bedroom, Angela was walking in from a smoke break.

"What's going on?" she asked, sensing the flurry of activity.

"Ethan's surprising me. Either that or abducting me."

Ethan chuckled and said, "Too soon." Angela didn't seem to find the humor. She crossed her arms, her face flushed from being outside.

"I don't know, Crow," she said, her tone beginning to sound more like an overbearing mother. "With what happened at the ven—"

"That's the thing, Angela, nothing happened at the venue. I get it, the threat was bad and obviously someone wants to freak me out, but I can't let that stop me from actually living my life. Being scared of my own shadow isn't the way to handle this. That just ensures that whoever is sending those weird notes ends up winning in the end, and I don't want that." Crow felt bad. He hadn't raised his voice, but it was clear that he was done talking about the threats. At least for the day. He was going to try and enjoy the rest of his time in Denver, especially since it was Ethan who seemed to be the most excited he'd been in a while. Crow knew it wasn't because the show had been cancelled, so what could he have been so happy about?

Could it be just because we're doing something alone together?

Is this a date?

Holy shit, I think this is a date.

Realization was dawning on him as Angela was shaking her head. She seemed disappointed but what was Crow going to do, especially now that he realized what this was? No way in hell was he going to tell Ethan no.

"Fine, I can't stop you." She stepped aside. Ethan looked between her and Crow. "I'm sending the security with you though."

"Sounds good," Crow said as he walked past. He didn't really care if he had an entire entourage following them. He knew his world was about to funnel in on one person, and one person only.

Ethan Winter.

(finished)

14 ETHAN WINTER

Crow read the words printed out on a big white banner out loud, trying to hold back a laugh, "The Denver Museum of Miniatures, Dolls and Toys." They were standing in front of a two-story colonial type house, a few white columns holding up the green-bricked roof. It looked much more like someone's home than a museum.

Crow loved it.

"Yup," Ethan said. "Excited?"

Crow looked from the white banner to Ethan, who was smiling like a kid on Christmas morning.

"Let's do this," Crow said, clapping his hands together and seeming to catch some of the excitement. Ethan had hated seeing him moping around and upset that his show had been canceled, so being the one to bring that smile back to Crow's face made Ethan's heart flutter a little harder. He also couldn't deny that this entire thing was very 'date-like' and Ethan was finding himself completely ok with that. He was excited to see how it would go, and wasn't as thrown off as he had been when Angela walked in on them. Over the past three days, Ethan had time to sit down and really think about what, or rather who, was holding him back from seeing all the possibilities with Crow in his life. He had to come to a place in his life where he wasn't feeling guilty about feeling happy, and he felt like today was a huge step in the right direction.

A blacked out sedan was parked on the street, two suited men standing outside of it and staring eagle-eyed at the museum, there fists hanging loosely in front of their silver belt buckles. Crow convinced them that they would be ok going in alone. The last thing he wanted was two men in black cock-blocking this, date or not. There was nothing — not even a neauralyzer— that could ever make Crow forget about that kind of missed opportunity. The crisp summer afternoon air was blown away by a rush of cool air-conditioning as Ethan opened the door for Crow. He got a whiff of Crow's scent as he walked by and was suddenly wishing this was a hotel room tour instead of a museum of unintentionally creepy toys tour. Ethan followed Crow in, entering a small lobby of sorts. The room was separated from the rest of the museum by a wall, with doors on either side leading into the museum. In front of the wall was the front desk, where an older woman placed her bookmark and set her book on the table, cover down.

"Welcome!" she said, her white curls bobbing as she greeted them. "Is this your first time visiting us?"

"Yes," Ethan asked, feeling like he wanted to run around the table and give the lady a huge hug. He had really woken up on the right side of the bed that day.

Or, maybe that's just what being with Crow does to me.

"Ooh, fun! Well, we have a collection of more than ten-thousand figurines and toys, some dating back to the 1600s. It's not a large museum, so no maps or anything, but you'll find yourself wanting to get lost amongst those dolls for a while." She smiled, softening the creepy factor of her statement. Ethan was starting to feel like he entered the Twilight Zone.

He was so fucking excited. He loved these weird little finds and he could tell Crow genuinely did too. Things were already off to a great start.

"Thank you," Crow said, pointing to either door. "Choose your own adventure?"

The little lady, Martha, according to her nametag, laughed as though Crow had just performed a killer stand-up set. "Both lead into the same room," she said, when her giggles died down.

"Perfect," Crow said with a wide grin. He looked to Ethan, who gave a tiny shrug. Crow nodded toward the right and started walking. Ethan followed, admiring for a moment how good Crow looked in a simple t-shirt and a pair of nice jeans. He definitely looked the part of a celebrity, with his blue cap tucked low on his head to give him some sort of cover from getting recognized and mobbed by a group of fans. Although, Ethan was pretty positive that most of Crow's fan base wouldn't be in a museum like this in the first place.

As they opened the door to the rest of the museum, Ethan realized that not only were Crow's fans missing, but so was everyone else. It looked like they had the entire museum to themselves.

And, boy, what a museum it was.

Right off the bat, they were greeted by life-sized porcelain dolls with cracked foreheads and chipped fingers, once bright red and blond hair, now faded by the years that passed on by. They were standing in front of a tall, all-glass cabinet that held a menagerie of tiny figurines.

"Holy shit," Crow said. "I love this place."

Ethan laughed, finding that he couldn't look at the dolls for too long before he got that weird tingly feeling down his back. And not the good kind. These were the kind you got when you heard the story about the babysitter asking the parents about the clown statue in their backyard and them answering that they don't own a clown statue.

Oh, you've never heard that story?

You're welcome.

"How did you even find this place?"

"Google," Ethan answered, leaning over a glass display that had caught Crow's attention. There was an extremely intricate and detailed town looking up at them. Ethan admired all the time that must have gone into creating it. From the tiny red bricked houses to the small football stadium outside of the local high school to the octopus man that walked the street.

"Wait, what?" Ethan looked closer. "Do you see that?"

Crow went 'whoa' when he saw the man wearing the suit and also sporting eight octopus tentacles as hands. On closer inspection, there were weird things placed around all over the town. A rainbow cat that was chasing after a duck with horns. A baby pushing a stroller holding his mom. A car with cheese for wheels.

"This is nuts," Crow said, pointing out more things. Ethan loved playing this I-Spy type game, but he loved that he was doing it with Crow more than anything else. This felt good. Laughing and exploring new things, making new memories that Ethan could look back on and smile. He hadn't done that in so long. His heart felt light as they made their way through the museum, his laughs coming easy and his smile never wearing out.

"You know," Crow said as they walked through a doorway and into a room full of toy trains, "I don't think I've seen you smile this much since we've met." Crow looked up from a railroad and locked in on Ethan's eyes. "I really like your smile."

"Thanks," Ethan said, feeling himself flush with warmth. "I don't think I've been this happy for a while now."

Crow gave a toying smirk. "Do trains make you really happy?"

"No, no I don't think it's the trains."

"Oh?"

"Could be the dolls. The porcelain ones."

"Yeah," Crow nodded. "Those do it for me, too."

Ethan chuckled, not even realizing that they had been moving closer to each other, like two planets pulled off track, on a slow but sure gravitational collision course.

"And you," Ethan said, feeling himself opening up on a new level. "You make me happy."

"Good," Crow said. They were inches apart now. "Because you make me really happy."

"More than the porcelain dolls?"

Crow cocked his head, the smirk playing wider. "Just about," he said with a sexy as sin laugh.

Ethan licked his lips. The air between them sparked with feeling. Both of them went in, their lips meeting slow and tender at first. Ethan reacquainted himself with Crow's taste—*fuck*, he missed that taste.

Ethan brought his hands up, encasing Crow's head. He moved up higher, digging his fingers through Crow's hair, gently tugging as the kiss grew deeper, harder, more passionate as their lips parted and their tongues danced. With every soft moan, Ethan felt more of his walls come tumbling down. His body felt like it was floating on a cloud of pure ecstasy, made even sweeter when Crow pushed his body up against Ethan's, making his arousal no secret. Ethan returned the favor, rubbing his hard bulge against Crow's, their tongues sparring, their body heat rising up through the ceiling, filling the tiny room of railroad replicas.

"I've been waiting for this," Crow said during a moment both of them were catching a breath. "I would have waited forever. You're incredible." His voice was low, but hit Ethan like a demolition crew tearing through the husk of an abandoned high-rise, only to build something bigger and better in its place.

"From the second you sat across from me at the bar, I wanted to do this." Ethan licked his lips, looking deep down into Crow's light brown eyes. "I shouldn't have fought it for so long. This bliss."

"It's ok," Crow said. "We all have a history that affects our present. I get it. And I hope that you'll be able to talk about it with me soon."

"I will," Ethan said, meaning it. He'd talk about it right then and there, but before he could spill his guts, voices drifted in from the next room. Now wasn't the time or the place.

Kisses were a different thing, though. It was always the time and place for a kiss, even if a family was walking through the aisles of toys collected from The Great Depression, most likely headed toward the very room they were in.

They kissed again. Lips found it hard to separate, but parted for their tongues. Another low moan from Crow, swallowed greedily by Ethan, right before they separated again. And just in time, too. The family, who seemed to be a little less impressed by the displays than the boys, walked through the door, surprised at bumping into two other people.

"Oh," the mom said, a quaint little thing with a white

shirt and a ruffled pink skirt that almost seemed to be swallowing her in reverse.

"Great museum, huh?" Crow said, smiling toward the family. Ethan cocked his head, feeling something odd in the air. The mother wasn't smiling back. Neither was the dad, who seemed to be pointedly looking in the other direction. Their son, who seemed to be in his early teens and much nicer than either of his parents, waved and nodded before narrowing his eyes.

Ethan realized then how close he was standing to Crow. And their faces were probably flushed, making it obvious that they weren't admiring the train sets.

"Let's go look at the dolls," the mom said, her accent placing her somewhere in the Midwest. She grabbed her son's wrist as though he weren't capable of steering himself out the room.

"Wait, mom, it's Crow!"

"Who?"

"Crow! I listen to his music all the time," the kid's eyes were bright with recognition.

"Well, we'll have to reconsider your choice in music," the dad said, turning and leaving the room, seemingly expecting his family to fall in step behind him. The wife did, but the son was resisting. He pulled his hand from his mother's hawklike grip and walked toward Crow. Ethan looked to his side, seeing Crow smiling but there was also worry in his gaze.

"Mind if I get a selfie?"

"Of course not," Crow said. Ethan glanced at the mother, who was spewing acid from her dilated pupils. He could see her gritting her teeth. "What's your name?" Crow asked.

"Nick," he said, smiling from ear to ear as he pulled out

his phone. Ethan noticed his bright green eyes were starting to well up with tears at the corner. "You're literally one of my heroes. Like the top of the list. Especially your new songs. They really hit home for me."

"Really? Thank you," Crow said, bending down so that they could be on the same level for the photo. With a few snapped, and the phone put away, Crow placed his hands on Nick's shoulders and looked deep into his eyes.

"Nick, you say I'm your hero, but I want you to know that you're mine. It gets better, ok, buddy? I can see what's going on, and it's going to suck for a while, but you're one strong kid. It's *so* obvious to me. You're meant for big things, and you're going to get past this."

"Nicholas, let's go."

"You got it?" Crow asked, ignoring the mother, who seemed to be getting redder and redder.

"Thank you," Nick said, the tears overflowing and running down his cheek.

"Here, have my number. If you ever need anything or feel like things are getting too tough, give me a call." Crow typed in his number in Nick's cell, handing it back to him. "Or just shoot me a text, maybe I can make it out to your graduation. Give a mini-performance."

"That would be insane." Nick smiled, his tears rubbed away. Ethan could see the pain. It was the same kind he felt when he was a young kid, hiding deep in the closet, afraid that one wrong flick of the wrist, or one little misplaced lisp would give it all away. The house of cards built around such a fundamental lie would come tumbling down. That was way too much pressure to put on any teenager. During an age when life should be the most carefree it could, before the hands of time start striking back, reminding you that there's no such thing as invincibility.

Too much pressure.

Crow said goodbye to Nick and they watched as he walked back, his shoulders held higher and his back straighter as he walked past his mom's furious whispers.

"Fuck," Ethan said when they were out of earshot. "Poor kid."

"Broke my heart. I could see it, right off the bat. He looked so much older than he actually was, and that comes from having to hide who you are *every. damn. day.* And then he brought up my new songs and what they meant to him and I knew for sure that he was closeted."

That was something Ethan had realized after maybe the second night of watching Crow perform. Before then, he had gotten so swept up in the talent and emotion filling the room, he honestly didn't even listen to the lyrics very closely. But when he had, he realized exactly what Crow was doing. He wasn't just singing pop songs with empty calories, meaning nothing at the end of the day except a catchy beat. Crow sang about the boy sitting across from him at the coffee shop, meeting him and rolling on the clouds afterward, a thinly veiled euphemism for romping around on pristine white sheets, sun streaming in from everywhere and lighting the scene like a dream. Crow never once sang about falling for a girl or the trappings that come with that. He was openly out and singing about it, and that gave a voice to an entirely new generation of LGBTQ kids that needed Crow like never before. In an age when bullying was as easy as typing out one-hundred and forty characters and hitting the blue 'tweet' button, Crow's voice had to prove stronger. And it was. Ethan saw it in that room, in the difference between the Nick who had walked in from the Nick who had walked out.

The Nick who walked in wasn't sure, wasn't seeing a bright future.

The Nick who walked out was filled with hope. He saw a future where he could take his boyfriend to a weird museum and enjoy the day, his disapproving parents nowhere in sight.

End of chapter

15 CROW KENSWORTH

The experience with Nick did equal works to both lower and lift Crow's spirits. He hated seeing the turmoil that raged inside the boy who just wanted to live without being judged, all while being able to love. Why was that so damn hard for people to understand? For *family* to understand? He hoped that he was able to give Nick some kind of look into what was possible for him. He wished he could do more. It hurt to know that his life wasn't going to change in the blink of an eye. His parents were still going to be terribly close-minded and potentially heartless while he struggled to find himself.

He looked to Ethan, the man who had the sapphire blue eyes capable of hypnotizing Crow on the spot. He found comfort in those eyes. A feeling of warmth that went beyond simply physical. He felt like he was finding his way back home, after years spent sleeping in empty hotel rooms. It was difficult to describe, but Crow didn't need to. He didn't care about putting names to the feelings, not yet. That would come later, when he was sitting in front of his laptop, typing away the lyrics to his next song.

"You changed that kid's life, you know?" Ethan said, his tone low as their faces drew back together. "You really are a hero."

"You're the one that literally saves lives." Crow bit his lower lip.

"You do too." Ethan pushed in, crossing the final inches between them, instantly filling Crow's body with a flood of ecstasy. Everything felt right when he was kissing Ethan. Fuck that, it all felt more than right. This was how it was all supposed to feel. He had been writing about love for a while, but never truly understood the kind of power a connection between two people can have.

He was quickly discovering that power. He had felt it the moment he laid eyes on Ethan, and it was only growing stronger and stronger by the second. He didn't care that Ethan still had things he was holding back on. He understood that people unraveled slowly. That was fine. As long as it was Crow he was doing the unraveling for, then everything was fucking perfect.

Crow broke the kiss for a moment, catching his breath. He looked into Ethan's eyes, feeling his heart skip a beat. "Let's go find somewhere less... uhh..."

"Sexual?"

Crow snorted. "Yes. *Much* less sexual. All these train tracks are really setting me off."

"Ah, so that's what it was."

"Yup," Crow smirked, unable to stop himself from stealing one last quick kiss. "That's all it was."

───────

THE MUSEUM HAD BEEN RANDOMLY TUCKED AWAY on a residential street, so they decided to hop in the car and explore the area a little bit further. To their surprise, just a few streets down, they saw a sign advertising the Denver Museum of Nature and Science. They both read the sign and looked at each other, grinning. Ethan drove the rental through the tree-lined streets, the security guard driving behind them, following the signs for the museum. Crow lowered the window, letting the cool summer air blow in, bringing with it the fresh scent of the trees and mountains that surrounded them. Denver had such a different feel than what he was used to back in Los Angeles. Things were much less rushed, for one. But things were also greener, more colorful. Trees were bright red and green and purple. They were on the tail end of spring, early summer, so everything still felt so fresh with life.

Not to mention, Crow had the best driver around. He couldn't help himself. He reached across the gear-shift and grabbed Ethan's hand. He twined his fingers through Ethan's, feeling that soft warmth rush over him, mixing with the cool breeze as he kept his gaze out toward the tall mountains in the distance.

"I lost someone," Ethan said as the car came to a stop at a red light. The words seemed so catastrophically different compared to the idyllic town that surrounded them. Crow looked to Ethan, his eyes wide. People crossed the front of the car, carrying cute little shopping bags from the tiny shops that lined the street. None of them aware of the pain feet away from them. The pain that was clear in Ethan's tense voice.

"Is that what you said you were running from?"

Ethan nodded. The light turned green. His eyes were pinned forward, Crow's on Ethan.

"Adam, my husband."

Crow felt himself give a sharp inhale, although he

hadn't even realized he needed to breath. He felt frozen. Unsure of what to say or do. He was still holding Ethan's hand, so he squeezed tighter. He had no idea what Ethan was holding, but he could feel that it weighed him down a great deal.

"We were married for a month before he was ripped away from me. And it was my fault."

"How?" Crow could feel emotions well up in his chest. This was not what he was expecting Ethan to talk about. He couldn't have seen this coming from feet away.

"Car accident. He was on his way to come see me present some dumb research thing. I guilted him into coming. He was feeling sick, he wanted to stay home. I wanted my new husband around me twenty-four seven. I wanted to hold his hand while my colleagues all stood around and discussed microsurgery and cellular reconstruction. I promised I'd make him his favorite chicken soup when we got home." Ethan shook his head. "I would have made it for him regardless. Fuck."

"Jesus..." Crow was at a loss. He couldn't even imagine the pain Ethan must have felt, and the scars something like that must have left. No wonder he had been so closed off. Crow wasn't sure how he would be able to recuperate from a loss like that.

"We had just come back from our honeymoon, too. A month before the accident, we were relaxing on the beaches of Santorini. Now, I'm starting to forget his voice. How fucked up is that?"

Santorini... that must have been why he freaked out back at the rest stop.

Fuck.

Crow squeezed Ethan's hand tighter as his heart strings thrummed harder. He saw a streak of sadness run down

Ethan's stubbled cheek. A tear's trail. "*Accident.* You said it yourself, it was a terrible accident, but it wasn't your fault in any way, shape, or form. Maybe he was going to go surprise you regardless of you pushing him to go there. You never know and you can't hold onto that." Crow took a deep breath and let it go. He rubbed his thumb over Ethan's hand, the slightly rough skin feeling familiar. "When one of my close friends passed a few years ago, I noticed the voice was the first thing to go. No matter how hard I tried to hold on, it just took on a sort of airy quality. Dreamlike. But you know what? I'll never forget Jeanie's smile. The way she lit up a room with a simple hello. She was a force and she had such a huge heart, that's what I won't forget. And I know there are things about Adam that you'll never forget either."

Ethan nodded, a thin smile working onto his face. He pulled into a parking spot, putting the car in park. Crow's phone buzzed in his pocket but he ignored it, this moment far too important. Ethan looked up from his hand in Crow's, meeting Crow's gaze. Crow felt the connection between them dig in deeper, the roots spreading out like a vast net encapsulating his entire being.

"I'm sorry for dumping this all on you now," Ethan said. He bit his lower lip, his brows scrunching together, as though he were regretting his words.

"Are you kidding? There's no need to apologize. None. This is what I'm here for. I want you to open up to me, I want you to share your pain with me. And your happiness. And everything damn-else in between." Crow was smiling now, matching Ethan's.

"I've just been so caught up in the pain. Guilt. I was fucked up for a while after that." Ethan swallowed. "From one day to the next, that was it. Such a bright, strong soul snuffed out. I felt like he had so much more to offer the world. He would have wanted to keep going."

"He also would have wanted for you to be happy." Crow felt words bubble up, as though he were writing a song. They flowed through him, on the river of emotion that connected the two men. "I never met him, but I can see him through the way you speak, and it paints a picture of a kind man who was full of love and compassion. A man who wouldn't want you to wallow in guilt and remorse longer than seconds."

"You're right," Ethan sat up a little straighter. "One-hundred percent. I was doing the exact opposite of what he would want me to do, and I didn't realize that until I stepped onto this tour bus with you. I thought I had been incapable of feeling a spark again. Castrated from ever connecting. But not with you. Everything was so easy, and I was reminded that I still have the ability to love and be loved. I just want to be happy again. And I am. You helped me find that happiness."

Crow felt Ethan's words plant themselves deep in his soul. He felt the air between them spark again, a precursor to another kiss that was sure to shatter their worlds. A kiss to seal their fates.

Knuckles rapped against the driver's side window, startling both of them and causing them to jump back into their respective seats.

Who the?

16 ETHAN WINTER

than looked out the window, surprised to see one of the security guards standing with his arms crossed, looking like an annoyed police officer busting two naughty teenagers. Ethan lowered the window, the fresh breeze carrying in through the car.

"Angela says we need to go. She said she tried calling you both but no one was answering."

Ethan could hear Crow give a sigh next to him. Ethan's mind immediately went to the stalker. He was slowly becoming more and more concerned with the stalker over the past few days. At first, Ethan thought that time would sort them out. Trolls get bored, the letters would stop. But now, venues were getting cancelled and Angela was moving them around ahead of schedule. Things felt off, and Ethan didn't like that. Especially not now, when he was finally finding his happiness again. He didn't need another threat to something he had an incredibly hard time of finding.

"Is everything ok?" Ethan asked.

The security guard nodded. "Sounds like it. She didn't

give me too much detail. Just wanted us to get back to the bus ASAP."

"Ok, thanks for letting us know," Ethan said. The guard left back to the blacked-out sedan, who had parked on the row of cars behind theirs. Crow looked worried, but not as worried as Ethan felt.

"She's probably overreacting," Crow said with a tired exhale. "The other day, when she kicked you out of my hotel room, I thought she was going to tell me something deathly serious with the way she looked. Instead, she talks about some lighting mix-up at the last night's performance."

Ethan wasn't so sure this was an overreaction. The security guards even seemed edgy, and that wasn't like them. His anxiety was bubbling up but he was determined not to show it. He had to keep calm, just like he would at Sierra View when he was handling a difficult case. He knew that sensing any kind of fear usually multiplied that fear tenfold.

"I guess we'll have to come back some other time," Crow said as Ethan pulled out of the parking lot. "Thank you for taking me to the first museum. Honestly, that was more than perfect."

Ethan gave a chuckle. It was him who reached for Crow's hand this time. He couldn't remember a time when he had initiated something like that with Crow. But after opening up about Adam and getting to talk to Crow about him, things felt different. Not only was there a weight lifted, but there was a space opened. "I'm glad I was able to finally say it all. I didn't want to feel like I was hiding something from you."

"Not at all," Crow said. "I understood that whatever it was, it was hard. I respected that."

"That's another thing about you," Ethan said. "Your

maturity level is a lot higher than what I would imagine a twenty-six-year-old pop star would have."

"And your maturity level is exactly what I expect a thirty..."

"Three."

"A thirty-three-year-old doctor would have." Crow laughed, spreading it on to Ethan. They continued talking the entire drive back to the tour bus, laughing random things and joking about others.

Aside from talking, they never stopped holding hands either.

"REMIND me why anyone here even has a cellphone?" Angela was clearly upset, and rightfully so. Apparently, there was a third threat and this one was more serious than the others. Ethan understood why her normally pale face was an off-shade of cherry red as she paced the tour bus, unable to sit down at the table with everyone else. There was room, especially now that Crow was sitting with his back against Ethan on the booth, Ethan's arm draped across Crow's shoulder.

This was the first time either of them showed any kind of physical connection in front of the group. Jordan's glares didn't go unnoticed, while Tony and Frankie both gave approving eyebrow raises toward the two. Ethan didn't care what anyone else thought, he was happy to have Crow in his arms.

"Sorry," Crow said, sounding sincere. Angela didn't meet his eyes, instead she looked at a letter in her hands. It was the first time Ethan noticed she was trembling.

"This came in an hour ago."

The bus rattled slightly as the driver kicked it into a higher gear while he entered the highway. The letter was handed to Crow, Angela's eyes pinned to the crumpled piece of paper.

Crow began reading it out loud, while Ethan read over his shoulder. Immediately, he felt the creeps. The font was in bright red, the grammar was atrocious, and the capitalization was all over the place, starting things right off the bat with an unnerving fear.

"Dear Crow, you'RE PeRFORMancEs have ALL been GreAT so FAR. Seriously., LOVE them. As much as I LOVe yoU!. U complete Me. So, I WAS obvioulSlY Upset when I Heard TONIGhts been CANCELLED."

Ethan had to look away. He couldn't keep trying to read the letter, so he listened to Crow instead.

"I was so upset, I made it all the way to your tour bus and I was so close to just talking to you and opening up and letting it all hang out, when... well, I saw you leave with a man. You both looked so happy. So fucking happy. Heartbroken. I watched you both leave, crying the entire time. I'm leaving this letter to let you know how heartbroken I am, and how I need you to stop hurting me. Please. I can't. You won't want to keep hurting me."

Ethan felt Crow shiver against him. He held onto him a little tighter, hoping the added pressure and body warmth would help soothe some of the anxiety he was sure to be feeling. This was no joke, and now Ethan felt like the crosshairs had grown double the size.

"No one saw anyone leave this?" Crow asked.

"The security guards were off with you two," Angela said, her hand covering her face. "I called the cops, but again, they said there's nothing they can do. One even said 'ma'am, we aren't CSI, we don't have fancy light-up machines,' fucking bitch."

Crow exhaled. Frankie and Troy were both looking at the letter on the table as though someone had let go of a live python. Jordan drank his vodka tonic, shaking his head almost imperceptibly. The entire mood was nervous and fucked up. This wasn't supposed to be how Crow's first national tour went.

Ethan clapped his hands around Crow, surprising everyone. "OK, we know someone is a little batty out there, but right now, there's nothing we can do about it. Absolutely nothing. I'll pay for added security at the rest of the venu—"

"No you're not," Crow said, cutting him off.

"Yes, yes I am."

"That's crazy, I'm not letting —"

"Don't worry, consider it going toward my bill. The one with the bottle of water I drank in your hotel room."

That got a laugh out of Crow. A big one. And everyone knows, when Crow laughs, the rest of the room laughs along with him. The shell of fear and anxiety that had been encasing them seemed to have cracked in that moment. Exactly what Ethan wanted to see happen.

"Anyway," Ethan continued. "I say we play some poker. Get our minds off things. It's still only seven, we're going to be on the road until tomorrow morning."

"Let's do it," Frankie said, slapping his hands on the table. "But none of that stripping bullshit. I'm tired of showing off my beer gut. I know it turns you fuckers on." He got up with a laugh and walked toward the cabinets, opening up the one with the stack of board games and card games. He pulled out the box of cards and walked back, throwing it down on the center of the table.

(End of Chapter)

17 CROW KENSWORTH

Crow was still feeling slightly shaken, but Ethan's idea of playing cards and getting their minds off it helped keep Crow calm. It also helped that Ethan and Crow were sitting shoulder to shoulder for the entire game, their thighs pressed together under the table, their feet bumping against each other at random intervals. Each time, Crow could feel a spark that would light up and clear away some of the fog of fear the note had left. It helped that they were on the road and heading to a brand new city. Maybe whoever the crazy fan was didn't have enough money to follow him from city to city. Maybe now that they saw he was with Ethan, they'll slowly start getting over Crow. That letter could have been a sort of purging of their emotions, that way they can start off on a new slate.

Jeez, I hope that's what happened.

Ethan yawned and stretched. A bump in the road sent his stack of red and black chips tumbling down, scattering across the table. They weren't playing with real money so Ethan shrugged and looked at his watch. "You boys can keep those, I think I'm going to take a quick shower and head to bed."

Crow felt a quick bolt of disappointment. It was only twelve, Crow was good for at least another four hours. He could spend the rest of the night just talking with Ethan. Not only did he love it, but he was still also on a slight adrenaline rush from that damn letter, meaning sleep was going to be hard to come by.

"S'ok, I'm clocking out, too." Troy stood up, stretching, his white t-shirt hiking up and showing a twisted scar on his hip. Frankie followed suit, throwing his hand of cards onto the table. It looked like everyone was calling it an early night by Crow's standard.

Damn it.

"Guys, please, I'm trying to sleep," Angela said from behind one of the heavy dark black curtains that separated the bunk beds from the rest of the tour bus. She had gone to bed pretty much as soon as they started playing, although she handled the boisterous noise pretty well until the last half hour or so when she made everyone drop down to whispers.

Crow slid out of the booth and let Ethan out. He went to the couch and flopped down, still not sure what he wanted to do. Except he was sure he didn't want to go to bed.

Maybe I can write.

He sat up and reached for the navy blue spiral notebook resting on the couch's armrest. He had been writing earlier in the day and had left the notebook on the couch with the pen tucked into the page he left off on. He went in and focused on the words, feeling the beat and hearing the flow in his head. He experimented with different phrases, swapped a few anchoring words around, changed up the rhyming structure a little.

He almost had it. He felt it running through him like a river.

And then he heard the door to the bathroom open. He looked up, on reflex, and saw a sight that made his mind go blank. Song structure was out the window. Rhymes were nonexistent. All he could think about was the perfect specimen of man that stood before him, lit from the side by the white bathroom light, the light playing off the beads of water that clung to hair on his chest, drops that fell off his flat stomach, down his dark happy trail, water sliding down the v-lines of his hips, holding up a precariously low white towel.

The sexy bastard grinned at Crow before reaching around and grabbing the stack of clothes he had left outside the bathroom. He went back in and closed the door, leaving Crow with his jaw cracked open and his boxer briefs feeling way too tight. Ethan was so damn perfect. He wasn't overly built like some of the obnoxious models he had dated in the past, nor was he a slob who let his body go downhill. He kept himself manscaped and fit and was entirely attractive. From his toes to those sapphire blue eyes, the man had it all and Crow wanted it.

He closed the notebook and set it aside. His ability to write songs was completely annihilated by the fact that all the blood was no longer rushing to the right head (the more literary one). He waited a few more minutes until he heard the door to the bathroom open again. Like it was a cue he had been trained to expect, Crow got up from the couch and walked straight to the bathroom. Ethan looked at him, seeming a little surprised at the conviction Crow was coming at him with. Crow didn't care. He grabbed Ethan by the hand and walked him past the drawn black curtains, straight toward his bedroom door. He pulled him in and shut the door behind them, dimming the lights before turning around and grabbing Ethan by the baggy blue sleeping shirt he had thrown on. He pulled him in, their lips crashing together in a display of unbridled passion. Crow moaned as Ethan parted his lips with his tongue, their kiss evolving into something deeper. Crow's hands glided over Ethan's back, pulling and kneading and tugging. Ethan's hands fell down to Crow's hips. Crow was wearing a pair of light blue gym shorts, which were quickly dropped by Ethan's hands, falling down to his ankles and revealing a bulging pair of gray briefs. Ethan's hand glided over Crow's hardening cock, squeezing through the thin fabric and drawing out another moan from Crow. He broke from the kiss and let his head fall back as Ethan palmed him harder, making the fire in his gut explode outward, consuming his entire body.

He wanted Ethan's skin on his. All of him. He had to get rid of these clothes. It felt like he was wearing a straight-jacket. He wanted Ethan that bad.

"*Fuck*, I want you," Crow said, putting his desires into low, husky words.

Crow pushed Ethan back onto the springy bed. He bounced slightly, a naughty grin playing on his chiseled face as he bit on his lower lip. Crow's knees always went weak whenever Ethan played with his lips. His jawline was perfectly squared and highlighted by the overhead lighting, set on a dim level. Crow licked his lips before climbing onto the bed, arms on either side of Ethan as he crawled his way up toward his face. He was finding that he couldn't get enough of Ethan's face. Of his lips. His tongue.

He had to taste him again. Immediately, one hand went to grab at Ethan's short hair while his left arm held him up. He picked Ethan's head up and brought him in for a possessive kiss that sent a message through the both of them. Crow felt Ethan's cock respond underneath him, jerking up, fighting against the shorts he had thrown on. Crow let go of Ethan's head, setting him back down on the pillow, and reached down between them. From the feel of things, Ethan had forgone the underwear for the night.

Fuck. Yes.

Crow pushed his hands down past the waistband, immediately feeling a soft tuft of hair before running his fingers over the long, hard shaft. Ethan pulsed in Crow's tightening grip. Their tongues lashed together, Crow thumbing the tip of Ethan's already leaking cock. He spread it around, pulling a moan from Ethan and greedily swallowing it.

He wanted to swallow something else too.

Crow pulled back with a sinful smile. He looked down at Ethan, who was grinning just as devilishly. They had both been waiting for this like that one Christmas you never fucking forget. The one with all the limited edition Power Ranger toys and a god-damned easy-bake oven thrown in the mix. (It was a great Christmas for Crow and also, surprisingly, no one was tipped off by the oven).

Yeah, that. It felt just like that.

Crow lowered himself on the bed, feeling the hum of the bus around them. He dropped to his knees on the floor, tugging on Ethan's pants as he did. Ethan already undid the zipper, allowing Crow to pull them off, releasing that thick, throbbing cock Crow was so ready to taste. He grabbed it with both hands, admiring the pure perfection of it.

"Fuck," Crow said with a breath, "I've never wanted to write a song about a dick, but yours is too perfect not to."

Ethan gave a delicious laugh, making his cock jerk in Crow's grip. "You can call it Winter's Staff."

Crow looked up, nodding his head with an overly impressed look. He loved how he was able to joke around while he held Ethan's cock in his hands. It was a level of comfort he had never achieved with any of his past hookups. He didn't even think that type of thing existed. "That's actually not bad. Poetic, almost."

"I want a cut of the sales," Ethan said, his eyes practically fucking glowing. "Although, there might be something else you can do. To, you know, prevent me from suing you and all."

Crow grinned, leaning in and licking around the crown, tasting Ethan's salty excitement. "Oh really? What's that?" He opened his mouth and wrapped his lips around Ethan's head. Ethan's head fell back on the pillow.

"You're already on the right track," he said, his voice sounding a little more strained. Crow felt Ethan's hands tangle in his hair, applying some pressure. Crow was up for the challenge. He opened his mouth wider and took in about half of Ethan's length, savoring the warmth and taste, relishing in the reaction it drew from Ethan, who was now lifting his legs a little higher on the bed, his fingers pulling tighter on Crow's hair.

He picked up the pace, slurping greedily on Ethan's cock, making sure he didn't get too loud with the rest of the crew sleeping right outside, but he was also making sure Ethan knew, without a shadow of a doubt, that Crow was abso-*fucking*-lutely loving sucking on his cock. Crow knew he could spend an entire day on his knees and he wouldn't care, as long as Ethan's dick was at lips-level.

He loved it. He loved trying to fit as much as he could before he had to come up for breath. He loved tracing lines down the velvet shaft, loved cupping Ethan's balls, loved tasting him, smelling him, feeling him.

Everything. He fucking loved it. And, from the sounds of it, Ethan did too. His grunts got deeper, more animalistic as Crow started swallowing more of Ethan's cock, looking up and locking their lustful gazes, Crow's mouth full of cock, saliva dripping down Ethan's balls, pure and primal and so damn hot.

Ethan's head fell back on the pillow, breaking the connection. Crow went back to dutifully sucking on his rod, using his hand to cover whatever area he couldn't with his lips, his tongue wrapping and swirling and lapping. Ethan was unravelling like putty. His thighs were tensing and starting to squeeze around Crow. His hips started to thrust a little harder, sinking his cock a little deeper, hitting the back of Crow's throat.

"Fuck, that's it, take it, Crow."

Crow moaned around Ethan's dick as he swallowed as much of it as he could. He pulled back for a breath, kissing Ethan's thigh before gently sucking and biting on the sensitive skin. "Come for me, Ethan," Crow said, rubbing the head of his man's cock against his lips. He opened his mouth and took him back in, thrusting Ethan over the edge. He said something that quickly transformed into a guttural moan as his entire body convulsed with the orgasm. Crow felt the first blast of seed hit the back of his throat, and he swallowed it back like it was the last fucking coke in the desert. He kept going, taking as much as Ethan was unloading, his entire body quivering around Crow's as the waves crashed over him, lessening with each passing second until Ethan was left twitching on the bed. Crow climbed back up, a smile plastered on his face, his lips plump and glistening wet. Ethan pulled him in for a kiss, his tongue taking back some of what he gave Crow.

It was insanely hot. Crow's cock pulsed almost painfully against his briefs. He had to get out of his pants before he broke right through them. He reached down between them and worked off his wet briefs, still not breaking from the hottest kiss of his life.

Crow dropped his hips, rubbing his stiff cock on a still very hard Ethan.

"Already down for round two?" Crow asked in a husky voice.

"I'm down for the fucking World Series."

Crow chuckled and locked lips, rolling their hard dicks together between them, Ethan still getting them both sticky and wet from some leftovers.

"I want you to fuck me," Ethan groaned as they broke for breath, their faces inches apart, their breaths caressing the others lips. "I *need* it."

The words could not have been hotter. Crow almost came right then and there. He had wanted this like nothing else, and now he was going to have it. Him and Ethan, one. Crow couldn't have reached for the bedside table fast enough, opening the drawer and grabbing a condom. Seconds later, the head of his cock was pressed against Ethan's needy ass. Crow looked down, deep into Ethan's eyes, finding a connection there unlike any he had shared with anyone else. Whatever was between them was some-thing incredibly special, and Crow felt like he was about to cement that.

He pushed his hips forward as he grabbed Ethan's legs and hoisted him up, aiming his ass higher in the air. Ethan's eyebrows drew together as his eyes lit up the moment Crow entered him. Slow at first. Very slow. Crow read Ethan's expressions, making sure he wasn't hurting him at any point. They hadn't used any fingers beforehand, but Ethan seemed relaxed enough to handle it. He also wasn't as big as Ethan, so he felt a little more comfortable picking up the pace as soon as Ethan started biting his lower lip, asking for more.

"Fuck, yeah, Crow, put it in."

It was so fucking sexy. Seeing this incredibly handsome man, his face shadowed with a light beard, his hair ruffled and his stunning blue eyes half-lidded, telling a story of pure bliss, his voice husky and his breathing heavy and his grunts deep.

"Fuck, Ethan, you're beyond sexy. You're everything. So fucking incredible."

Crow wasn't much of a curser, but his mind was no longer holding the reigns. This moment was being driven on a wave of passion, a current of lust. He wanted to be buried balls deep inside his man, claim him as his own, make him want more. He wanted Ethan in every way he could get him, for however long they could go for.

He thrust, finding a rhythm that had both their eyes rolling backward. Crow reached down between Ethan's legs and grabbed his thick bouncing cock, giving it a few strokes before Ethan reached his hand out to stop him.

"You already have me so fucking close," Ethan said. "I don't want to come yet."

Crow slowed down, bending down and taking a pebbled nipple between his teeth, rolling it and sucking it and feeling Ethan's ass clench in response, his calves pressing harder against Crow's head. He pulled back and turned his head so he could kiss Ethan's calf, feeling the soft hair against his lips. He kept kissing, higher and higher until he found Ethan's feet, which he still kept kissing. And sucking. And almost unwinding the both of them right then and there.

But not yet. They both weren't ready.

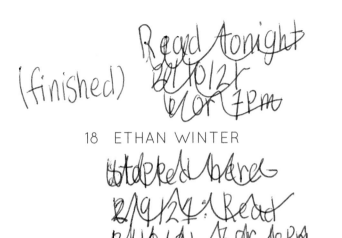

18 ETHAN WINTER

Ethan's entire world was being rocked. His legs were up over Crow's shoulders, his thighs quivering with every thrust, his cock still leaking onto his belly. He hadn't realized how starved his body had been for this type of connection. Not even just his body. His damn soul. He felt alive again in a way he hadn't for the past two years. This was the first time he had ever let anyone inside of him since Adam. This was special in so many different ways.

He looked up into Crow's eyes and felt such a safety, such a comfort. He was letting this man inside him, and he was loving every damn second of it. Ethan let his head fall back, his eyelids shutting as Crow slowly drove himself deep into Ethan. He could feel Crow's balls press against his ass, making Ethan's own cock throb. He reached down and gave himself a stroke in an attempt to alleviate the building pressure. He looked back up, locking in with Crow's eyes. He was biting his lip, his breaths coming out hard whenever he thrust.

"Come here," Crow said, pulling out of Ethan and

leaving him suddenly feeling empty and in desperate need of the remedy. "I want to see you riding me."

Ethan was more than up for it. Crow laid down on the bed, spreading some more lube on his cock as Ethan took his position, both thighs straddling Crow's firm stomach. He reached behind and grabbed Crow's dick but Crow grabbed Ethan's hips first and pulled him up, lining his hard cock up against Crow's lips. Crow looked up and licked the tip, smiling as Ethan felt his entire body quake. He was still so sensitive from coming moments before that the slightest touch sent him into overdrive.

Ethan let himself go. He closed his eyes and let the soft, warm, wet sensations coming from Crow's tongue transport him to a different place. It was heaven. Ethan hadn't thought he would experience this again. He didn't think he'd *let* himself experience this again.

"Oh, fuck," Ethan groaned, the words escaping his lips without a thought behind them. They were primal in their need to be heard. A way to spur Crow on, making his mouth open wider, his head bobbing down farther until almost all of Ethan's cock was swallowed. He was a big guy — thicker than average — so he was even more turned on by watching Crow greedily gobble him up.

Well, at least trying to. Ethan started to push his hips up, tightening his ass as he thrust his cock a little deeper down Crow's throat. Ropes of saliva coated Ethan's hard cock as Crow came up for air, stroking Ethan's length in the process and sending a bolt of pure electricity straight to the base of Ethan's spine. He felt his balls tighten as Crow went back to work, worshipping him with his mouth. It was surreal. Ethan let his head fall back as another groan escaped him, rising up from his balls. His toes curled as the pleasure enveloped him. The feeling of Crow's lips on his cock, along with the soreness of his just worked-out muscles and the warmth of Crow's throat, it was all too much.

Too fucking much.

"Fuck, stop, stop," Ethan pleaded, feeling the crest of the tidal wave. His thighs tensed as his fingers tangled in Crow's hair, his balls almost disappearing inside him. He pulled himself out of Crow's mouth before he blew. He still wanted to give Crow the ride he asked for. He moved back, feeling the head of Crow's throbbing cock press against his ass. He reached back around and grabbed the thick shaft, lining it up with his hole. He sat back, Crow's cock sliding in without any resistance. Ethan took him all, sitting down and filling himself full with Crow. It was ecstasy. Pure, unfiltered ecstasy. Ethan rose back up, watching as Crow's lips tried to form words but let out moans instead. He smiled and chewed on his lower lip as he sank back down onto Crow, impaling himself. He stayed there and rolled his hips forward, rubbing his own rock-hard erection onto Crow's tight abs. His ass clenched around Crow's cock, feeling himself reaching the edge whether he liked it or not.

He started bouncing on Crow's dick while stroking his own. Up and down. Crow looked like he was transported to another dimension. His expressive brown eyes glazed over and seemed drunk with bliss. Ethan must have looked the same. His hands pressed down on Crow's sexy chest, feeling the soft dusting of hair under his palms.

That was when Crow started to thrust up and all bets were off. His cock was hitting Ethan's P-spot with every push, rubbing over the swollen gland and sending shock-waves throughout Ethan's body.

"I'm gonna come," he warned, unable to hold it back any longer.

"Fuck, yeah, come for me. I want to see you shoot it all over my chest."

That was all Ethan needed. His balls tightened as he unloaded exactly where Crow wanted him to. Even though he had just come moments before, he had plenty more to give. Rope after rope landed on Crow with every wave. The moment must have been too much for Crow, because his entire body tensed as his thrusts became erratic before he gave one final push and buried himself deep in Ethan, holding him there while he came inside him.

In that moment they were one, and they would forever be one after.

Ethan came crashing down on Crow, breathless and still moaning and beginning to chuckle. This was all so fucking incredible. Even the fact that he was currently being cemented to Crow's chest by his drying come. He figured if he had to be cemented together with one person, it would definitely be Crow.

"That was..." Crow was catching his breath. It sounded like the one with all the words was speechless.

"Mind blowing," Ethan said, helping him out. They kissed, tasting each other, melting into each other. After a few more moments, Ethan got up and wrapped a towel around himself so he could sneak off to the shower and rinse off. It was a tiny bathroom so they could only go one at a time and they had to be quick. Crow went in right after Ethan and came out five minutes later. They got back into bed, naked and dewy, both smelling like sex and coconut shampoo.

"So are you usually a top?" Ethan asked playfully, their noses touching, their lips giving out random kisses between words.

"Yeah, I prefer it. And you make such a good bottom," Crow teased. Just talking about it was giving Ethan a chub again. "I might play around back there if you want me to."

"I'll see what I can do," Ethan said. They laughed and went back to kissing, their bodies pressed against the other under the thin white bed sheet.

"You know...You're the only other person I've ever had sex with." Ethan was feeling so vulnerable, he felt like he had to peel off another layer to the wraps around his heart. He wanted Crow to learn every about him over time, and there was no better time to start than the present.

Crow's eyebrows rose before settling back down almost immediately. "Really? I mean not that I have a ton of bedroom encounters, I guess I was just blindly assuming that a guy like you had to have had his time around the block."

"Nope," Ethan said. "Adam was my first and then I just never found anyone else. Until you barreled into my life."

"I've had a few, ehm, bedfellows before, but you're my first real boyfriend. And I don't see a second ever coming along."

Ethan's heart gave a flutter. It was like a programmed reaction for whenever he heard the 'B' word.

Next up, H-town.

They fell back into kissing and ended up with round three on their (sticky) hands. After that, they talked some more about their pasts and their futures. About how one of Crow's biggest fear was heights and how he wanted to conquer it before he was thirty. They talked about Ethan's secret crocheting skills, skills so secret that Crow was the first to hear about them. They discussed how Animal Planet only plays crappy fish tank shows and talked about their mutual love for Big Brother. There conversations were random and all-encompassing and always entertaining.

They laughed and talked and laughed and kissed and spent the rest of that night wrapped up together, pure happiness surrounding them the entire time.

ONE WEEK LATER

Tall buildings stretched above them, creating a sort of junglescape out of slabs of concrete and walls of glass. Sunlight bounced between the buildings like it was playing a solitary game of tag. Crow and Ethan walked down the busy Chicago streets, admiring all the influential architecture and enjoying the summer breeze. The windy city wasn't exactly blowing them over (that would come in the winter, when the thick ropes anchored on the streets were used so people weren't knocked down) but there was a gentle wind, which made the day more than perfect to walk around and explore the city. Crow had performed the night before to a sold-out crowd and was still riding the high. That, mixed with the high he got from holding Ethan's hand, and he almost couldn't even believe this was all real. Two years ago, no one could have ever told him how happy he would be in the future. How perfect everything would seem. He also wasn't the type to think about the possibility of the rug being pulled out from under him, and so he wasn't worried about things feeling *too* perfect, as if his happiness needed to be knocked down or something.

"You sure about this?" Ethan asked as they stopped in front of a towering skyscraper. Crow looked up, quickly looking back down before he got too dizzy and chickened out.

"Yes, positive."

"Because I'm totally fine with just grabbing something to eat."

"Nope. I'm doing it."

Ethan cocked his head. Those baby blues were bouncing between Crow's eyes, searching for any sign that said Crow wanted to back out. He wasn't going to, though. He was going to conquer one of his biggest fears, all while Ethan stood by his side. He was ready. He was going to stand in the all-glass box that jutted out from the topmost level of the skyscraper.

"Alright, let's do it." Ethan pumped his hand around Crow's and led them through the sliding glass doors, entering into a huge, modern lobby with glass accents and massive screens that gave a colorful rundown of the building they were currently in. There was a line of people waiting to buy tickets at the booth. Ethan was a planner, though. He had bought their tickets online, so they walked to another line that was waiting in front of a group of four elevators. One of them dinged open. Staff members counted and guided a group into the elevator, staying with them as the door closed. Crow and Ethan waited for a couple more groups to be escorted before it was their turn.

By then, Crow's anxiety was starting to bubble up. He absent-mindedly played with the brim of his LA Dodgers cap, tucked low on his head. He was trying to listen to the staff member in the elevator with them. She was a bright-eyed college student who was rattling off facts like she was practicing for a final. All Crow heard was 'tallest' before he tuned her out. There was a screen on the elevator that showed them how high the elevator was climbing, compared to other well-known landmarks.

And we're now higher than the Statue of Liberty.

Great.

Ethan must have sensed Crow's rising tension. That was something Crow noticed about Ethan; he was very intuitive to the emotions around him. He could read a room like he was reading a medical chart. Quick, efficient, and knew exactly what to do.

Ethan let go of Crow's hand and wrapped his arm around Crow's lower back. He pulled him in and kissed the side of his head. He didn't do that often, but the few times he had, Crow would instantly melt. No more worries. No more fears. Heights? Pft, Crow could climb Mount Everest. Ethan's kiss had the power to make him feel invincible.

And just in time, too. The elevator, after climbing for what felt like minutes, came to a smooth stop at the top, opening up to another lobby of sorts. Another staff member, wearing a bright purple shirt, came to greet the group and take them over to the glass box. There were a few glass viewing areas, and they were all occupied by smiling couples and giggling teens snapping selfies. Crow, meanwhile, was trying to not look out the windows. The feeling of invincibility from Ethan's kiss wasn't permanent, that was for sure.

"You ready?" Ethan asked as a couple stepped out of the glass box, both looking wide-eyed and giggly. Crow looked to Ethan, finding strength in that blue gaze. How could anything go wrong when Ethan was smiling like that? His eyes crinkled at the edges and seemed to glow like stars. Nothing could go wrong. Crow took a deep breath and nodded.

"Come on," Ethan said, twining his fingers through Crow's. He had slightly smaller hands than Crow, his fingers a little finer. A perfect fit. Crow jokingly called them surgeon fingers before Ethan told him that was actually a thing. Ethan's hand also felt incredibly comforting, surgeon fingers and all. They walked toward the box, Crow already seeing way past the city of Chicago on the horizon. That had been one of the facts. They were so high up that they could see the three neighboring states; Indiana, Wisconsin, and Michigan. He remembered that one.

It's ok. I'm fine.

He kept his eyes peeled straight as they entered the glass box. He heard Ethan give an excited 'whoa' as he looked down, which Crow was certain he wasn't going to do. He knew that the moment he looked down, his fear of heights would hit him with a brick to the gut. He looked straight ahead, controlling his breathing, holding Ethan's hand a little tighter than he normally did.

"Look down, baby, it's fine."

"Please don't call me baby, it creeps me out," Crow said in a spurt of fear filled honesty. "Sorry. I mean, you can call me donut hole and it's totally fine. I just can't look down."

Ethan laughed, squeezing Crow's hand. "Ok, *donut hole*. I won't make you look down, but I promise you, it's ok. It feels like I'm looking down at an anthill. I can see people getting into taxies, and cars clogging the streets, people walking with their dogs. But they're all so small. Like toys."

"See, you're painting a perfectly clear picture. No need to look down."

"I think you should."

"Nope." Crow could feel his knees locking as his body tensed. He wasn't going to look down. Looking straight ahead was hard enough. Ethan's presence could only be so calming before actual paranoias started taking over. This was something Crow had to overcome himself, even if Ethan was being an immense help. Crow took another deep breath.

"Speaking of toys, can we just go back to the toy museum? That place was fun." Crow sighed. "And on the ground."

Ethan chuckled next to Crow. "It had its own appeal, that's for sure. Although the only thing I can really remember from then was that kiss."

Crow's pulse quickened, but it wasn't from fear this time. Ethan bringing up any kind of kissing had that affect on Crow. It was strong enough to momentarily push the fear away. "That kiss was nice. The ones that followed were better, though," Crow said.

"You know what would be even better?"

"What?" Crow asked, peeling his eyes off of the cloudless horizon and looking into Ethan's eyes, tunneling in.

"A kiss on top of the world." Ethan smirked before he leaned in, grabbing Crow by the lower back and pulling him in for a surprise kiss that swept Crow off his feet. It was so passionate and powerful, Crow momentarily forgot that there was still a crowd of people waiting to enter one of the glass boxes. Nor did he remember anything about his fear of heights or his determination to not look down. He forgot it all.

They broke apart, leaving Crow slightly flushed. He straightened his back and tried to tamp the smile down. He grabbed Ethan's hand again and said, "I'm doing it. I'm looking down."

Ethan's eyes opened wide. Crow moved his gaze from those blue orbs, down to Ethan's chest, his jeans, his navy

Converse, and then down, through the glass floor they were standing on.

It was mesmerizing. Crow felt a rush of fear and excitement and awe flow through him. It was simultaneous and instant. And then the fear was gone. Completely and totally. He was looking down through the thick glass with childlike fascination, feeling safe with Ethan's hand on his back (along with the immense testing he had presumed was done on the glass balcony by award winning scientists... and if they didn't have awards, they damn well should). He could see what Ethan had described. It looked like a technologically blessed ant farm was sprawling underneath him. Everyone walked around, seemingly so small and inconsequential and yet Crow knew that was far from the case. Every tiny person below them had something going on; something to worry about, something to be happy about, something to cry about. If he looked further out, he could see the Chicago River, slithering like a dark blue snake around the tall anthills.

"Do you guys want a photo of the two of you?"

"Yes, that'd be great," Ethan responded, handing over his phone to the upbeat tourist, her hair pulled through her Las Vegas emblazoned cap in a ponytail. Crow went to stand up but it seemed like Ethan had different plans. He tugged on Crow's hand and pulled him down so that they could sit. This was infinitely more trying on the 'fear of heights' thing, but Crow was able to handle it. He sat cross-legged and smiled for the camera, a hand placed on Ethan's knee.

With the photo snapped, they both stood. Crow looked at the photo while Ethan shielded the screen from the sun.

"We look good! Send it to me," Crow said, admiring how bright Ethan's smile was in the photo. It was also one of the first photos they had together, and Crow was going to be sure to hold on to it. He didn't even look nearly as scared as he thought he would. Both of their smiles were wide and their eyes beaming. Knees were touching and hands holding as the entire city opened up underneath them, while the rest of the world stretched out behind and below them.

Crow's phone buzzed in his pocket. He pulled it out, answering it as they stepped out of the glass box, a pair of young twins running past them to take their spot, not a fear in the world.

"Hey, Red!"

20 ETHAN WINTER

"Red!" Crow called, his arms outstretched as he grabbed Red for a hug. They were standing next to a wall of tall, well-kept hedges that bordered a Michelin three-star steak house. The valet had already taken Ethan's rental. Ethan looked around, admiring the interesting, all black exterior, broken by sections of one-way windows, blocking anyone from seeing inside. When Crow had said where they were going, Ethan thought he had misheard. He knew about The Block from a friend of his who was a big foodie. He said it was one of the best steakhouses he had ever been to, and that was coming from a man who ate around the world for a living. He had also said the prices were through the roof but the experience made up for it.

"Red, this is Ethan." Crow stepped aside and motioned toward Ethan. "My boyfriend."

"Hi," Ethan said, sticking his hand out and trying not to overload from hearing Crow call him his boyfriend. He had known that's what they were, but they hadn't really said the title out loud. Not until then. "Nice to meet you."

"So you're the one that got Crow up higher than three

stories." Red smiled, his face sharp but warm. "You'd think with a name like *Crow*."

"Yep," Ethan said, laughing and forgetting for a moment that he was meeting an international celebrity. Red was genuinely warm and seemed much more grounded than Ethan had unfairly presumed he would be. And then he turned to his fiancé, smiling with a glint in his gaze as he introduced him, "Ethan, this is Caleb, my fiancé."

"We've met," Caleb said, matching Red's grin as he shook Ethan's hand. "We work at the same hospital."

"Oh, that's right! Duh." Red palmed his forehead.

"That's ok, I don't think we've ever really talked though," Caleb said.

Ethan nodded. They had chatted once before in a break room, but his rotations never brought him around the same floors as Caleb, or at the same times as him. Even then, everyone at the hospital knew who Caleb was. He was already pretty popular simply because he was such an incredible nurse and a great person. Ever since he and Red had gone public, Caleb climbed up a level and turned into a mini-celebrity in his own right. He had a quarter of a million Instagram followers and was constantly being pictured out with Red, whether they were on a date at some trendy new restaurant or vacationing in Cancun. "Looking forward to talking over the steaks at this place," Ethan said, genuinely excited to share some good conversation and some good meat.

"Right?" Red said, excitedly.

Crow chuckled as he reached for Ethan's hand. Their fingers locked together, Crow's warmth feeling exactly right in Ethan's. He had been slightly nervous about meeting Red. It wasn't even so much the movie star aspect, although that part was also a little surreal. It was more about how close Red and Crow were and how important Ethan thought it was that he make a good impression.

"Alright, we've got a nurse and a doctor. Now all we need is a priest. Let's go find one," Red said with a laugh, slapping a hand on Ethan's shoulder and leading them toward the heavy black doors that marked the entrance to the steakhouse.

"What does that even mean?" Crow asked, chuckling, the sound resembling Ethan's favorite song.

WHO KNEW HELPING someone overcome their fears struck up such a big appetite? Ethan was more than happy to be sitting down on solid ground, looking over an expansive menu while trying hard to ignore the expensive prices along the side. Red had insisted on treating them, so it was all going on his check.

The place was quaint... in an expensive, world-renowned steakhouse kind of way. The lighting was low, and candles were lit. The tables, about fifteen of them, were all draped in silky soft white cloth, the plating and silverware feeling just as expensive. Their appetizers were brought out on plates decorated with exotic nuts and a palate of different color sauces, one plate even having rose petals adorning each corner. It could have easily gone over the top, and maybe some of it did, but Ethan was so hungry he couldn't care less. Plates could have been brought out by dancing bears and Ethan wouldn't have thought about the overkill, he would have only focused in on the food.

And Crow, of course. He was the one person who could distract him from his quest to eat everything in sight. Crow had the ability to distract Ethan from just about anything.

Right then, Crow was distracting him by recounting a story from the other night about two drunken fans who had climbed up onto the stage and proceeded to give Crow a lap dance. It was all clearly in good fun, and Crow then turned it around and gave the entire audience a mini-Magic Mike show. The security team was not thrilled that night.

"Everyone was cracking up and cheering," Crow said, smiling at the memory. "Maybe if singing doesn't work out, I could go into exotic dancing."

"That could work," Caleb said, agreeing with a nod. He drank the rest of his wine, placing it down just as the sommelier brought over another bottle. He showed the all black bottle to Red, who had charmingly said to the sommelier that he wanted the most expensive red they had (and saying that in a charming way was *very* difficult). The man then uncorked the wine and poured a small amount into a glass, swirling it a little before handing it for Red to taste. Ethan watched, wondering where the whole tradition of appreciating wine started. He had a flash back to his college days, before medical school, when he could afford shooting back shots of vodka and glasses of wine without ever appreciating any of it's various 'notes' and 'textures', or whatever words were used to describe the things Ethan could never taste.

They all thanked the sommelier once he was done refilling their glasses. He had left the rest of the wine on the center of the table, next to the bread basket. Ethan grabbed a slice of toasted bread, spreading some of the olive oil and rosemary mix as Crow's knee rubbed up against his under the table. They weren't sitting too close together, but just like magnets, they somehow ended up touching one another.

"So, Ethan, how's it been touring the country with this

one? I remember taking him for a world wide press tour once. Never again." Red laughed, winking at them. "So damn demanding. I thought I had hired Kim Kardashian as my assistant for a second."

"Stop flattering yourself. You're no Paris Hilton," Crow shot back, smirking from across the table. Ethan loved that about him. He was quick with quips that never failed to draw a few laughs, even if the reference may have flown over Ethan's head.

"It's been great," Ethan said. "I was a little apprehensive at first, but it's honestly been an unforgettable experience. We get to see all these different cities, and they all start feeling like their own little worlds even though they're only a day-trip away." Ethan drank some of the wine, finding it incredibly smooth. "And Crow hasn't had too many weird demands."

"Too *many*?" Crow asked, turning on Ethan. "I haven't had any!"

Ethan gave the face that said "eh... I don't know about that".

Crow crossed his arms and faced Ethan in his seat. "Really? What have I asked for?" Red and Caleb were both laughing, while Ethan was trying to hold it in. He loved playing around with Crow. He hadn't joked around with someone in a while, not like this, with all his walls down. He just never felt happy enough. There was a certain level of happiness you had to be to be able to joke around and genuinely laugh, and he hadn't felt that for years.

Until Crow came along.

"Well, you do always ask to make sure we have coconut water and sour skittles in every green room."

"That's for my health! My physical health, hence the coconut water, and my mental health, hence the skittles."

Crow shook his head. "Jesus, you think you know someone." Then he started laughing, causing Ethan to crack. They laughed as Ethan leaned in and stole a quick kiss from his boyfriend.

Fuck. I'd never thought I'd feel this again.

They continued to joke around a bit, all of them having a great time. The steaks had arrived by the time the laughs were dying down, which was perfect. Ethan dug into his juicy medium-rare filet mignon, serving Crow a piece when he asked to try some. He even held his hand up to Crow's chin and everything

Boyfriends.

The title rang through his mind again. This time, it hadn't struck him with the same stab of sad guilt he would feel in the past whenever that term was brought up. He was proud to be Crow's boyfriend. And beyond that, he was *happy* to be Crow's boyfriend.

When the steaks were done and the desert menus laid out, the conversation started to turn toward a more serious topic. Red was the one to bring it up. "So," he started, his amber golden eyes examining the sorbet list, "anything else on the whole stalker situation?"

Ethan immediately felt the air in the room get ten degrees cooler. He could sense Crow tense up in his chair. "Not since the last letter back in Denver. It's crazy and all, but the more time passes, the less freaked out I get."

Red nodded, his eyes coming up from the menu. "Yeah, it's always upsetting, man. You saw when I was getting all those weird fan letters and 'gift boxes' filled with bras. One or two had jockstraps, but still, my point stands. Creepy."

"Why don't I get sent jockstraps?" Crow asked, sounding offended.

"Be careful what you wish for," Caleb said from across

the table. The waiter came and took their desert orders before they got back into the conversation. The classical music played lazily over the speakers, adding to the din of conversation from the other tables.

"Seriously, though, are there any more details about the canceled show? I saw it blowing up on Twitter, except no one seemed to know why it was cancelled." Red's brows turned downward. He must have known how much Crow hated having to cancel the show.

"Yeah, we don't want to freak fans out so we're keeping the reason kind of hush for right now. No new details on it either. Thank god for Angela, though. She was able to schedule another date a few months from now. So I'll just fly out from LA and make up for it."

Red's slight frown turned upside down. "That's great! Text me the date later and I'll try and make it out. Hopefully my new assistant doesn't mess up my schedule some how."

"That bad?" Crow asked.

"I ended up in a petting zoo on the day I was supposed to be meeting with the head of Paramount. Yeah. That bad."

Crow couldn't hold back a laugh, which in turn had Ethan laughing. "A petting zoo?" Ethan asked. He was amazed at how many crazy stories these guys had to share. It was clear that Red and Crow had grown close as friends, and they both had the gift of gab.

"A petting zoo," Red emphasized. "Meanwhile, the exec was over at the restaurant, wondering where my dumbass was. Little did he know, I was trying not to get my kneecaps busted by a crazy goat." Red sighed. "I'm trying to find a new assistant."

"They just don't make them like they used to," Crow said, smirking that sexy little smirk of his. Ethan could barely contain himself. He wanted to lean over and suck on Crow's neck. He could see the slight rise and fall of his pulse. A perfect spot. A bull's-eye for his lips. Not to mention, their knees were still pressed together under the table, anchoring them to each other.

Ethan adjusted himself in his seat, using his elbow to discreetly move his growing cock so that it wasn't a clear bulge. He felt like he was a kid on his first ever date, popping random boners left and right at the slightest shift in the breeze. He couldn't help it, and no one could blame him. Crow was one sexy mother fucker, and it didn't help that Ethan already knew how he looked like naked.

His firm, muscular torso. Those broad, solid pecs. The pebbled nipples, perfect for biting. The toned body and sexy trail of hair that led down to Crow's meaty cock. Ethan could practically feel the weight in his hands. He grabbed his wine glass, drinking the last of his wine, hoping it would somehow stifle the flickering flame in his gut that was soon to become a forest fire.

Except, the attraction went past the physical. Ethan was also intensely attracted to Crow's personality, and that only made his boner even more persistent. Sure, he could see when guys were physically attractive, but he was reacting to way more than that when it came to Crow. They could fuck in the pitch dark for the rest of their lives, Ethan never having to see him, finding bliss from simply being one with him.

"You know," Caleb said, leaning back as the waiter brought the deserts. A decadent chocolate cheesecake was slid in front of Ethan, two spoons placed on the side of the plate. Crow grabbed one, Ethan grabbed the other. "I watch a lot of those weird ID channel shows, with the unsolved mysteries... that, and a lot of Judge Judy."

"*A lot*," Red cut in.

Caleb cleared his throat. "And, I don't want to creep you out or anything, but, have you considered looking into the people closest to you first? I know it could seem like a crazy fan, but these things are sometimes closer to home than people realize."

"What were you saying?" Red asked. "The part about not creeping anyone out."

"Sorry," Caleb said, his brows coming up with a chuckle. "It's the truth, though."

"He's right." Crow said, surprising Ethan. They had never talked about that possibility. "I've thought about it."

Ethan looked to Crow, who was rubbing the bridge of his nose, climbing up to the corners of his eyes. "Who?" Ethan asked.

"Well, I mean Jordan's had a crush on me for a long time, and he did start acting a little off when you showed up." Crow let out a breath and shook his head. "But then I feel ridiculous. I've known Jordan for six years now. I've known everyone on the tour for pretty much the same length. We all know where we stand with each other, and Jordan knows I can't ever give him what he wants."

Red tilted his head, chewing on his lip. "Desperation is a thing."

"Thank you, Dr. Freud," Crow threw back with a sarcastic smile. "But no, I don't think he's desperate. He's a good-looking guy, he can find anyone he wants. He's probably just waiting until the tour is over to settle down."

Caleb cut in then, "A wise lady once said; if it doesn't make sense, it's not true."

The crowd had blank stares until Caleb clarified, "the wise lady is Judge Judy."

Red couldn't hold back his laughs as he pulled Caleb in

for a kiss. Ethan loved seeing how happy they appeared. It was clear that their stars were meant to collide. Both were perfect for the other. They were constantly smiling and laughing and stealing quick touches from each other. It was beautiful to see.

Ethan squeezed Crow's hand a little tighter, feeling overwhelmed with love. He was not only surrounded by it, but knee-deep in it. He could barely even focus on the rest of the conversation before they noticed the time and decided they should get going.

"I'm not ready to go to sleep, guys," Red said, checking his watch. Looked like it was a Rolex from where Ethan stood. "Where's the after party?"

"Our hotel has an incredible rooftop bar and garden mashup thing. Let's check it out," Crow suggested, putting his arm around Ethan as they walked out of the quiet, dim restaurant and into the busy world. The restaurant was in a pretty busy part of Chicago, surrounded by a ton of other restaurants, office buildings, and world-famous improv theatres. It seemed like a show had finished just as they wrapped up their dinner, a flood of people coming out of the doors to the building across the street.

"I really want to see a show there; we're going to have to come back." Crow said to Ethan, almost like an afterthought.

Except, for Ethan, it was no afterthought. *Come back.* Crow was already thinking of the future together, with a vacation already in the works. It filled Ethan's heart with a sense of blissful certainty. They had really discussed their future after the tour, but Ethan had always felt like it was already understood that this was no fling, and Crow seemed to have just confirmed that.

They were on the street, waiting for the security guy to

bring around the car, when Ethan heard Crow's name being called from across the street. It was getting late into the evening but there was still some light out. Ethan could make out an excited girl, jumping up and down and waving frantically, her group of friends seeming to catch on. One of them spotted Red and the entire group had a complete meltdown. Ethan thought they were about to run into oncoming traffic just to get to them in seconds flat.

Thankfully, they waited until the red light.

"Holy shit, it's you!" One of the girls exclaimed, staring at Crow with wide green eyes before turning to Red and saying, "it's you!"

A boy in the group, who was also on the same level of 'holy shitness' as the rest, turned to Crow. "Can we get a picture with you guys," he managed to squeak out.

"Of course," Crow said with a smile. Ethan could practically feel the tensed body guard, who was standing feet away from them. He started to move toward the group to intervene but Crow waved the man back. "They're ok. Just fans."

The fans seemed unfazed as they launched into a mini photo-shoot with the two guys. Caleb had even been asked to be in some. Ethan wasn't exactly known yet, and he was totally fine with that. He didn't crave the spotlight, sometimes he didn't even like it.

He helped take some of the photos, unable to avoid catching the excitement from the kids. It was overwhelming. They almost looked like they were meeting some kind of royalty. He knew Crow was loved, and for good reason, but seeing that affect out in the real world was infectious. He smiled as he took the photos, happy to be helping them capture a memory.

With the photoshoot wrapped, the kids started saying

goodbyes. One of the girls seemed a little more reserved than the others. She almost looked a little upset toward the end. It was then that Crow seemed to recognize her.

"Hey, you... you stopped at my tour bus right? At the beginning of the tour?"

The girl nodded, looking down at her feet. "That was me. My name's Tricia. I've loved the tour, been to every show so far except one."

"That's awesome, thank you," Crow said. Ethan watched him, wondering if there were any alarm bells ringing in his head. Ethan wasn't an overly suspicious person, but those letters had put him on high alert, and this girl was clearly bothered by something.

"Alright, we should start heading back, the driver should be pulling up any second," Ethan said, nodding his head toward the curb. "Angela's going to have our heads if we don't leave for the next stop on time."

"True," Crow said, smiling at the group of kids. They started to leave when the one girl who seemed bothered separated from the group and came back to Crow. She looked like she was about to say something but stopped herself. And then their ride pulled up on the side of the street, giving Ethan the opening to grab Crow's hand and tug him toward it. The girl turned back to her group of friends, who were calling her to run across the street before the light changed.

Ethan and Crow got into the car, followed by Caleb. Red took the front seat.

Crow had rested his head on Ethan's shoulder as they drove back to the hotel. Ethan had been lying about Angela watching their time. They actually had an entire night in Chicago before they had to leave, and so they had planned to spend it on the hotel's rooftop bar, popping champagne with Red and Caleb. Ethan was grateful for the champagne, because his nerves were starting to fray at the edges. He was used to high-pressure situations, but this stalker thing was making him more frightened than he could show. He didn't want to project that fear onto Crow, who was already having a rough time, all while he still had to put on a good show for his fans. He enjoyed being Crow's solid support, the face he could look to for comfort. Crow was that for him, but in a different way. Crow's smile brought him a sense of freeing joy. It was like every time those dimples popped up, Ethan was being reminded of happy he was and how far he had come. There was a buoyancy in his life now that kept his head far up above the clouds, when only months ago, he could barely look up far enough to even see the clouds.

End of chapter

ONE WEEK LATER

The crowd was clapping and cheering and hollering for an encore. Crow stood on the edge of the stage, waving out to the thousands that showed up to hear him. It was insane. Security was pissed and had a hard time controlling things, but thankfully everything had gone off without a hitch. The show had been one of the biggest so far. He had been worried because Asbury Park had been one of the bigger venues he was performing in, and the tickets had taken a while to sell out. Angela had been right about the east coast being procrastinators thing. But New Jersey ended up showing in force, filling up the outdoor venue and giving Crow one of the best nights of his life. At one point, he had even brought Ethan up on stage, something he had never done before. It was during his song, 'Angel Scars', and he had become so wrapped up in emotion that he just needed to have Ethan with him. He looked backstage, where Ethan usually stood, and ran over as the drummer tapped out a slow beat to the beginning of the song. Crow grabbed Ethan's hand and pulled him out to the stage, the crowd breaking out into a roaring cheer. They may have thought Ethan was a special celebrity guest, so Crow clarified things further.

"Everyone," he had said into the microphone before the song started, "meet my boyfriend, Ethan."

Crow thought the crowd couldn't have sounded louder. He was wrong. They all roared as Crow pulled Ethan in for a quick kiss, one that was displayed on the two massive screens that bordered both sides of the stage. Their love was being magnified and played out so that even the people at the very farthest corner of the venue could see them. And more than that, Crow knew this moment would be filmed and uploaded to the internet in seconds flat. He wanted that. He wanted his kiss to go viral, so that struggling kids out there could see that open love and pride is possible, all while thousands of people cheer you on. Crow wished he had someone show him that when he was growing up, so now he was going to be the one carrying the message. Him and Ethan. They would bring that message together. Role models for children who otherwise thought the entire world was against them. Crow remembered that feeling. When you don't see anyone like you anywhere else, you start thinking maybe you are the problem. Maybe the mean kids with their meaner words are right.

But, no, *fuck that.* A small-minded asshole does *not* represent the entire world. Bullies and thugs don't represent what's good about life. The world is much bigger, and much brighter. Sometimes that light can fade, but it never goes out.

"Thank you, guys!" Crow said into the mic as he took another bow, feeling a swell of gratitude rush over him. How did he get so lucky?

THE MEET and greets after his shows were one of Crow's favorite parts of touring. He loved every opportunity he got to reach out and connect with his fans. He absorbed all their stories and tried to send them home with a memorable experience. He had heard horror stories of celebrities standing feet away from their fans for the photo and then having them rushed away. No way was that going to be Crow. Security had everyone standing in a separate room, coming in one by one. Crow stood by the white paper backdrop the photographer had set up against the far wall. The first meet-and-greeter walked in with a wide smile and eyes that resembled that of a baby fawn imprinting on her mother. She was shell-shocked at being able to meet Crow.

"Hi," Crow said, excitedly. It broke the spell. She jumped up and started saying hi repeatedly as she walked over, her hand outstretched. Crow rejected the hand and pulled her in for a hug instead. She was freaking out by the time they had to take the photo.

"Oh man, everyone's going to be so jell," she said as they turned toward the camera. "My entire calculus class like *worships* you."

"Calculus, huh?" They smiled for the photo, the flash going off like a white bomb. "I hated math. It was my worst subject."

"Ugh, me too!" Her smile grew wider, if that were even possible. Crow loved it, that moment he made a genuine connection with a fan. He could see how blown away she was by simply finding out she had something in common with Crow.

It was that girl he had seen on the street. The same one who had been at the tour bus.

"I'm sorry," she started, waving off the camera, "I just

have to ask, please tell your manager to never contact my family again."

"Huh?" Crow, along with the rest of the room, were thoroughly confused.

"Yeah, I don't know, she somehow figured out who I was and told me to stop coming to the shows. Must have been through ticket sales, I guess. She found my home address and sent a letter to my mom, saying I needed to be better. I was going to bring it up the other day when I bumped into you, but freaked out."

"Shit, I'm sorry." Crow was genuinely confused and also felt bad for what this girl must have gone through. Why was Angela harassing a fan? Crow understood that the stakes were raised with the letters, but that didn't mean she could bully people away from seeing his shows. It wasn't unheard of for fans to road trip it cross the country with their favorite band.

"It's ok. I was bummed for a little, but it's fine. I think my mom understood that I was telling the truth when I said I wasn't stalking you. The cops even questioned me, dude. It sucked."

"I'm really sorry," Crow reached out and pulled her in for a side hug. Frankie stood in the corner, watching the time and signaling when he was beginning to cut into another fan's time. The finger swirl went up in the air, warning Crow that he needed to somehow wrap things up.

"Here, let's grab a photo and then I'll get you a VIP pass to a future show, your choice."

Her eyes lit up. "Really?!"

"Hell yeah, just leave your info with Frankie over there and we'll be in touch."

"Ugh, this is why I love you."

They posed for a photo and Crow said another apology

before the next fan was brought into the room. There wasn't much time between smiling faces and hyperly enthusiastic conversations to think about what Angela had done. Another hour of meeting fans passed when things quickly soured. He was in the middle of taking a photo when the devil herself stormed in through the door, followed closely by a worried-looking Troy.

"We need to go," Angela said, her voice pointed, her eyes ignoring the young fan at Crow's side.

"What's going on?" It was Frankie. He was asking from across the room, setting down his beer bottle and walking over toward the group. Crow eyed his friends, sensing fear in the way they stood, in how quickly Angela spoke and how shaken Troy seemed to be.

This felt wrong. He had to go. Crow said a heartfelt sorry to the fan for having his time cut short and then left the room. He promised to reach out to everyone still waiting in line with a personalized message and free tickets.

"Where's Jordan?" Angela asked. "I want to leave tonight."

Crow shrugged, having seen Jordan for a second back stage before he went out to the bar for drinks. "I'm not sure, he was out dancing I think." They continued on through the back hallway, the thumping of the music in the club getting farther and farther. It never disappeared though. In fact, it almost got louder the second they opened the door and exited out into a parking lot.

As they walked toward the parked bus, Crow could see the damage that was done. One of the side windows was shattered, heavy chunks of glass strewn about the dark gravel of the parking lot. Whoever had done it must have climbed onto some kind of step stool and smashed the window with a rock, because there was no way a regular punch would have broken through. Crow reflexively looked around the private lot, seeing the security tower in the distance.

"And no one saw this happening?" Crow asked in disbelief.

"The security guard says he stepped out for three minutes to the bathroom, came back and it happened," Angela said, a hand to her mouth. "Everyone else was inside the venue. This must have happened while we were all inside." Jordan came out through the back door then, followed by a sweaty Caeri who had joined them for the east coast leg of the tour. She looked pale, her dark blue hair making her elven features pop in contrast, her big green eyes wide in fear.

"Jesus..." Caeri said, her voice trailing off.

This was an escalation. This was someone who was desperate to send a message.

"Did they take anything?" Crow asked. He could hear police sirens in the distance. Familiar sounds now.

"No," Angela said. "But they did leave something on your bed."

"My bed?" Crow felt bile climb up his chest. "They were in my room?"

Crow had to see for himself. He needed to go inside. He walked toward the bus, the door already open. He climbed the steps, Ethan and Angela close behind him. The security guards nodded when he asked if they had cleared the bus.

"Maybe we should wait until the police get here," Ethan said, but Crow was determined. This message was for him, so he was going to see what it was. He took a deep breath as he pushed open the bedroom door. His room was exactly as he had left it, the bed made, clothes thrown on the back of a chair, underwear piled in a corner by the hamper, some of them inside the hamper.

One thing was different. An addition. A doll sitting on the center of the bed, propped up with the pillows.

"Fuck," Crow said, feeling himself break into a cold sweat. How could he be so hot and cold at the same time? He could feel Ethan wrap an arm around his lower back, like a hook pulling him onto shore, an anchor to keep him grounded. Crow felt sick. The doll was one of the small porcelain dolls that had been on display at the Toy Museum they had visited. It meant that whoever it was had been watching them even when Crow thought he was safe. They had gone to some random museum without anyone spotting him or tweeting out his location, he thought he had nothing to worry about.

Ethan had been there. He was sure he had nothing to worry about.

He took a breath, trying to regain the blood flow to his extremities.

There was something else about the doll that felt off. It was cracked, all over. The porcelain skin was held together with sloppy pieces of tape, making the smiling baby with the bald head seem even more demented.

But why was it broken?

Crow walked toward the doll. Every step felt like his shoes were filling with cement. He could hear Ethan advising him to stop, to leave it for the police, but Crow needed to see this for himself. He could see a corner of a piece of paper sticking out from one of the cracks. Before anyone could tell him others, he grabbed the corner and pulled. The doll came undone, porcelain chunks falling onto the bed, still taped together in parts.

Crow stepped back from the bed, a folding up piece of

paper in his hand. He looked to Ethan, whose expression was unwavering. He really did do well in high pressure situations.

Crow, on the other hand, was shaking slightly as he unfolded the note and started to read it out loud.

"I feel broken. Just like little Amy here, the doll you have in your hands. Amy. I like that name. It could be the name of our daughter one day. Wouldn't that be nice? Little Amy. Hell, we could even name our little teacup piggy that. I know you want one of those. Just like you're going to want me. You want that, I know you do. So STOP breaking my heart. I see you with that man, and I can't have it anymore. Break things off or Little Amy won't be the only thing being held together with tape."

Crow felt his blood pressure plummet. He was close to passing out. This was no longer some dumb online troll who didn't mean any real harm. This was someone who was clearly unhinged and also close to Crow in one way or another. This person knew that Ethan had taken him to the toy museum.

"And teacup pigs," Crow repeated. "That's not something everyone knows. I think I said it in one random interview like a year ago. And that was to some unknown blog which probably doesn't even exist anymore. What the fuck..."

Ethan must have felt the fear sticking to Crow like a film of cold sweat. He felt Ethan's hand rub his back, the spot between his shoulders, exactly where Crow loved being rubbed. It helped calm him down, and the fact that it was Ethan who was doing it increased the calming effect.

Until his mind snapped back to the note.

Break things off or else...

Crow shook Ethan's hand off his back. It was making

him sick. This entire thing had him physically ill. He stumbled to the bathroom, the world funneling in like a fucked-up haunted house attraction, where the walls are programmed to collapse. He made it to the bathroom in time, emptying his stomach into the toilet. Ethan came in with a glass of water and knelt down, his hand returning to that one spot. Crow looked up from the toilet, silent tears running down his cheeks.

"Everything is so good. Why? Who would do this?"

Ethan put on a strong face. Those baby blues were as soothing as looking out onto a calm ocean, the water serene, gentle waves breaking through on occasion. Except now, Crow had to look away. He felt like he was seconds from drowning. Another wave of nausea hit.

"You're ok. Everything's ok. Listen to me, Crow, nothing is going to happen to either of us."

"They were in our room. They knew where we were. They broke in and I'm sure didn't leave behind a trace of anyway to find them. That's what the cops are going to say. That's what they've said each and every other fucking time. 'Nothing we can do now, except keep an eye open.' Well *fuck*, my eyes are wide open, Ethan, and I really don't like what I'm seeing."

"Neither am I, Crow, but we aren't going to let this fuck things up. I've had my life get completely thrown off the rails by circumstances I couldn't control. This, though? We can control this. Together."

Crow grabbed the cold glass of water. He sat up and away from the toilet, drinking the water, feeling comfort in sitting cross-legged on the bathroom floor with Ethan across him.

"But being together is the problem. Ethan, if anything ever happens to you, I —"

"You don't need to think about that," Ethan said, cutting him off. "I had to work real hard getting rid of that thought pattern, so don't even start going down that path. We can't live life like that, and we definitely aren't going to live life in fear of being together."

"I'm scared," Crow said, feeling a moment of vulnerability rush over him. He felt like a jellyfish without the stingers and washed up on shore; limp and useless.

Ethan put a hand on Crow's face, his thumb gently rubbing the ridge of his cheekbone. Crow found the courage to look into Ethan's eyes, and those sapphire eyes staring back somehow managed to lend him even more strength. "We're going to be ok," Ethan said, wearing a smile that seemed indestructible. "You know why?"

"Why?"

"Because our love is too strong for any other outcome."

(End of Chapter)

(finished)

22 ETHAN WINTER

TWO DAYS LATER

2/18/21

(Read tonight — 8 or 7pm)

They were all lounging around the living room area as the bus drove down the highway. They were luckily able to find someone who could fix their window in record time. He was Troy's cousin, so he gave the group a discount, which Angela had greatly appreciated. Now, Frankie was at the table, Troy across from him, Crow and Ethan cuddled together on the couch, Angela pinned to her iPad on the chair across, and Jordan sitting on the floor, cross-legged and chewing on a pencil, a Sudoku puzzle book open on his lap. The mood on the tour bus had substantially shifted. Things had escalated far past the point anyone was expecting. This was all supposed to be some bored troll, sending weird messages just to freak Crow out. The letters were supposed to stop and that would be the end of that. Everyone would have gone on living their happy little lives.

Instead, someone broke into the tour bus without anyone seeing, and entered into Crow's bedroom. It was a violation and a threat. Ethan was scared, but he felt more worried for Crow than anything else. He didn't want this casting a shadow on what was supposed to be one of the

Stop @ 8pm

best times of his life. Everything outside of the stalker situation was going so well, for both of them. And now, he could see the fear in Crow's soft brown eyes. He didn't express it and had barely talked about it over the last few days, but it was clear that the entire thing weighed heavily on his mind. His golden laughs were few and far between, and the nights they spent together were soft and warm, with a lot of spooning and cuddling and not much else. They both were worried, but Ethan had to remain solid for Crow. He knew that the moment he cracked the façade and revealed how anxious he really was, Crow would feed off that and become ten times worse.

There was another facet to this. A fear that was growing larger and larger every day. Ethan was scared he was going to lose someone all over again. The thought was unbearable and never put Ethan into a good headspace, but he had been able to work out of it by reminding himself that not all stories had to end the same way. Some of them did have happy endings, and he was determined to make that the case for theirs. He couldn't imagine the world giving him another blow like it already had. How cruel would that be?

The world's a cruel place.

He had to snap out of it. He shifted on the couch, bringing his head closer to Crow's. The scent of his fruity shampoo drifted up from his messy bed head. They had spent the entire morning laying in bed, watching old Nanny episodes and enjoying each other's presence.

"Anyone down for some cards," Ethan asked, not getting much of a response from the room. "Ok, never mind."

"Sorry, bub, I'm just not in the card playing mood," Crow said, sounding down. Ethan hated hearing that in his voice. Crow had such an exceptional voice, whether he was singing or reciting a damn recipe. Ethan never wanted that voice to fill with sadness, except he was finding that there was little he could do except just be there for Crow and make sure he knew he wasn't alone in this.

"It's alright," Ethan said, bringing Crow's hand up to his lips and placing a gentle kiss on the back. "We can just hang out."

"How about some Smash Bros?" Frankie said. "You know what they say about bros before hoes." He gave a pointed look to Ethan before he cracked into a smile.

"Alright, alright, let's do it." Crow perked up a little. "I call Pikachu."

"I thought you were more of a Jigglypuff kinda guy," Ethan noted.

Crow put a hand up. "That's offensive."

Ethan and Crow both laughed as they got up to make some room on the couch. The TV had been mounted on the opposite wall and was already plugged into the gaming console, so they didn't have to do much before the three guys were in a virtual world beating each other up with cartoon characters.

It was a pretty great stress reliever.

After a few rounds, Jordan came from the table and asked to join. He sat on the other side of Frankie, jumping in and slaughtering everyone with his surprising skills as Mario.

"Ok, I'm bored, you guys are no challenge," Jordan said, getting up once a couple of rounds had finished. "I'm almost finished with my crossword; I'm going to work on that."

"A crossword?" Frankie asked. "When were you bitten by a weremother?"

"A weremother?" Crow asked. Ethan had a feeling he knew where this was going.

"Yeah, you've never heard of it?" Ethan asked, jumping

in for Frankie. Crow shook his head, genuinely interested. "It's an old ancient Nordic sickness. Was discovered a few years back after some ice melted. All over the news, too. You sure you hadn't heard it?"

"No," Crow asked, sounding a little frustrated. He was looking to Ethan, so he didn't see Frankie starting to crack on his other side.

"Well," Ethan started, not even sure what he was about to say, "a weremother is when a grandmother crochets, or works on a crossword puzzle in this case, under a full moon until the sun comes up, turning her into a monstrous beast that can then spread her banal interests through a quick chat at the bus stop."

"You're a fucking asshole," Crow said, shaking his head and smiling as he realized the joke. "I mean... I honestly should have seen that coming."

"You were so interested, I had to," Ethan said, smiling as he leaned in to kiss his man. Once again, he found himself surprised as how happy he was feeling. Even with all the shit surrounding them, Ethan still felt like he was floating along on Cloud Nine, with Crow at his side.

They lounged around for a little longer, the bus going on down the highway toward their next stop. Ethan couldn't believe they were already on the last leg of the tour. It felt like years ago when he was in Sierra View's break room, getting asked to say yes to something that was going to change his life in so many different ways. He remembered how much doubt he had about taking the job. He had been fine with his routine. Sad, but fine. He was so close to saying no. That thought scared him. He realized now how much he needed this, how much he needed Crow. A reminder that the world wasn't supposed to be a dark place, it just had its dark moments. And even then, there was always a light switch to be found.

"Ok," Frankie said, cutting through the silence. "Honestly, it's been bugging me. Can we talk about this whole stalker thing? Maybe we can Scooby Gang the shit out of it and figure out who it is."

Ethan tensed, feeling Crow shift next to him. "Let's do it," Crow said, clapping his hands, apparently choosing to put on a strong face. Ethan admired that about him. "Staying quiet about it isn't helping, so maybe some more talking will help."

Ethan nodded. "Talking usually does. Anyone have any ideas?" Ethan looked around the room. Jordan didn't look up from his puzzle, while Frankie was looking out the window in thought.

"Hmm," Frankie said, clearly taking the Freddy role. "Crow, you don't have any exes that maybe didn't take the break-up so well?"

Crow shook his head. "Nope. I've never really even had a serious boyfriend. Not until Ethan."

"Ethan, you say?" Frankie looked toward Ethan, arching a playfully suspicious eyebrow before he smiled and went back to looking out the window.

"And those notes. Is there anything you recognized in them?" Frankie asked. "Handwriting or something?"

"Nothing," Crow said, a hand messing up his hair. "Besides the teacup pig thing, which could mean they either fell down a deep internet hole and found my random interview where I mention it, or..."

"Or it's someone that knows you well." Frankie finished Crow's sentence, the words sounding more ominous than when they were just thoughts in Ethan's head. Just like Caleb had suggested at the dinner.

"I feel like it *has* to be someone you know, or at least that you've seen," Jordan joined in then, looking up from the puzzle. The pencil's pink eraser was all chewed up. "They were close enough to you to see that you and Ethan were together before it was ever publicly announced. Are there any faces you can remember from the earlier crowds? Faces that kept popping up?"

Ethan looked down at his hands. He remembered that one girl from the random street encounter. He had already talked about her with Crow, though, and he insisted that she was just a super fan. Ethan had argued that the line between super fan and stalker was getting thinner and thinner, but Crow didn't see it. He just thought that Angela had overreacted with everything going on and intimidated her, thinking that maybe she was the culprit. Ethan thought that they should talk to Angela about it, but she had been so busy with everything going on, Crow had kept putting it off, thinking it wasn't very important. Now, he sat up on the couch. "I can't say for sure," he said, sounding stressed. "Fuck, if only I paid more attention."

"It's ok," Ethan said, reaching a hand out and rubbing Crow's thigh, his sweatpants soft under Ethan's touch. "No one's saying you have to remember every face. There was that one girl who bumped into us on the street though," Ethan said, bringing her up again incase anyone else had a story to share. He was going to bring up the meet and greet situation, but with Angela sitting right there in the middle of the group, he thought it would be wiser to wait until she was alone. She was the type of person that would shelter in place, shutting things out if she was overly stressed and put on the spot in front of other people.

"Yeah, but she just seems genuinely excited to be following the tour, I don't know, maybe it's naive of me, but

I don't get a 'breaking and entering' kind of vibe from her," Crow said. Ethan noticed Angela perk up, but the conversation kept moving before she could ask anything.

"Beside," Frankie chimed in, "it's not unheard of to have people following a musician around the tour. Groupies are still a thing."

"True," Jordan said, looking back down at his puzzle before popping back up almost immediately. "Although, the whole broken porcelain doll thing is unheard of. Just sayin'."

Ethan felt a shiver crawl down his spine at the mention of that doll. If the stalker wanted to send a clear message, they had certainly done that. Crow and Ethan had talked about the message during one of the nights neither of them could find sleep. Both had been tossing and turning, keeping quiet in hopes that the other could at least find some peaceful shuteye. After an hour of this, Crow spoke first, in a small whisper. "You awake?"

"Yes," Ethan said, foregoing the whisper. They both chuckled and turned toward each other. Ethan remembered how happy he was to see Crow's face etched in soft whites and barely-there oranges from the residual light sneaking in from the lampposts.

"I spoke with the sheriff," Angela chimed in, breaking Ethan out of his thought. She was still looking down at her iPad, "before we left, he told me that they had a decent lead. Apparently there was a traffic camera across the street that might have caught whoever did it. They said they'd be in touch as soon as they have news."

"Really?" Crow asked, "that's incredible, why am I just learning about this?"

"Because it's not a sure thing yet. The angle might be covered by the bus itself, and then they'll be back at square one, especially if whoever did it was smart enough to sneak by with a hoodie or something." Angela sighed, her eyes looking more tired than ever. She must not have been getting much sleep either. "I didn't want to get your hopes up, Crow."

"It would still be good to know," Crow said, frustration playing in his voice. This entire situation was causing more and more friction. The stress was hanging in the air like a dense fog.

"Sorry, Crow, I wish I could just stop it all with the press of a button," Angela said, putting her iPad down. "Trust me, seeing you like this isn't fun for anyone. We're all on this tour for you, and it all started off on such a great note. Then, from one second to the next, things turned to shit. It sucks. I wish there was something more I could do."

"Seriously," Frankie joined in. "This sucks for all of us, but I can't even imagine what you must be feeling, Crow. Fuck, man."

"It's not the best, that's for sure." Crow held his shoulders high, even though Ethan could see the weight of this all wearing him down. Ethan was just like the others. He wished there was something more he could do to keep Crow from having to go through this. He was happy that he got to sleep next to him and make sure he felt protected, but that still didn't feel like it was enough.

Silence soon followed, the Scooby Gang seemingly disbanded. It wasn't like they had a long list of suspects to look through. Ethan felt a twist of helplessness grab at his gut. He looked around the room, everyone else trying to get lost in something but their eyes still holding on to that worried feeling.

"I need to go lay down," Crow said, getting up from the couch. He didn't look back at Ethan, just started walking toward the bedroom. Jordan caught Ethan's eye and nodded in Crow's direction. He was thinking of giving Crow a little space, but fuck that. He was going to hold Crow in his arms and kiss the top of his head until that man felt ok. He wasn't going to let him feel this fear on the last few stops of his first national tour.

Ethan got up and followed Crow to the bedroom, leaving the rest of the gang in their silence.

(End of chapter)

23 CROW KENSWORTH

He felt like shit. Crow couldn't shake it off. He was normally good about letting things roll off his shoulders, like water off a damn duck's back. He didn't like stressing out about things he couldn't control, and this was something that was incredibly out of his control. But it wasn't so much that part of it which caused him the anxiety. It was the fact that Ethan was involved, and from the sound of it, he was becoming a bigger and bigger target. It had all started off feeling like a creepy, off-color joke. Now it was beginning to feel more like a horror movie, complete with the nightmare-inducing porcelain dolls.

He rolled into bed and threw the comforter over his head. He felt the bed sink moments later when Ethan got in, an arm coming over Crow's side. Crow felt silent tears start rolling down his cheek, a trail of wet fear rolling down onto the pillow. He didn't want this to end, and he didn't want to be forced to end it. On the same token, he was now risking Ethan's life just by being with him. How fucked up was that? They were supposed to be each other's saviors, not executioners.

They laid there for a while, Crow trying to control his emotions while Ethan was pressed against his back, his body warmth coming through the covers. It was exactly what Crow needed, but also a reminder of what had him scared in the first place. He was beginning to think that he didn't care what the stalker threatened to do to himself, all he was thinking about was what they had planned for Ethan if their relationship continued.

If.

Another stab of sadness brought more tears. These weren't as silent. Crow's shoulders shook as he tried holding them back. Ethan must have sensed something, because he held Crow even tighter and kissed the back of Crow's head, which was peaking out from the covers.

"I'm here, it's ok."

"That's what I'm scared of, Ethan." Crow's voice was tight. He swallowed back more tears. He pulled the covers off his head and rolled over, face to face with the man of his dreams. "They want us apart."

"And we won't give them what they want. For what? So we could live without each other, feeling worse off than before? Giving power to some crazy person who's going to get caught sooner or later? Absolutely not. I refuse. You're my world, Crow, and I'm not going to let anyone hurt you."

Crow wanted to fall deep into what Ethan was saying, but he knew the universe could have a very fucked up sense of humor. He felt like Ethan understood that too, and maybe that's why he was so certain that he could protect Crow. Maybe because he felt like the universe already fucked things up once, twice would just be overkill.

Crow took a breath. There were no longer any tears, but there was definitely sadness and fear. Ethan brought a hand up to Crow's face, his soft palm encompassing Crow's slightly wet cheek. His thumb rubbed softly. The physical contact helped bring Crow down from his anxiety trip. The serene blue eyes staring back at him helped end the anxiety all together. Ethan was right. As scared as Crow was, he had to believe that the stalker was going to get caught and that nothing was going to happen to them. There was that one traffic camera the police had to look over, and Crow was sure that couldn't have been the only mix-up. The cops had checked the tour bus over for any evidence and didn't find any, but that didn't mean something couldn't turn up.

Crow sighed. "What a fucking mess."

"For real." Ethan cracked a gentle smile. He looked so good, even though the bedroom lighting was dim. Ethan had the ability to look good in any lighting. "At least you'll have material for your song writing."

Crow chuckled, surprising himself. "I could become the Stephen King of the pop charts."

"Imagine?" Ethan asked, playing along. "All your songs could be crazy upbeat, but the lyrics get more and more fucked up until you end the song with an alien invasion sent over by Satan himself."

"I think I've read that one."

"Or, you could make a love song and people end up realizing that you're singing it from the perspective of a crazy clown monster. Leave hints like 'I'll always love you under the big top' or 'baby, run with me through the field of fun house mirrors,'. And then end it with the clown eating someone but make it sound romantic. People will eat that shit up."

Crow was laughing now. "We're on to something here. I could call the album.... 'Stephen's Throne.'"

"I like it. Obscure enough but still poetic. Stephen King. A throne. Perfect."

Crow chuckled at the absurdity. Ethan was smiling, his eyes glowing bright every time the bus drove past a streetlight. Neither of them could hold back the urge. They both pushed in at the same time, their lips coming together and their bodies moving closer on the bed. It was soft, almost delicate. No tongues, just lips. Slow. Soft. Started at the tip of their toes, climbed up through their thighs, hugging their backs, warming their necks. Crow swallowed a soft moan from Ethan, who's hands were beginning to explore more of Crow's body, running over his shorts, past his hip, setting on Crow's chest. Suddenly, his t-shirt felt like a prison. He had to strip it all off. He had to feel Ethan's body against his. It was an urge so primal it almost surprised Crow how badly he felt he needed it.

He sat up in the bed and grabbed the bottom of his shirt. He pulled it off and threw it to the side. Ethan followed suit, throwing his in the pile. They worked on each other's shorts next. Crow reaching in and grabbing the zipper, pulling it down gently over the already massive bulge. Ethan's dick gave a rogue throb against the white briefs that were left once the shorts were off. A dark spot stained the tip where Ethan was already leaking. Crow licked his lips and rubbed Ethan's erection over his briefs, causing him to drop his head back with a groan.

He wanted to have him in his mouth again. He went down, pulling Ethan's briefs with him, tugging them off his ankles and throwing them to the side. Ethan's fat cock bounced free, begging to be licked. Crow more than obliged, running his tongue up and down the shaft, licking around the head, tasting the salty sweetness before sucking Ethan into his mouth, immediately eliciting a grunt and a tensing of thighs. "Fucckk," Ethan hissed into the air. Crow reached

down and pulled his own underwear off, letting his dick out
of the tight fabric.

Who knew this was exactly what Crow needed?
Ethan's dick in his mouth and he was calm as a fucking
button. All he was focused on was pleasing his man, making
him writhe on the bed as he slobbered on his dick.

He kept going for a while longer, savoring it all, coming
up for breath to then move down and pop one of Ethan's
balls into his mouth. This had Ethan's toes curling as Crow
played with his balls, licking the sensitive flesh just underneath, causing Ethan to buck up in pleasure.

"I want to be in you," Crow said, kissing his way back
up to Ethan, who moaned a 'yes' in response as Crow's dick
rubbed against his ass, pushing his balls up. He reached over
and grabbed a condom from the nightstand. Their lips
locked, moans and grunts mixed, Ethan was pushing his
hips off the bed, rubbing his ass on Crow.

It was so fucking hot, Crow knew he wasn't going to last
long. He looked down and held his cock down at the base as
he pressed the head against Ethan's pink hole. Ethan was
holding his ass open for Crow, which drove him completely
fucking nuts. The view was almost enough to undo him.

He looked back at Ethan's piercing sapphire blue eyes
as he pushed in past his tight entrance. Ethan gasped as he
adjusted to Crow, who continued to push a little deeper. He
pulled back before sinking a little more. The warmth and
tightness that surrounded him was beyond words kind of
good. It was the kind of thing that inspired an artist to write
a Grammy winning record and paint a fucking Mona Lisa
type masterpiece all in one night. It felt *that* fucking good.

He pushed in deeper, feeling the warmth envelope him
entirely. He shut his eyes and stayed there for a moment,
relishing in the feeling, hearing Ethan's breaths and feeling

his channel tighten around him. Crow pulled back and then thrust in deep, sinking his cock into Ethan until his balls were slapping against Ethan's ass. He was going harder now, drawing whimpers of pleasure from Ethan. It was one of the hottest sounds a grown man could make, and Crow didn't want it to end. He kept going, reaching down and grabbing Ethan's hard cock as he continued to fuck him. Ethan's eyes were rolling back. His hands grabbed fistfuls of the sheet. Both of the men were getting close. The edge was near.

A few more deep thrusts. A few more groans. A few more whimpers.

"Fuck, you're going to make me come," Crow growled, still pounding into Ethan.

"Do it," Ethan begged. His own orgasm took over as Ethan's cock throbbed in Crow's grip, shooting out ropes of comes. The sight and sensation combined to throw Crow off the highest ledge he had ever climbed. Crow's orgasm rocked through his every muscle as he pulled out and ripped off the condom, squirting all over Ethan, some of it getting on his chin, and turning him into an even bigger sexy mess.

"Wow," Ethan said with a chuckle. "I'm... a mess."

"You're welcome," Crow toyed, smiling as he came down for a kiss. "It's not a bad look for you if I'm being honest."

"What? Being covered in come?" Ethan smirked. "Thank you, I'm thinking of wearing this look out to one of our dates."

"You can rock it," Crow joked, laughing and feeling like his body had turned into play-doh in seconds flat. With their bodies spent, Crow managed to roll out of bed and grabbed a soft white towel from the closet. The bus was equipped with a shower, but it was outside and small and also limited use. He did have a separate bathroom with a sink in his bedroom though, so he wet the towel with warm water and used that to clean up. Ethan's mess was a little more intense, so he hopped in the shower for a few quick minutes before coming back.

By the time they crawled back into bed and nestled up next to each other, Crow's entire universe felt fuzzy. Like a soft blanket that he could reach out and wrap around him, tighter and tighter. He felt so safe, with Ethan's arm thrown across his side, his firm chest pressed against his back, his soft cock tucked against Crow's ass, the heat that came off of Ethan and warmed Crow. Everything about it felt so right. Nothing was out of place. Everything right where it needed to be. He took a deep breath, held it, found his center, and exhaled, feeling happier than he had ever been. His tour was coming to a close and he felt like his music had been pushed to an entirely new level, but even beyond that, he connected with his soul mate that first night at the bar. He was never going to forget the feeling he got when he looked out into the crowd and connected with Ethan's steely gaze. Just like he'll never forget the nights they spent up laughing together, watching dumb YouTube videos until they fell asleep. Or like how he'll never forget the first time he pushed inside of Ethan, deep and passionate and raw and everything Crow ever fucking wanted. He'll never forget being one with Ethan, and he knew he was always going to want it.

"You feel so good in my arms," Ethan said.

"I was just thinking about how good it feels to be in your arms," Crow said into the dark room. The bus sped on down the highway. They were supposed to be crossing over into North Carolina, on their way to it's Southern cousin.

"Ok, good, I was scared my arm was too heavy or something. Your breathing got funny."

Crow chuckled. "I forgot you were a doctor for a second. It's like you're hyperaware of my body."

"Is that a bad thing?" Ethan asked mischievously, pushing his hips forward a little.

"Not in the slightest," Crow said, loving how Ethan's chubby dick felt against him. He felt his own cock start waking up again, even though he thought he was spent from their last fuck. "That was just me doing a breathing exercise some yoga teacher had me do once. It was for one of Red's movies. About finding your center and really reveling in it, kind of visualizing the air as a river going through you, and then replacing that thought with a river of all the happy things going on in your life. I don't know, when we had tried it back then, there wasn't really all that much in my life I could be happy about. I was still working as an assistant and living in the closet. I put up a smiling face, but that wasn't always the case. And I could never really picture the river, so I thought it was all just dumb. It didn't work for me."

Ethan pressed his lips to the back of Crow's head. "And now?"

"Do I see the river?"

"Mhmm."

"I see a whole damn ocean," Crow said. He rolled over, facing Ethan now. "An ocean of happiness. An ocean full of love. How can I not? Your eyes alone are like little windows over the calmest ocean ever. So *blue*. And your heart, it's so damn big. You make me laugh and you're also incredibly intelligent. And, let's not forget," Crow's hand slipped down between them, running over Ethan's soft dark pubes, cupping his cock, giving a gentle squeeze, "you're also crazy sexy and your heart isn't exactly the biggest thing about you. How can I not be happy?"

Ethan was grinning. The room was dark, lit only by the passing yellow highway lights outside that broke in though the sides of the thick brown curtains. But Ethan was definitely grinning. Crow could see that. Hell, he could practically feel it. Ethan's smile was so damn special, it filled a room and it made Crow's heart skip a beat every damn time. "Well let's hope my cock isn't bigger than my heart because we'd both be having problems."

Crow laughed, feeling that ocean of happiness rise up inside him, the tide swelling. "Ok fine, *second* biggest thing... well, wait, I think a penis is longer than a heart, right? Isn't a heart the size of my fist."

Now Ethan was laughing. "About the size, yeah, but I guess I'm thinking girth. My cock isn't exactly fist-sized either."

"You're right, you're right... thank god." They were both laughing. "I can't believe I just had a scientific discussion about which is bigger, a heart or a dick."

Ethan pushed across the distance between them, catching them both in a smiling kiss. Their lips were curled at the corners as their tongues danced, their heads lifting from the pillows so that they could work the angles. It was soft and slow. Two naked men laying in the dark, displaying their intense attraction and complete devotion to each other with soft lips bites and tongue swirls, in ways only the other would ever know or feel.

They kissed for another eternity. Crow pulled back for a breath, his eyes finding Ethan's in the passing flashes of light. Blue. So... damn...

"Blue," Crow said in a low voice.

Ethan winced. It was hard to see in the low light, but

Crow didn't miss it. "Has anyone ever called you that?" Crow asked, seeing the turmoil that flashed for a second in the calm seas of Ethan's eyes. Something that told him there was a past linked with that name.

"Adam," Ethan confessed. His voice was tight, but he wasn't drawing away either. There were none of the walls that Ethan had previously fortified and built around him. Crow sensed an openness. "He called me Blue from the get. From the day I met him, sitting in the same exact booth that you and I met in."

24 ETHAN WINTER

E than felt a second of sadness swell up inside him before it was tamped down, replaced by an acceptance that soon made way for the happiness Crow gave him. He knew he would never stop feeling that pang of pain in his chest whenever something reminded him of Adam, but he also knew he couldn't be a slave to it either. Adam would have hated that. And so Ethan took a breath and found strength in the man laying next to him, their bodies only inches apart, their legs tangled together at the ankles, their feet lazily playing with the other.

"I met him at that bar in Santa Monica, the one you had your opening night at. I think that's why I started going back to it a few months ago. It felt like I was moving on without leaving him behind. I don't know, it was weird." Crow shook his head, ready to interject, but Ethan kept going. "There's a palm tree etched into the corner of the table we were sitting at. He got a tattoo of it on his side. Said it symbolized his move to Los Angeles and his meeting the love of his life. I was supposed to get a similar tattoo but never got to before the accident. And then I was just torn up for so fucking long... And then you showed up, and suddenly nothing made sense anymore. I was used to living with nothing much to look forward to. And yeah, that sounds *really* fucking shitty —and in hindsight, it definitely is — but back then, it was my reality, my normal. But the moment you started singing, I felt something shift. It was like a reminder of everything I had been denying myself. Happiness, thrill, bliss. All of it. And then we talked, and we clicked, and *fuck* did I want to see you again. But I thought that I wasn't, and I felt myself going back into my routine. Sinking back down to the part of myself that forgot what joy felt like. Tasted like. Sounded like." Ethan's thumb rubbed Crow's cheek, feeling the slight stubble. "And then I got booked onto this tour and the rest is history."

"Jesus, Ethan," Crow's eyes were filled with a sense of sadness. "I never want you to lose this happiness again. Your smile is too big, your eyes too bright. I'm swearing, right here and right now, that I will keep on singing as long as I physically can as long as it puts a smile on your face."

"And I'll keep listening until I can't anymore."

Crow's eyes searched Ethan's. "How long were you both together, if you don't mind me asking?"

"Not at all," Ethan said. He actually appreciated Crow's question. He never wanted Adam to be forgotten, and the only way that was going to happen was by talking about him. It helped Ethan obtain a sense of peace and didn't make it feel like it was some big fucked-up secret between him and Crow. "We met two years before we got engaged. He had just moved to Los Angeles from Portland and was going out by himself so he could make friends. He wanted to be a producer. He had an eye for talent, that was for sure."

"He sounded like a great guy."

"He was," Ethan said. He hadn't talked this much about Adam to anyone. It felt therapeutic in a way. Like sharing this wonderful person who had made such an impact on his life was somehow setting him free. Ethan felt his eyes water but no tears flowed. He was filled with emotion, and of course sadness was there, but there was an overwhelming happiness that was mostly in part because Crow was the one listening to him speak. He could feel his warmth under the sheets, see his eyes glow with the passing lights.

Ethan felt lifted. He was somewhere above the clouds. He was sure he would never have felt like this again, not after Adam. Ethan moved for a kiss, goosebumps spreading down his back. The good kind. The warm kind, that send a soft desire pulsing through you.

"I love you," Ethan said, the words flowing like a river.

"I love you, too," Crow said, his soft breath caressing Ethan's lips. They were so close, in so many different ways. The night was late but their life together was just beginning. Ethan felt his heart fill with that familiar warmth that used to hug him to sleep and wake him up as one of the happiest people on earth.

"So now you definitely have to write a song about me," Ethan toyed, running a thumb over Crow's soft lips.

"I have an entire library of songs about you already."

"You do?"

"Mhmm," Crow answered mischievously. "You've been a storm of inspiration. Every time I get a minute alone, I'm writing. I think I have an entire album by now."

"That's incredible," Ethan said, "and not even because the songs are about me. I just love how talented and dedicated you are to your music. I always admired people who could sing and write, and you can do both so damn well. How are you even real?"

"I guess this is the moment I tell you I'm actually an android hell-bent on taking over this world."

"I knew it."

"You did?"

"Yeah," Ethan said, smiling playfully as they kissed. "There's no way a regular human can be as talented and smart and funny. You're also one of the sexiest androids ever."

"Thank you," Crow said, mimicking a classic robot voice.

They both broke down into laughs and kisses and tangled limbs.

(End of chapter)

(finished)

25 CROW KENSWORTH

It was midday, Crow and Ethan were lounging naked in the bedroom as the bus rolled on through Pennsylvania on the way to New York. The blinds were half shut, letting them see out the darkly tinted windows at the vast countryside they were cutting a path through. They had planned a day filled with Netflix and chill (emphasis on the chill part). Crow couldn't have been happier. It was paradise. He could have been told he'd just won a million dollars and still not feel as happy as he did just laying naked in his man's arms, watching old Friends episodes and stealing kisses whenever he felt like it.

"Wait, I don't think we've even discussed this yet," Crow said, propping himself up on an elbow and pausing the episode. "Who's your favorite friend?"

"Uh oh," Ethan said. "This could be a deal breaker, couldn't it?"

Crow arched an eyebrow. "We'll see."

"Phoebe, obviously."

Crow nodded, his lips pursed. "Ok, ok, I can respect that."

"What?! You mean she's not yours?" Ethan sat up on the bed, looking more shocked than Crow's grandmother when she found out he was gay. He couldn't hold the face as long as she could though, his breaking down into a smile.

"I'd have to throw my vote in for Rachel."

Ethan shook his head. "You think you know someone."

The phone rang from the bedside table. Crow leaned over Ethan, stealing a kiss from him on his way, and grabbed it. The number was unknown. Crow considered silencing it and getting back to cuddling with a very handsome and very naked Ethan, but he pressed answer anyway. It could have been the police calling to say they found something.

"Hello?"

"Hi, Crow! This is Deena, the manager over at The Raging Saddle."

"Oh, hey, Deena. Listen, thanks for understanding about canceling the show. Angela said you offered the deposit back but we felt terrible about taking it."

"Don't even worry about it. I was just calling to see how you're feeling?"

Crow took a breath. Ethan was looking at him with a questioning glint in those blue eyes of his. "Better," Crow answered. "A little shaken but every day is getting better."

"Ok good. Angela scared me a little when she was talking to me."

"I can't even imagine what you must have felt." Crow rubbed his brows with his fingers. "It was your venue."

"Don't even think about me. You're the one going through it." A child's voice could be heard in the background, asking for the remote control. "Sorry, the little guy is begging to change my Bones marathon."

"Turning him into a detective?"

"He says he wants to be a veterinarian, so fingers crossed."

"I'm rooting for him," Crow said with a chuckle. "Thanks again for calling, you really didn't have to."

"I just got a little nervous, that's all. My husband actually just went through the same thing."

"He did?" Crow sat up straighter in bed. Maybe this was somehow connected to his situation.

"Oh yeah." Deena huffed on the other end of the phone. "Worst week of our lives."

"What happened? Did they find the stalker?"

Silence on the phone. "Stalker? No, no, my husband came down with a terrible strain of the flu... what do you mean stalker?"

"A flu?" Crow was thoroughly confused. Ethan could probably read it on his scrunched up facial expression. Ethan sat up in bed, putting a hand on Crow's thigh, searching his eyes for an answer to what was going on.

"Yeah... Angela said you had caught the same thing. She told me there was no way you'd be able to perform."

Crow wasn't computing. He could literally see his brain going into the 'blue screen of death' mode. The one there was no recovery from. What the hell was Deena talking about?

"Deena... was there ever a threat against your club the night I was supposed to perform?"

She huffed on the other end. "A threat? No, thank god, everything was fine. We had a backup performer lined up, although the crowd was definitely disappointed you couldn't show up."

Crow felt a pang of disappointment at failing his fans, but it was clouded by the intense confusion he was feeling.

"I'm going to have to call you back," Crow said, shaking his head as if it would clear the daze over his head.

"Yeah, of course. Good to hear you're well."

Crow hung up the phone and dropped it on the bed, his jaw falling along with it.

"What happened?" Ethan asked.

"Angela canceled my Denver show, saying I had the bird flu or some shit."

Ethan shook his head, clearly as confused as Crow felt. "Maybe she knew something that she didn't tell us? Or maybe Deena's the one that's confused?"

Crow shook his head. One thing was certain, he wasn't going to get any answers by sitting around and staring at Ethan's handsome face all day. He got up, threw on a pair of gray shorts and a tank top and started walking right to the living room. Ethan got up behind him, "Whoa, where are you going?"

"To ask the one person who can clear this entire mess up."

———

"I CAN'T BELIEVE THIS." Angela's face matched the shade of her blouse. Red. She was angry. They were in the living room. The bus had been parked and so the rest of the crew was out exploring the city. Crow was standing across from a steaming Angela, her arms crossed against her chest. "You honestly think I'm somehow involved in all this shit?"

Crow shook his head. He wasn't sure if approaching her out of the blue and asking her if she was the stalker was the right approach, but he was so caught up in the moment, he had to get it out. Crow knew Angela, or at least he thought he knew her, and he was sure that throwing her off balance would be the best way to figure out if she was actually involved in all this. To her credit, she didn't seem to act like someone who had just been called out on some twisted shit. Crow expected a guilty person to stammer and become nervous, trying to find immediate ways out of the conversation. Angela just seemed pissed. Hurt. And Crow could understand why. They were close friends and now Crow was accusing her of being a psycho stalker.

For a moment, Crow wondered if he had gone too far.

"We just want to have a few questions answered, Angela, that's all." Ethan spoke in a tone meant to calm a rabid dog backed into a corner. "There are some things that smell a little fishy."

"How dare you," Angela said, tears pricking at the corners of her eyes, threatening to well up over the dark eyeliner. "All I've done is try and keep Crow safe while turning him into a household name." She looked to Ethan, waving a hand in his direction. "What have you done, Ethan? Besides keeping me awake with your grunts, I don't think you've done much to help Crow. Yes, you're here because we need you, but that's it, Ethan. I can fire you just as quick as I hired you. So maybe reconsider the next time you want to accuse me of stalking Crow. Calling me *fishy*."

Crow stepped in, feeling like this was about to spiral out of control. The last thing he wanted was to turn this into a fight over who got a piece of Crow.

"But why did you cancel Denver? Why weren't you honest with anyone involved? You lied to me and to Deena. Was there ever a threat?"

Angela took a heavy breath out her nose. "You won't get it."

"Try me."

"I had a nightmare, ok? A really bad one. The premoni-

tion kind. Looking back, it might have been extreme paranoia, but I just had a really bad feeling about that night and
I knew I had to do something. I knew we would make up
the show in the future, and I balanced all the books to make
sure any hits to our ticket sales were doable. I thought that if
we needed to stretch, I would have added money in from
my own pocket. It would have been fine, my choice, my
consequences. At the time it felt like the right thing to do. I
couldn't, nor would I *ever*, fake a threat so I had to tell
Deena that you had gotten sick." She shook her head. "I
don't know what got into me, but that was my fault.
I'm sorry."

Angela sounded sincerely pained. The look in her big
brown eyes looked like that of a fawn staring down a wolf,
just before it takes off running. "I'm sorry," she said again,
dropping her head. Crow looked to Ethan, who didn't seem
as affected by Angela's apologies. His face was stone-cold,
like he was about to deliver some kind of terrible diagnosis.
Crow could empathize with Angela a little more, though.
He knew how influenced she was by those mystical type of
things. If she did have a vivid nightmare, he could see her
acting on it out of fear.

"What about that one girl?" Ethan asked, pressing on.
"Tricia? The one from the beginning of the tour? She went
to Crow and said you were harassing her? Why are you
harassing a teenager?"

Angela's eyebrows shot up. "Seriously?" she turned on
Ethan. "You still don't get it. I'm doing this to *protect* Crow.
That girl has been to juvenile lock-up *twice*. Once for
beating up a classmate until he couldn't breath and another
for stealing her neighbors' Lexus. She's bad news, and with
everything going on around Crow, the last thing he needed
was more bad news. You know how I found out about her

past? Because her mother reached out to *me*. She knew that her daughter was chasing Crow around the country, and she wanted me to intervene. Jesus. I stopped her at one of Crow's earlier shows and told her to leave him alone and go back to her mother before I get the cops involved. Whatever else she told you two is a complete lie."

"What the fuck," Crow said, starting to feel like he had made a huge mistake in confronting Angela. All she had done during this entire tour was try and keep things running smoothly without having Crow offed by some crazy stalker fan. "I'm sorry, Angela."

Ethan took a step back, giving Angela some space. She turned back to Crow, who opened his arms and took her into a hug. She was stiff at first, but soon warmed up, her hands coming up to Crow's shoulders.

"I'm sorry," Crow said again, feeling terrible for accusing one of his friends of something so terrible. "The pressure of this is getting to me."

They separated, Angela's eyes moist and pink at the corners. "No, it's ok. I understand. I should have been honest from the beginning. Things will be different," she said, managing a smile. "I promise."

"Ok," Crow said, taking a deep breath, feeling like he avoided a crisis. The last thing he wanted to do was lose a good friend because of a bad bout of paranoia.

I just need to chill.

He looked over Angela's shoulder, catching Ethan's sapphire eyes. He glanced up at the clock on the wall. They still had two hours before Crow had to be at rehearsals for that night's show.

I know something we can do for two hours to help me chill.

(End of Chapter)

26 ETHAN WINTER

(finished)

Crow was sweaty and flushed from finishing up his performance, and Ethan loved it. They were in Crow's private room backstage, just the two of them sitting on the couch and talking about what an incredible night it had been. The energy from the New York crowd was absolutely explosive and had left Ethan winded, he couldn't even imagine what Crow was feeling after being the one on stage, all that energy directed straight at him. He had controlled that entire club, a crowd of at least half-a-thousand, all there to celebrate Crow's incredible talent for writing songs and bringing them to life with his voice. At one point, Ethan remembered seeing a few fans breaking down into tears as Crow sang one of his slower songs, about his coming out and how strong it made him. It was beautiful to see what an impact Crow was making on people's lives.

On Ethan's life.

"Did you see Frankie on the drums tonight?" Crow asked, taking a chug from his water bottle. Ethan watched his throat bob, his mouth suddenly starting to water.

"Yeah, he was really feeling it tonight," Ethan said, grabbing an ice cold Corona from the cooler next to the couch. The room wasn't as equipped as some of the other green rooms they've had, so instead of a mini-fridge stocked with alcohol, they had a big blue cooler. Crow put his water down and reached over Ethan to grab a Corona. Ethan couldn't help but get a whiff of sweat and cologne. A perfect mix, especially when it was coming from Crow.

Damn, he's so hot. How can he be so hot?

Ethan's dick gave a rogue throb of greedy need. He had spent hours earlier with Crow, playing around naked in the bus, and yet he still couldn't get enough. Crow might as well have been a controlled substance. Something Ethan would have needed to prescribe to avoid addiction.

It was too late, though. Ethan was already addicted. All it took was one hit, and Crow was all he could think about.

"I can't believe the tour's almost over," Crow said, taking a chug of the ice cold beer. Ethan followed suit, feeling the smooth bite of the beer down his throat. "And I can't believe it's only been months since it started. It feels like we've been on the road for years."

Ethan laughed at that. "I definitely think I've lived more in these past few months than I've lived in the past entire two years. Plus, I think the fact that it feels like we've known each other for years has something to do with it. It warps the perception of time."

Crow nodded. "You're giving me an idea for another song."

"About time? Perception?"

"Yeah, I can hear it now." Crow whipped out his phone and started typing out lyrics, half-speaking, half-singing them out loud. "Time heals all things, time makes all change. Blue makes me see, calm rivers and evergreen trees. A forest of peace and tranquility. Love heals all things, love makes time tick."

Ethan was shocked at how fast Crow could flow with the words. He was truly a force to be reckoned with, and it was obvious to see why he was such a success. Crow put the phone down, chewed on his lip as he thought of more lines, and then took a drink of his beer, finishing it up.

Ethan decided to throw in some more inspiration. "Try to fit in how time is a big ball of wibbly-wobbly, timey-wimey stuff."

Crow arched an eyebrow, stumped at what Ethan was referencing.

"You mean you've never seen *Doctor Who*?" Ethan asked, a hand coming up to his chest. "Pfft, we aren't going to sleep tonight."

"Oh?" Crow asked, seeing where this was going.

"Nope. We're binging as many episodes as we can get through. You're going to be TARDIS-certified by next week."

"Tar-wha?"

"Don't worry about it," Ethan said, smiling as he leaned in to steal a kiss from Crow.

"I'll watch whatever you want me to, Ethan." Crow was smiling from ear to ear, his lips slightly wet from beer and Ethan's kiss. The room was lit by two floor lamps on either side of the room, so it actually made for a romantic experience. It didn't hurt that Caeri had reached her slow songs, serenading the crowd outside with her angelic voice.

Ethan had to kiss Crow again. He pushed back in, setting his Corona aside and cupping Crow's hand in his hands, feeling the freshly shaved cheeks, the sharp cheek

bones, the diamond-cut jawline. Their tongues danced to
the music that pumped in from outside. Their bodies moved
closer on the couch, until Ethan was pushing onto Crow,
leaning him back down on the couch.

Crow's hands slipped under Ethan's t-shirt, finding his
lower back and sending fireworks shooting through him.
That was his spot, and Crow knew it. Ethan pulled back,
opening his eyes, Crow doing the same. He smiled up at
Ethan mischeavously, his fingers gliding over Ethan's lower
back and making his knees shake. Then, Crow slipped a
hand underneath the waistband of his dark jeans, under his
briefs, and finding a handful of Ethan's ass, squeezing him
and pulling him down onto him. Ethan immediately felt
how hard Crow was through his jeans. Their cocks rubbed
over the other's as they continued their kiss, clothes beginning to feel like a jailcell.

Fuccckk. I want him so bad.

Ethan was hungry for cock. Crow's to be specific. He
couldn't handle the deep urge he had to see Crow sitting
down on the couch, legs wide and throbbing hard dick in
the air. He needed it. His hands went to working on Crow's
zipper, pulling it down over the already growing bulge.
Ethan fucking loved getting Crow hard from just kissing
him. Crow had the same effect on Ethan. It was potent. A
bond that sparked the air around them. They could hear the
music thumping outside of the green room as the crowd got
hyped up by Caeri's performance, the slow portion of the
song kicking back up again. Instead of opening tonight's
show, they decided to give her a chance at closing it.

Ethan pulled Crow's jeans off and threw them to the
floor. He crawled off Crow and repositioned him so that
Crow was sitting with his bare feet planted on the floor, his

thighs opened wide. Ethan fell to his knees, getting face-level to Crow's glorious fat fucking bulge. He couldn't stop himself from leaning in and mouthing on it through the fabric, taking in the scent of man, worshipping him, relishing in the feeling of Crow's cock struggling against the thin, wet white briefs. Ethan wanted to give him exactly what he was asking for.

He stopped mouthing the soft fabric and put his fingers in the black waistband, pulling them down and watching as Crow's rock hard cock bounced out of its confines. The tip was already wet with precome. Ethan leaned back in, his tongue flicking across Crow's slit, lapping at the clear juice as Crow moaned above him. He felt Crow's fingers thread through his hair, pulling him down harder onto Crow's cock. Ethan opened his lips, taking the velvety soft head into his warm, wet mouth. His tongue drew circles around the sensitive tip, drawing out more moans from his man.

Ethan fucking *lived* for this.

He opened his mouth wider, trying to take more of Crow inside. His cock was big. Ethan loved it. He almost felt addicted to the taste, the feel, whether he was soft or hard. Ethan could play with Crow the entire day and never get bored. He could have stayed between Crow's muscular thighs for the rest of his goddamned life.

Just then, Ethan heard the door open behind him and froze.

"Whoa!" the door slammed shut again. Ethan looked up, feeling his cheeks rush with red. Crow was blushing too, but he was also smiling. He put his fingers back through Ethan's hair and guided him down onto his cock, clearly showing that the interruption didn't bother him. Whoever it was didn't leave, though.

"Sorry, Crow, but, uhm, you're being asked to get back on stage in, uhm, five." The girl's voice on the other side of the door was nervous. It was probably too quick for her to have made out any explicit details, but it was obvious she had walked in on something. It wasn't like most guys hung out between the other one's thighs just for giggles.

"I thought I was done," Crow said, his head falling back as Ethan licked him up and down. He smiled up at Crow, feeling a hot rush come over him.

"Caeri just finished up. The crowd's, uhm, ready to riot. They want at least another song from you."

"Ok," Crow said, biting back a moan as half his cock disappeared down Ethan's throat. "Be there in five," Crow said, his thighs tensing around Ethan. He returned his attention back down to the man sucking his dick. "You do that so fucking good."

"It's because your cock is so fucking good," Ethan said when he came up for breath. "I can't get enough of it."

"Good," Crow said, grinning wide before biting his lower lip as another intense wave of pleasure took him over. Ethan was fondling Crow's tight balls now. He felt his own needy cock pulse against his jeans, his briefs getting slick with precome. And he didn't care. All he wanted to focus on was Crow's tasty cock and heavy balls.

"It's going to have to wait until after the encore," Crow said, thrusting his hips slightly up, burying his cock deeper down Ethan's throat.

Ethan came back up, a rope of saliva trailing down Crow's shaft. Ethan grabbed him in a fist and jerked him off as he came up for a kiss, letting Crow taste himself on Ethan's tongue. They stayed like that for a few minutes before Crow started pulling back.

"Wait," Ethan said, getting up and walking over to his

backpack. His hard-on was clearly visible, pushing against the front of his jeans as he walked back with the backpack. He unzipped it and pulled out a black velvet draw-string bag. Crow looked from the bag to Ethan, confused.

Ethan, with a smile, opened the bag and flipped it over, emptying it onto his hand.

"Is that a... dildo?"

"A butt plug," Ethan said, "but close enough."

Crow chuckled, his head shaking. "You're crazy."

"I got it one-dayed from Amazon. I wanted to play with you, and I think now might be the perfect time. I want to see you up on that stage, and I want to imagine you with this inside."

Crow's eyes went from Ethan's to the toy back to Ethan. His smile grew wider as he shrugged.

"Put it in me, doc."

Ethan laughed, biting his lip as he grabbed Crow and positioned him on the couch so that he was on his fours, ass in the air. The plug wasn't overly large or anything, but it did have a surprise feature Ethan was going to hold off on telling Crow about. Instead, he grabbed the soft navy blue silicon plug and spat in his other hand. He used his finger tips to get Crow's ass nice and wet, drawing a few moans from the sexy man melting at his touch.

Crow gasped as Ethan pushed the tip of the toy in. "Breathe," Ethan reminded him. With a few more breaths, Crow relaxed enough for Ethan to slip the toy in until the rounded end.

"Oh fuck," Crow said.

"How's that feel?"

"So fucking good," Crow replied. Ethan gave his ass a hard slap and stood up next to the couch. Crow stood up too, his eyes opened wide as the sensation rocked through him.

"Ok, I should take it out now."

"Take it out?" Ethan gave a chuckle. He stepped forward and kissed Crow, reaching down and giving his exposed, still-wet cock a few good strokes. "Crow, you're singing to me out there with that plug deep inside you."

(End of Chapter)

(finished)

Read tonight
12/23/21 - 6 or 7pm
STOP @1:00pm
PRM LOD

"I heard all of y'all wanted an encore?!" Crow said into the microphone as he bounced onto the stage. The crowd roared. It was the after party, so the entire audience was made up of drunk people ready to butcher the lyrics to his songs and sound so confident doing it. Alcohol had that affect on people.

Something else that had an affect on people?

Butt plugs.

Crow couldn't believe it. He walked over to the micstand, grabbing it and looking out into the crowd, his ass clenching around the small blue silicon plug Ethan had put in only moments before. He was aggressively fighting back an erection at that point. Tensing his thighs and trying to reroute blood flow away from his cock, focusing on the crowd instead of the delicious sensation of being secretly filled. Only one other person in the entire building knew what was really going on, and he was currently standing front row at the VIP section, glass of champagne in his hand and a knee-quaking smile on his face.

Fuck, he's perfect.

He thanked god he didn't go commando that day. His briefs were tight enough to hold back his cock from announcing itself as a surprise guest. As the music kicked in, he brought the micstand in closer, using it to block his crotch from view. The club was dark anyway, the only lights that were on were changing between blue, red, and purple and shining out into the crowd from behind Crow. To them, he must have looked like some godly figure, crooning into the mic before the beat dropped and he tore into a set with more upbeat vocals. They wouldn't have been able to make out how hard he was getting from feeling the plug filling him. It was an entirely new sensation for Crow, too. He had only bottomed once before and it was for an overly-aggressive top who had a massive dick. It wasn't the best first experience and had turned him off from exploring it any further. But with Ethan, he wanted to do it all. He felt comfortable enough with him to bend over and have him work a butt plug inside of his ass. And, *damn*, did this feel good. It wasn't painfully large and Ethan had been so gentle with putting it in. Once inside, Crow was surprised at how great it felt. He couldn't wait to get off stage and play even more with Ethan.

It was during the chorus when his world was rocked to an entirely different level.

Suddenly, without any warning, the plug began to vibrate. Gentle and steady and completely electrifying. Crow looked out at the crowd, locking eyes with a grinning Ethan. He held up a remote and bit the end of it, his lips curling up higher.

That...oh fuck... that fucking... shit.... Bastard.... Fuck.

Crow couldn't sing. He had to turn the mic around to the crowd, letting them take the chorus. His cock was rock hard now. He was beginning to get nervous that it would be obvious, but everyone was so drunk and lost in the song and the lighting was terrible. They all knew the words and drunkenly sang the chorus. Crow lifted an arm and started to pump it in the air, fist clenched, to encourage them and also give him a way of releasing the extreme tension that was building in his body. It was a tension that wound tight in his gut and only got tighter with every pulse of vibration the plug gave. His ass clenched tight around it, almost involuntarily pushing it directly against his P-spot, the vibrations rocking him to the very core.

His knees shook for a second before he aimed the mic back to him. He had to look away from Ethan. He glanced to the side of the stage and noticed a big guitar propped up against the wall. It was an arm's length away. Crow reached for it and threw the strap over his shoulder, all while keeping the micstand from blocking any visible penis lines. He felt his thighs twitch as the plug gave a particularly intense pulse. Ethan must have been turning it up.

That fuck... the fuckking, oh fuck, that fucking bastard.

He thumbed at the guitar, his erection now safely and fully covered. He pressed it against the back of the guitar as he tried to hit a high note but had to turn away toward the end, giving it back to the crowd as the plug began to vibrate consistently. Crow could barely see straight. Thankfully, he had been playing the guitar since he could walk, so his muscle memory kicked in and took over the chords.

And then it turned off.

How considerate of him.

Crow grabbed the mic and sang the chorus, driving home the song, keeping his eyes shut as he pictured Ethan being the one inside him. The crowd roared as Crow hit his note, trying not to focus on the intense feeling of being filled while being in front of so many people. He looked back to

Ethan, immediately recognizing his mistake the moment they locked eyes.

It was too much. Crow was about to come. He was going to lose it in front of all these people. Frankie kicked in with the drums behind him then as the song continued, except his edge was right around the corner.

And then, as if a look wasn't enough, Ethan turned the vibrations back on and completely rocked Crow's world. He turned the microphone away from himself and back toward the crowd, letting them sing the song as his orgasm blossomed up from his toes to consume his entire body. He shut his eyes tight and tried to play it off like he was loving the music and not like he was blowing a load into his briefs against the back of a guitar. His knees quaked, but his legs had to stay loose as he tried to jump up and down, hiding the spams. He couldn't, so he flipped the guitar around over his back and leaned down on his thighs, acting as if he needed to catch his breath for a second while the crowd continued to rock it out.

When the wave had crashed, he opened his eyes and took a deep breath before bringing the mic back to his lips. He found Ethan's gaze and gave him a look that said it all. Ethan smiled back and mouthed out 'I owe you'. Crow went on with his song, wrapping it up without anyone but Ethan knowing that he was a sticky wet mess underneath his dark black jeans.

It was one of the hottest nights of Crow's life.

(End of Chapter)

"It's not exactly a creepy toy museum, but I hope you like it just as much." Ethan stepped aside and let Crow take in the scene in front of him.

There was an archway made by thick, twining branches and emerald green ivy, looped through with twinkling fairy lights. Beyond the archway was a square patch of grass, right smack in the center of the private garden, surrounded by round rocks in all kinds in shades of tan and gray and white. There was an antique streetlamp next to the square of grass, it's arched neck hanging over the patch and shining down with its soft orange light. The garden itself was walled in by tall Wonderland-looking hedges that were filled with blossoming roses in all kinds of different colors, giving them a fantasy book feel even though they were still in the middle of New York City. A small pond bubbled in the corner as a bamboo fountain poured water into the pond. The garden was located inside the central courtyard of a five-star hotel, and so it was pretty well insulated from the sounds of the city. Since there was no ceiling, some sound did drift in, but it was worth it so they could look up at the night sky, framed by the building. There were no windows looking down at the picnic area, so they didn't have to worry about any peeping toms.

"This is..." Crow looked from the picnic to Ethan. "Beautiful. Thank you."

"You deserve it. Something completely private, completely serene, and completely for us. Besides, I did say I owed you yesterday." Ethan wrapped his arm around Crow's lower back, pulling him in and kissing the side of his head. He couldn't get enough of having his lips somewhere on Crow's body. Anywhere. He didn't care, so long as it was Crow he was kissing.

"This is perfect." Crow started in through the archway, Ethan right next to him, his hand finding Crow's. Their fingers locked together. They walked to the patch of grass first, going toward the pink and white plaid blanket that had been laid out in the center. There was a heavy whicker basket in the center, opened up with three different trays coming out of it. There were all kinds of cheese, meat, crackers, and spreads. He had found out about the private garden only a few days ago and was lucky to have been able to book it on such short notice.

"You're crazy," Crow said, shaking his head while wearing a wide, sexy smile. "I don't deserve all this."

"Are you kidding me? You deserve this and more. If I could hand you the world right now, I would."

Ethan chuckled, his eyes taking on a devilish glint as his mind went reeling back to yesterday's after show, when Crow was performing to a crowd of hundreds while Ethan controlled the vibrations in his ass. It had been insanely hot and left Ethan with a lasting boner he was sure he would have to see a physician for.

Then he remembered he was a doctor and went back to lusting over Crow.

The wind picked up then, a gentle breeze caressing them. It was summer in New York, and so the days were hot but the nights were bearable. It helped that the both of them were in jeans and a t-shirt. Ethan considered dressing up in a suit for the surprise, but he thought he would be running the risk of turning into a sweaty mess before the part of the night when being a sweaty mess was hot.

Then again, Crow could sweat at anytime of the day and I'd still find it so fucking hot.

They walked hand in hand to the picnic area. They sat down and enjoyed the cheeses and wine, laughing and talking about anything and everything. They talked about Ethan's missionary trip to Haiti and Crow's volunteer trip to plant trees in Australia. They laughed over the prank they had pulled on Frankie last week and they discussed what they thought about Jordan's new-found upbeat atti- tude. By the end of the picnic, Crow's head came to lean on Ethan's shoulder and their conversation turned a shade deeper. Ethan's hand glided higher, reaching Crow's neck and giving him a gentle massage.

"Thank you," Crow said. "For showing me that I actu- ally have the ability to love."

"What do you mean?"

"Before you came along, I swore I was broken. I wrote about love and finding someone's soul mate, but I felt like that would never happen to me. I dated some pretty good guys, but none of them ever lit me up in the way I sang about. Yet everything seemed fine on paper. It should have all added up and I should have at least felt a spark. But I was always pretty bleh about them. Just empty. I guess in your case, you blocked yourself off from love. In mine,"

Crow took a pause. "I was scared I couldn't feel it in the first place."

Ethan kissed the top of Crow's head. "We both had lessons to teach each other."

"It all started with that whiskey," Crow said with a chuckle, reminding them both of that night they first met. "And with this whole stalker thing, you've been nothing but amazing. I don't think I'd be nearly as sane as I am now if you hadn't been around to hold me down. Without you, I know that I'd be obsessed with it. It would have driven me crazy. I'm normally a pretty big scaredy-cat, but you give me a strength I never realized I had."

Ethan stomped down a tendril of fear that crept up at the mention of the stalker. He wasn't going to allow himself to feel that fear. It only gave the stalker the power they were looking for. Instead, he was going to hold on to the hope that the police would figure out who it was soon. He would focus only on Crow and making sure he was ok, in every sense of the word.

"Well hopefully we won't have to deal with it much longer." Ethan held Crow a little tighter. Crow practically melted into his grip, molding to his body. They made a perfect shape together.

A few moments of silence followed before Crow looked up into Ethan's eyes. There was a deep connection there, one that Ethan felt so fucking lucky to have. It was love. Ethan could see it plain and clear. Pure, unadulterated love.

Ethan had to seal the moment with a kiss. He brought his fingers to Crow's chin and lifted his face higher so their lips could meet once again. The kiss was warm and quick to burn, like a brush fire tearing through a drought stricken countryside. His insides burned with a need to have Crow.

To become one with him. He wanted all of Crow. Needed it.

The kiss grew stronger. More passionate. Fingers started pulling at clothes. Tugging until buttons popped loose. Rubbing over growing bulges, grabbing zippers and pulling them down. Soon, both men were standing naked under the light of the streetlamp. They smiled as they pressed their bodies together, kissing once again as their cocks crossed and pressed against the other and heat rolled off them both in waves. Ethan's hands came down to squeeze on Crow's juicy ass, giving them both firm holds before he slipped a finger between the crack. Crow jerked at the feeling, but he didn't pull away. Ethan continued to play with his hole as their kiss grew even more fiery. Ethan could feel Crow's precome smear across his belly as their hips pressed toward each other.

Ethan glanced toward the entrance of the garden, making sure he had thrown the lock on. He went back to kissing Crow before he took a step back, admiring the sexy musician underneath the artificial light. The shadows high-lighted all his muscles, making them pop, his tan skin glowing underneath the light, his fat cock jutting out ahead of him. Ethan couldn't help but reach out and grip him tight.

"I want you to fuck me," Ethan whispered, biting Crow's earlobe in the process. Crow's cock gave a throb in Ethan's grip.

"Let me play with you first," Crow said, "give you a little taste of what you did to me." His voice was gravely and so damn fucking swoon-worthy. Ethan smiled as Crow guided him back down onto the soft plaid picnic blanket. Crow grabbed their discarded shirts and bundled them up, placing them underneath Ethan's head so he had a make-shift pillow to lay on.

Ethan looked up at a smiling, dreamy-like Crow. The night sky painted the background a dark blue. A few stars surprisingly managed to twinkle through the city's light pollution. Well, one was a plane, but *still*, it was romantic and perfect and everything Ethan ever wanted. He looked into Crow's eyes, seeing a deep pool of love reflecting back at him. Ethan pushed up and kissed Crow. Their lips crushed together. Possession and love. Lust and passion. Promises and hopes. Everything was shared between them in that moment, and Ethan knew that there was so much more to come.

Crow pressed his stiff cock against Ethan as they kissed. Ethan felt his body cry out for Crow. He felt every muscle in his body relax as he pushed his ass against Crow's cock. Feeling the slick tip pressed against his hole was pure bliss. He wanted it all and he was so close to just digging his fingers into Crow's hips and pulling him in.

"I need you inside me," Ethan whispered as they caught their husky breaths. They had gotten tested already and so the lack of condoms wasn't a concern. "Please."

Ethan was fucking begging. He wasn't one to plead, but the word came out of his lips without any thought except that Crow needed to get inside of him. Crow brought his hand to his mouth and spat, using it to get Ethan nice and wet, spreading his cheeks with his fingers, sliding them across Ethan's tight hole, teasing him with a tip before pushing a finger in past the knuckle. Ethan gasped, spreading his legs a little wider, his cock giving a rogue throb and leaking a rope of clear precome down onto his belly as Crow sunk his finger in deeper.

Then came the 'come here' motion, and *fuck,* did Ethan

almost come right there and then. A man's P-spot was no joke, and Ethan was certainly not laughing. His eyes shut tight as his hips bucked up, his ass tightening around Crow's finger as he pushed on the magical button that sent every man over the moon and back, again and again.

"Fuck, Crow, that's it. Finger my ass," Ethan managed to say, encouraging Crow to go a little harder. "Fuck, right there. Yeah, use two fingers."

Crow slipped his finger out, leaving Ethan feeling empty and needy, and spat on his hand again, bringing his fingers back to Ethan's ass. He pushed two in past the tight ring of muscle, causing Ethan to moan and roll his eyes back. He tugged on his cock, but stopped short of jerking himself off. He didn't want to blow too early, and with the way Crow was fingering him, he felt like that was a very real possibility.

"Please," Ethan said again. "Fuck me."

This time, Crow seemed happy to oblige. He pulled his fingers out and grabbed his own cock, lining it up with Ethan's tight, wet hole. Ethan's eyes rolled back as Crow pushed in, sinking halfway into Ethan. Both men groaned in pure ecstasy as Crow pulled back out. And then went right back in. Out. In. Out. In. They built a rhythm that rivaled that of one of Crow's hits. Ethan felt Crow's balls slapping against his ass as he thrust balls deep, burying himself inside of Ethan and giving him exactly what he needed. He cried out in pleasure, bucking up as Crow continued to fuck him, hard, giving him all he had. Ethan's legs shook with every thrust, the intense pleasure over-whelming him.

"Oh fuck, fuck," Ethan said, the entire English dictio-nary escaping him at the moment. The only words he could manage to say were 'fuck', and that was barely coming out.

They both turned into grunts and moans. Sweat beaded across Ethan's forehead as his toes curled in the air. Crow held his feet up higher, giving him better access.

Ethan started jerking himself off. His eyes were shut tight as Crow pounded into him. It was bliss. His balls tightened as his body quivered with an impending explosion that was set to rock Ethan's entire fucking universe.

"Ethan, I'm going to come," Crow grunted, his thrusts sporadic, some deep, others shallow. Ethan pushed his hips up, impaling himself on Crow's cock, pushing him over the edge. Ethan clamped his legs around Crow, locking him inside as he unloaded in Ethan's ass. Crow spasmed above Ethan as he filled him up with his seed. Shot after shot, Ethan could feel Crow pulsing inside him, giving him more and more of what he wanted. The feeling was enough to catapult Ethan over his edge. He shouted as the climax blasted through him, shooting ropes of warm come onto his belly, his ass clenching with every shot around Crow's still-coming dick.

When the moment was over, Crow collapsed onto Ethan, his cock popping out of Ethan's ass. They were both breathless and giggling like they were naughty teenager all over again. That was the kind of rush that came over the both of them. It was the type of rush that took you to a completely different time and place. Crow was everything to Ethan, and he was so fucking excited to have this every single day of his life.

"I love you so much," Ethan said, kissing Crow as they laid down on the pillow of shirts. "You were thanking me earlier, but I should be the one thanking you." Ethan swallowed back a sudden cry. The range of emotions he was currently riding were pretty extreme. He felt so relaxed, laying across from Crow and looking deep into his eyes, his body feeling like jello. That also brought other emotions. Intense relief and a powerful happiness. "I don't know how much longer I would have been able to keep things together. I'm positive I was on the road to becoming an alcoholic physician. Someone who ends up getting their sad lives' discovered because they were secretly drunk when they made a mistake on one of their patients. No exaggeration, that was where I was headed." Ethan took a breath. He had never said that out loud. It was one of his biggest fears, and during the time, he was blind to see that it was happening. He would come home from a long shift and knock out an entire bottle of wine by himself. It had started as only a weekend activity until it began creeping into the weekdays. "I was just so damn sad. I didn't know how to handle it. I thought there were no second chances and that I'd never be happy again." Ethan smiled, a real, true smile. One that wasn't propped up on a bottle of pinot. "You showed me that happiness is only one random bar performance away."

A tear rolled down Crow's cheek, wetting the white shirt underneath him. "Jesus, I'm sorry, Ethan."

"It's ok," Ethan said, feeling for once in his life that things were truly ok. Hell, they were way better than just ok.

Whenever Ethan looked into Crow's big brown eyes, he could see that things were truly perfect.

(End of chapter)

(clone)

29 CROW KENSWORTH

THREE DAYS LATER

Read This Part 6 Or 7PM

U *ghhhhhhh.*
　　　Dizzy. Nauseous. Feverish. Crow felt sick. He wasn't sure what was going on, but the motion of the bus wasn't helping. Ethan had him take two aspirins before he crawled into bed and knocked out.

(done)

E than was lounging on the couch in the living area. They were two stops away from finishing off the tour. They still had to perform at a college in Georgia and then move on down to Miami to close off the show. Ethan couldn't believe that it was almost done. He tried remembering how he felt on that first day, way back when, on the day he walked onto the bus and saw the man he thought he'd never see again. He was used to that. Ethan wasn't used to getting his happy ending, though, and this was certainly a happy one, but it wasn't necessarily an ending. Ethan felt like it was quite the opposite. He felt like as soon as the bus dropped him off back in LA, an entire new story was about to begin, and Ethan couldn't wait.

Frankie, who had been arguing with Troy about that damn golden dress from years ago (Frankie swore to his unborn children it was blue and black), seemed to have decided he had enough and shuffled over to the couch. He plopped down, the cushions sinking in with his weight. Ethan sat up a little, looking out the window across from them as they drove through Asheville, North Carolina. There were mountains bordering them on every side and bright green landscaping that popped off the rocky backdrop mixing in with the busy streets and small town rustic feel of the bracketed buildings and wide streets.

"What a trip, huh?" Frankie said, shaking his head. "Can't believe it's almost over."

"Me neither," Ethan said. "Three months never went by so fast."

"And you and Crow, huh? You two are good for each other." Frankie patted down the back of his head, controlling his thinning hair. "I've been working with him for years now and I don't think I've ever seen him this happy. He's constantly smiling and joking, even his singing has changed. It's more... I dunno, soulful? Like he feels the words now. You've done him good, Ethan."

"He's done me even more."

Frankie arched an eyebrow, a smile playing on his face.

"Done me more *good*," Ethan said, chuckling as he realized what he said. "I was in a bad place when I said yes to this. I, well, I lost my husband a couple of years ago and I had a really difficult time. I didn't know how I was getting out of the hole I dug myself. At one point, I didn't really even care about climbing out. Exactly what Adam wouldn't have wanted, but I was so deep into the dark, I didn't care. And then Crow came along. It wasn't dark anymore." Ethan took a deep breath. He had never really spoken about Adam like that without being asked. He would always hold his death close, like a fucked-up secret that was only meant for Ethan. It was weird and messed up and the weight of it had clearly affected Ethan, but no more. Ethan had to honor Adam's memory with endless smiles and belly-busting laughs, unforgettable dates and uncontained love.

"Sorry about Adam," Frankie said. "I lost someone, too. A long time ago. That ache never goes away, but the world does regain its spark. It took me a while to find it, like you. I don't know, it also makes me love in a different way. Stronger, almost. Not that I loved Lisa any less than I love Cristina, but there's something different. Like I learned how to love in those years I thought I was an empty husk. I appreciate every damn second of my time with her, and I don't care about the little shit nearly as much as I used to."

Ethan nodded his head, understanding where Frankie was coming from. He had no idea he had experienced something similar. The big ol' jolly drummer always had a smile on and a joke at hand. He seemed like one of those people who were lucky enough to never be touched by tragedy. "Same," Ethan agreed.

Just then, Troy came out of the bathroom, drying off his hands with a paper towel before throwing it out. He came over to the couch and sat down between Frankie and Ethan.

"How's Crow been feeling, doc?" Troy asked.

"He's been ok. After a bit of nausea, he said his head's been killing him so I prescribed him some heavy duty aspirin and a few hours of seclusion inside his dark bedroom."

"Sounds like a solid plan." Troy reached for the Wonder Woman comic book on the table. "Sucks that he got sick at the end of the tour."

"Yeah, I think it's something he ate."

"But we haven't had much, except those pancakes Angela made us and then the sandwiches Jordan put together. Maybe we've just got stomachs of steel."

"Maybe, although he did have also have a leftover taco from last night," Ethan said, his phone buzzing in his pocket. "He's a garbage can when it comes to food sometimes. I don't know how he still has the body of Adonis. Although I'm not complaining." He pulled his phone out, realized it was another depressing political headline, and put it back in his pocket, turning his attention back to Troy. They continued to talk for a while, the bus rattling on down a particularly rocky North Carolina road. Ethan would constantly find himself looking out the window, getting lost in the beautiful scenescape that unrolled like a film camera opening up to them as they drove on through.

Angela pulled aside the curtains from where the bunk beds were. She walked out to where the boys sat, an anxious look on her face. For the past week, Angela had been on permanent anxiety mode. More so than usual. Ethan considered taking her aside and asking her if she wanted to talk, but he didn't think Angela was the type of person to respond well to those kind of things. She seemed like someone who would gruffly say she's fine and then storm off, offended that she was offered help. As if it were a sign of weakness or something. So, Ethan just gave her space. He figured that closing off a cross-country tour and having it go without a hitch, all while some crazy stalker fan kept popping up, was most likely extremely stressful. It had also become a little awkward between them after Crow had confronted her.

"Guys," she said, a hand running through her hair. "I'm sorry, I totally forgot to get all the stuff we need for the surprise party. Can you all run out and grab some stuff while I get to work setting up. With Crow asleep, now's a good time as any."

Ethan sat up, excited to help. Angela had brought up the idea of a surprise congratulatory party so that they could lift the morale up and show Crow how much they appreciated him. He was already getting a tour-closing party, so this one was meant to be more intimate with just the crew and cake and party games.

But, apparently, they were missing most of those things.

"Just tell us what you need," Troy said.

"Perfect." Angela handed him a list, "I'll tell the bus driver to take us to the nearest supply store."

———

THE NEAREST SUPPLY store was a small supermarket in Asheville, a historic-feeling city tucked away in North Carolina's Blue Ridge Mountains. Ethan had stepped off the bus and immediately started taking photos of the tall brick buildings set in front of breath-taking green mountains that cut across a dimming orange sky. Even the supply store was photo-worthy, causing Ethan to stop at the front and snap a few before running in to catch up with the gang. They had all walked around the block from the parking lot to the store, leaving Angela behind to set up with whatever little things they did have.

They were immediately greeted as they stepped inside of the supply store, something Ethan wasn't totally used to yet. In Los Angeles, you barely got an acknowledgement unless someone thought you were there to steal from them. But Asheville felt so different in that regard. Everyone was genuinely warm and willing to say a hello.

Honestly? He wasn't entirely sure which one he liked more yet.

"Ok, let's split up?" Troy asked, looking at the list and then up at the aisles. All of them were labeled by hanging wooden plaques, letters scrawled in dripping white paint.

"That's the first thing you're not supposed to do," Frankie said.

"Yeah," Troy's eyebrows drew together, "if you were in some horror movie? Which this is not. So I'm going to go right, you go left."

Frankie shook his head and raised his heads. "Don't say I didn't warn you."

"Stop being stupid," Troy said, both the guys breaking into laughs as they walked their separate ways. Ethan took the center aisle, looking for the chips and salsa Angela had asked them to bring. Of course, the store carried none of the brands Angela suggested, so Crow settled for one that seemed like it would be close enough. He turned back around, ready to go and find the guys, when he saw someone that surprised him. "Hey, Rod, what are you doing here?" It was the security guard that had been following the bus down the East Coast leg of the tour. Ethan was curious. He knew that Rod was supposed to be shadowing Crow at all times. He normally drove behind the bus and slept in hotels whenever they stopped since there weren't enough beds on the bus. Ethan had gotten pretty close to the security guard over the last couple of weeks, and he knew that Rod wasn't the type to slack off on the job.

"Huh? Oh, Ethan, have you seen Crow? Angela said he snuck off to hang out with you guys, but I haven't seen him. Haven't seen Jordan either, thought they came here together."

Ethan narrowed his eyes. "No, the last I knew, Jordan was taking a spa day for himself and Crow was in his room sleeping off a headache. Did you check in there?"

"No, Angela was practically chewing off my head, telling me to get the hell out and to find Crow. That she doesn't pay me to stand outside of an empty bus."

Something wasn't making sense. Was Angela just mistaken? Did she not spot Crow under the covers? Or maybe he did sneak out and just didn't go to where Ethan and the rest of the crew was?

Ethan took a breath. He reached inside his jeans and realized he was missing his phone.

Fuck.

It must have fallen out on the bus, probably slipped between the cushions on the couch.

"Can I borrow your phone?" he asked Rod.

"Sure."

He grabbed Rod's phone and pulled up his contact list. He still didn't have Crow's number memorized, but Rod had it already programed. He found Crow's name and tapped. It immediately started ringing.

Ring. Ring. Ring.

"Hey, you've reache —"

Ethan tried again. And again. Nothing.

That was weird. Crow was really good about answering his phone, even when he was sleeping. Ethan had joked with him about it one day, calling it his lame superhero power. Everyone had one. Ethan admitted his was being able to write his name with his foot. Crow had just called that weird. They laughed and laughed, falling asleep in each other's arms. Just like most nights had been.

"We need to get back to the bus." Ethan turned and hurried out of the store, Frankie and Troy following behind them, neither of them knowing what Ethan was running for.

It took them three minutes to get back to the parking lot where the bus was parked.

Where the bus *had* been parked.

Ethan whipped around the corner, following Rod, to see

the parking lot empty. The bus was no where in sight. Ethan double checked the street signs, making sure they were at the right lot. There was a guard's booth but no one was in and the gate had been set to open.

Something was wrong. Something was terribly, terribly wrong.

Crow has disappeared, or has he been kidnapped?

The mystery / story continues...!!!

31 CROW KENSWORTH

(finished)

The world was hazy. Crow tried to rub the sleep out of his eyes, but he couldn't move his arms for some reason. He blinked away the blurriness and looked down, trying to figure out why his hands weren't coming up to his face. What he saw shocked him. Leather straps, tied tight around his bloody wrists, the material rubbing his skin raw as his seat jerked up and down with every bump in the road.

"What the..."

He looked up, out the bug smeared windshield. He was sitting in the passenger seat of his tour bus. It was dark out, and they were barreling down the highway, headlights beaming bright and wide ahead of them.

Why were they going so fast?

He looked to the side.

"Angela?" Crow couldn't believe it even though there was no doubt. Angela was sitting in the driver's seat, her hands on the wheel, her hair pulled up in a ponytail. She looked oddly comfortable for someone hijacking a bus, in a pair of black sweat pants and a loose white t-shirt.

"Oh good, you're awake." Angela gave him an

unnerving smile, lit up by the streetlights whipping past them. Crow felt a wave of nausea hit him. What the fuck was going on? "I wasn't sure I could do the rest of this drive by myself... I also wasn't sure if I put too much Benadryl in your pancakes this morning."

"What drive? Where are you taking me? Wh — Holy fuck... it was you. It's been you this entire time." The dawning hit Crow like a wrecking ball.

"I've had such a difficult time keeping it from you, Crow. Hiding my feelings. I've been trying to be professional, hell, I even tried stopping for a little while. I swear, I got so close to quitting you, Crow. But then you'd take the stage and sing your songs and god damnit, I wanted you all over again. All to myself. Crazy, huh? You guys almost had me, too. Had to make up some stuff on the spot. Couldn't let you figure things out that way."

"What other way did you want me finding out? Angela, what are you thinking?! We're friends, you're my tour manager, I'm *gay*." Crow could think of a million other reasons why it would never work out between them, but his tongue got twisted as his throat tightened with fear. He was strapped to a seat inside a bus that was racing down a dark highway with increasingly sharper twists and turns as they drove through the mountains.

I'm fucked.

"I know all that, and I don't care, Crow. I feel something deeper than all that bullshit. You know, when my husband cheated on me with my sister, I swore to myself I was through with men. After almost marrying a man jailed for attempted murder, and then marrying another actual *monster*, I decided I was finished. I was done with men. And sisters, too. Everyone. I was finished. I didn't care. Then, I find out that my niece was his daughter this entire time. Can you imagine that? Married to the man for three years, meanwhile my sister gets pregnant at the same time, a week after our wedding day if I'm getting the dates right. A week. That was all it took for him to come inside my sister. So yeah. I hated men. Didn't want anything to do with anyone." She chuckled and shook her head, looking over at Crow while still keeping the bus at a heart-pounding eighty miles per hour. "Then, the same day I decided to kill myself, I get a job offer to be your tour manager. You saved me. We had been friends for years, but it was then that I really saw what we were meant to be. And then your music spoke to me. It changed me."

Crow had his eyes pinned to the front of the bus, expecting a car to get in their way at any moment, causing them to crash and burn and end it all. Angela would slow around the curves but pick up speed on the straightaways. The curves were beginning to come more frequent as they climbed.

Ethan.

Crow's heart swelled, cracked, and disintegrated. He couldn't do this to Ethan. He couldn't sit back and not fight. Ethan's words came into his head like a loudspeaker clicking on from far, 'our love is too strong for any other outcome'. And it was true. So *fucking* true. There was no way Crow would let this be the end of their story. Not when everything was clicking into place so damn well. Crow found someone who fulfilled him on every single level, while Ethan found someone who reminded him how good it was to love and be loved.

Another thought struck him like a brick across the face. "Where are they? Where's Ethan?" Did she do something to them? If she had even touched a hair on Ethan's head,

Crow was sure he would have found the strength to rip right through the leather binds and tear her apart.

"They're fine," she said, shrugging it off. "I sent them away."

A truck blared its horn at them as they blurred past, going much faster than a bus should be, especially since the roads were beginning to get more and more narrow, ready to wind through the mountains that bordered whatever town they were currently in.

Holy fuck, what the hell.

"All those letters..."

"Were from me, from the start. I didn't even show the cops most of them. Sure, I said I did, but I had to keep some things secret. I didn't want anyone getting in the way. And then... well, Ethan came along. *Completely* fucked things up. You know? I had laid it all out. I was going to have you loving me by the end of the tour. I was going to have everything go off without a hitch and make you see me as the one for you. But then Ethan walks onto the bus and your eyes go all starry and hazy. You look at him the way I wish you'd look at me. It hurt."

"And the cancelled show? And that girl? Tricia?"

"The cancelled show was a little punishment. I was just getting so upset seeing you and Ethan together, I had to knock things down a notch. Then you go on a crazy cute date to the creepiest museum ever. I had such a difficult time tailing you that day. Thankfully, I hired the security off of Craigslist, those men were pretty useless as guards. They never suspected a thing. You almost saw me twice, though, but I'm pretty quick. And then Tricia? She was just someone I could point to if things ever turned sour and I wasn't prepared for it. She was at every show and continued to go to your shows, even after I warned her to stop. I didn't let security know so that they wouldn't stop her from attending."

"You wanted her present for everything that went wrong."

"Ding, ding, ding." The bus gave a rattle as Angela kicked it up another gear. "Not only that, but I managed to grab a few strands of her hair. All I needed was to write another note and drop those babies in there. She would have been screwed."

"You didn't."

"Nope. I saw things turning too fast. I saw the tour finishing and you leaving with Ethan and my chances being completely over. I had to act. I had to do something. So I did. Fuck the consequences, Crow. It's like your new song 'Confidence' where you say 'Looking up at you and falling into blue, don't think of the consequences. A kiss. A touch. Break all the rules, because, babe, it isn't lust when it feels this much like love.' I see what you mean now. Break the rules and fuck the consequences as long as it's for someone you love."

"Angela, please. Stop the bus. Please."

It was all Crow could say as he dug his finger nails into his palms out of nerves, his knuckles paper white, his jaw clenched as the dark world whizzed by them outside. He had written that song for Ethan. The man of his dreams. And now he was going to die and he was going to devastate Ethan again. Crow felt a torrent of emotions pounding into him. He couldn't let this happen. He had to find a way out of this alive.

The moon was full, shining bright rays through the tall trees that bordered the highway. Thankfully, no one seemed to be out on the road at this time of night. They were also driving away from the city, so less and less people. He had no idea where Angela learned the ability to drive a bus, but she was shifting gears and steering like she was a fucking NASCAR driver. That's when he remembered her asking the bus driver for random lessons around the parking lot. He thought it was because she had gotten bored. She slowed down as they turned a corner, climbing higher into the mountains. The roads were noticeably thinner. The steel rail was low on the edge of the road, stopping no one from veering off and plunging to their deaths. Crow was suddenly taken back to watching Red drive his stunt cars across empty parking lots, practicing as wheels screeched and smoke billowed. Then he remembered Ethan taking him up to the Sky Tower in Chicago, a place where he had overcome one of his greatest fears with the greatest man at his side.

Jesus. Is this my life flashing before my eyes?

He felt it. Deep down, he felt like there was no getting out of this.

"Just pull over and we can talk," Crow said, trying to get words past his dry lips. Maybe if he could get her to slow down and think things through, maybe then he could get out of this alive.

Maybe wasn't good enough. She didn't stop.

That's when Crow looked over his shoulder, toward the back of the bus. What he saw made his blood freeze in his veins.

"You killed him." Crow couldn't believe it. It was Greg, the bus driver. He was lying face down in a pool of his own blood, his arms had been outstretched. "Holy shit." Crow's mouth was desert dry. He almost passed out, but held onto consciousness by a thread.

"Ugh, I know. I wasn't happy about it, but he wouldn't

get off the bus and I didn't have much time before the boys at the supermarket realized what was going on."

Crow gagged. He kept his eyes straight ahead, his mind taking him back to the nights he and Ethan would spend talking. A brief escape from the horror that currently surrounded him. He cried. He felt like it was over so soon. Too fucking soon.

Blue. All he wanted to see again was the color blue.

Angela has kidnapped Crow and has killed the bus driver...

will Crow ever be rescued...

The "James Bond" / Mission Impossible bus chase adventure is about to begin...

Read tonight 6 or 7 PM —finished

E than's heart was pounding in his throat. He white-knuckled the steering wheel, taking turns like he was a trained stunt driver, which he certainly was not. On two occasions, Ethan felt the cheap rental lift up on its wheels and slam back down as he took a corner. He only pressed on the gas harder. He threw glances at the map displayed on Rod's phone, making sure to never lose the blue dot that signified his phone. He was so fucking happy he dropped his phone in the bus, because the Find my Phone app was now leading him directly to Crow. He had left a copy of the app on Frankie's phone so that he could give it to the cops when they showed up. For Ethan though, they were taking too long. He grabbed the keys to the car and took off, the group protesting behind him but Ethan peeling out of the parking lot anyway. There was no way he was going to let this happen. He was not going to lose Crow.

The roads started getting more serpentine as they climbed in altitude. The bus had gotten a head start, but Ethan was now only a mile behind it. He stepped on the gas, passing around a lone car that had ventured out onto the roads this late at night. Ethan saw the man flash his headlights at Ethan as he sped past, but there was nothing he could do except say a sorry out loud and continue speeding.

"There you are."

The bus was just ahead of him. The rental's headlights lit up the back of the all-black tour bus. It was driving fast, but slowing down now that the roads were much more treacherous. Ethan matched the speed, tailing as close behind the bus as he could.

Fuck. What do I do now?

He had to get the bus to pull over. He had no idea who was even behind the wheel, but he needed to see if he could yell some sense at them. He sped up and pulled into the other lane, making sure there were no oncoming cars. The road started to curve in half a mile, so he didn't have much time.

He matched the bus's speed and looked across, shocked to see Angela in the driver's seat. She looked strangely calm for someone hijacking a tour bus. It took her a second to see Ethan. He lowered his window in hopes of yelling for her to stop. She flipped him off and sped up the bus. The curve was coming. Ethan had to pull back. There could have been another car turning that corner and neither would ever see each other coming until they crashed headfirst.

"Fuck, fuck, fuck," Ethan said. He made a split second decision. He gripped the steering wheel tight and pressed down on the gas. The car shook and the engine groaned as it accelerated. A shitty car was still faster than a huge bus. He managed to cut in front of Angela just before the turn hit. A car came around the bend right then, its headlights almost blinding Ethan. His blood pressure was through the fucking roof, his pupils were probably the size of quarters; he was sure of it, his doctor instincts kicking in.

Being in front of Angela gave Ethan some control. He slowed the car down, hoping that he would force Angela to do the same. There was no way she could switch lanes anymore. The roads were too narrow and curving way too frequently. She would tip the bus right over the edge.

She started inching to the left. That bitch was going to risk it.

"Fuck," Ethan sped back up again. That's when he looked in his rearview mirror and saw Crow for the first time. He was sitting in the passenger seat, fear painted across his face, his hands tied behind him. It made Ethan want to stop the bus with his damn fist, Superman style. He was filled with powerful adrenaline. It coursed through him. Fueling him. His senses were sharp and his reflexes quick.

He knew he had to do it. There was a wide bank of bushes to his right where the mountains opened up onto a valley. He significantly slowed down, almost braking, but not stopping so that he wouldn't get rear-ended. Angela spotted it and did exactly what Ethan thought she would do. She swerved the bus to the right, away from the edge and into the bank of bushes. They weren't going as fast as earlier and so the bus managed to come to a stop in a huge cloud of dust and dirt, bushes trampled flat in its wake. Ethan pulled over onto the dirt, the car bumping along the bushes as he raced to where the bus had stopped.

He pulled up and practically fell out of the car. His first instinct was to vomit, but he held it back and straightened up. There was no way he was showing an inch of weakness. He had to stay strong. For Crow.

He hurried around to the door of the bus, but before he

got there, he heard it hiss open. He turned the corner and saw Angela holding up Crow, a knife pushed against his throat.

Ethan swallowed back the fear. He stuck his hands out, as if he had bumped into a rabid dog. "Calm down. No one needs to get hurt, Angela."

"Oh please, Ethan. You're a smart cookie, you know how this has to end. I've already been hurt enough. It's your turn."

Crow's eyes were wide with dread. It made Ethan feel like that knife was pressed against his throat, like it had already cut through. It was pain. Pure and simple. He felt physical pain at seeing Crow in such a state. This was his worst nightmare personified. He didn't think the world could be this cruel. Could take two loves away from him.

No. No. It's still not over.

The look in Crow's eyes made him want to fight until his very last breath. He was going to get them out of this alive.

"Fine," Ethan said, taking a step forward. Angela took three steps back. The cops were on there way, but Ethan felt like he had to finish this before they even showed up. He was scared that Angela would end it all at the sight of flashing red and blue lights. She lost it. The thread that tethered her to humanity was snapped. Ethan wasn't sure when it happened, but he could tell in her eyes. "Take me."

"No," Crow managed to get out. Ethan could see a scarlet ribbon form across his throat.

Angela didn't seem as put off by the idea. Ethan saw it in her eyes. A weakness. He needed to work at it. "Take me. I'm the one that fucked it up for you, wasn't I? I stole your man, accused you of being a psycho. I'm the one you want to hurt."

Crow was shaking his head as much as the knife would let him. Crow's hands were free but it was clear there wasn't much he could do with a knife ready to slice off his Adam's apple. There was no way he could fight his way out of this. Ethan needed to get in there. He had to swap places. If the cops did get there and Angela was willing to end it all, he wanted to be the one that was in her grips, not Crow.

And for a moment, Ethan thought his plan was working. She smiled and shook her head. "No." With a chuckle, she moved back a few more steps. "Although, you're right, you are the one I want to hurt." Her grin was maniacal. "And I know exactly how to do it."

She raised the knife. The blade reflected the moonlight in a morbid display of beauty. Ethan had seconds to react. He jumped the distance between them, using all the force in his legs, and outstretched his arms. By doing so, he was able to push back on Angela's shoulders, knocking all three of them down toward the ground. He used a free hand to push Crow to the side, away from the sharp blade.

It was exactly what Ethan wanted to happen. He also knew what would happen next. With Angela still holding onto the knife and all three falling, Ethan was exposed. He felt the searing icy-hot pain first before he realized it had actually happened. Angela, who was laying on the ground with Ethan on top of her, was looking up with glee as she blew a kiss and pushed the knife deeper into Ethan's back.

Ethan cried out as the pain intensified.

"Ethan!" Crow cried out. He was on his feet. Ethan could see him from the side of his eyes, except they were beginning to cloud over from the pain. Angela gave a twist. Ethan had to fight back. He grabbed her by the throat and tried to squeeze, but the pain in his shoulder was unbearable. Angela pulled the knife out. Ethan gave another scream as the blade exited flesh, blood flowing down his side. He knew what was coming next. He tried to roll over but couldn't get enough strength in his arm to manage it. Angela was going to plunge the knife right down Ethan's neck and end it all.

"Fuck you!" Crow cried. He grabbed Angela's wrist and yanked it back, the sound of snaps soon following. Angela's face contorted with pain. The knife dropped to the ground as she writhed on the ground, her knees coming up to hit Ethan. He managed to roll off of her then, feeling the grass underneath his back. He looked up at the night sky. Police sirens started echoing through the mountains. They were getting close now.

"Holy shit, holy shit." Crow ran to Ethan's side. He knelt down. Ethan looked up, wincing as a pulse of pain shot through him. The adrenaline was doing a decent job of tamping down the pain, but it was impossible to shut it all out. Even with Crow's big brown eyes looking down at him, making him feel like everything was going to be ok. "What do I do? Are you ok? Can you breathe?"

Ethan shook his head. "She didn't puncture a lung," he said, gritting his teeth as another wave of pain hit. "I'm almost positive she didn't get anything vital. If she hit an artery, I'd be done by now."

"Fuck... Ethan."

Ethan worked himself to sit up. Crow helped him. "Can you wrap your shirt around it? Add some pressure."

"Of course, of course." Crow sounded scared out of his mind. He practically tore off his shirt and tied it as tight as he could around where the blade had entered. "You know you didn't have to go through all this to see me shirtless, right?"

That actually got a laugh out of Ethan. It was fucking

painful, but oh so worth it. Even in Crow's freaked out state, he still knew exactly what to say. Angela groaned from the ground nearby, holding her broken wrist in her hand and beginning to cry loudly. Crow held onto the knife with one hand and Ethan with the other. His wrists were raw and bloody from where the straps had been tied. Angela must have cut him free to get him out of the bus.

"Are you ok? Did she do anything?" Ethan asked, concern in his voice. He didn't care about what happened to himself, he wanted to make sure Crow wasn't hurting.

"I'm good."

The cops pulled up then, bright lights shining on the scene, flooding the entire valley in eerie white and black shades. Ethan looked up at Crow. With as much pain as he was feeling, he still couldn't help but feel a sense of relief.

"It's over," Ethan said. Crow came down to sit on the ground next to Ethan. "She's done. We're together and no one's ever going to change that."

Crow smiled, tears running down his cheeks. "You saved my life."

"And you saved mine." Ethan smiled. "We're even."

"I love you, Ethan Winter."

"I love you, Crow."

EPILOGUE

A YEAR LATER

Crow Kensworth

Paris felt like it had been pulled straight out of a fairytale. Every street felt magical, like there was a story underneath each and every brick, maybe a little fairy that would barter away magical jewels for French baguettes.

Crow had read two Harry Dresden books on the flight over, so his imagination may have been running on over-drive. It didn't hurt that he was holding hands with the best muse anyone could ever have. The prince that rode in on his white horse to defeat the terrifying dragon and sweep Crow up off his feet. He couldn't believe it. He was walking down Rue du Louvre, a narrow street filled with boutiques and businesses of all kinds, with the man of his dreams at his side. They walked past fancy glass displays, some with mannequins dressed to the nines, some with store names scrawled in a gold script above their entrances. Some of the storefronts were below balconies that lined the rows of apartments above. It was a sunny Sunday afternoon, so many of the residents were sitting (if they had the space) or standing outside on their balconies, watching the people go on with their lives below. Those that didn't have balconies did have their windows open, letting the fresh air billow against their curtains. Crow let his eyes wander, admiring the old styled architecture and wondering how it must have felt to call this place home.

"Holy shit, it's Crow!"

Crow turned at the mention of his name, a young fan jumping in place as he realized who had just walked past him. Crow was wearing dark jeans and a dark black shirt, with a blue LA Dodger's cap pulled down over his eyes, but that still didn't make him invisible. His parents stood behind the young fan, recognition dawning on their faces as well. They were all dressed pretty sharp in nice polos and shorts, the mom sporting a necklace of pearls, like a rich American family taking their first Euro trip.

Over the past year, Crow's star had only climbed, and now it seemed like everyone was aware of who he was. Even if they weren't a fan of his music, almost everyone had heard the story of Crow being abducted and subsequently rescued. It was the only thing the news channels could talk about. At least for an hour or so, before they moved on to dissecting ridiculous tweets for information. And when the news stopped talking about him, social media only kept the conversation going. It was definitely an odd time in his life, but the outpouring of love and support he had received from people all across the world helped him keep it together.

"Can I grab a picture with you?" the fan asked.

"Of course," Crow said, extending an arm out so the boy could run over. He dropped his Nike backpack and ran over. Ever since Angela was revealed to be the stalker, all of the threatening notes stopped and Crow didn't need to suspect random fans of being crazy psychos. It was such a relief. Crow hated living a life filled with fear and suspicion. Of course, there were crazy people everywhere, but Crow didn't feel like he had to constantly be looking over his shoulder anymore.

"What's your name?" Crow asked.

"Steven," he said, staring up at Crow like he was looking straight into the sun.

"Great to meet you, Steven." They turned to look at the camera his mom was holding up.

"Thank you!" the fan said once his mom had snapped the photo. "Seriously, thank you."

Crow brought the kid in for a hug before he went back to his parents. Crow thought the interaction was over, but then the boy's father stepped forward, his hand outstretched. Crow smiled and returned the handshake. That's when he noticed a tear in the man's brown eyes.

"I just wanted to personally thank you for what you do. Your music helped Steven when he was going through a really difficult patch. His mom and I felt so damn helpless, we didn't know what to do. Doctors, medication, therapy. Then he heard your songs, and he felt like there was so much hope. After what happened to you last year, Jesus, and you *still* finished your tour. You're an inspiration for all of us. Thank you."

Crow swallowed back his emotions. He drew the man into a hug. "I'm glad things are good."

The man smiled a genuine smile and returned to his family. No one else stopped Crow as he went back to Ethan's side, fingers locking together like magnets.

"That was amazing," Ethan said as they continued to walk down the street. "You have such an impact on people. It's beautiful to watch."

Crow couldn't stop himself from leaning in and stealing a kiss from Ethan. He squeeze his hand tighter as the street opened up wider. Crow looked straight ahead and spotted the Louvre in all of it's glass majesty. The pyramid jutted up from the middle of the square, surrounded by a building that resembled a palace on all three sides. The shops and apartments disappeared as the street opened up into a garden that marked the beginning of the square.

"Speaking of beautiful," Crow said, his jaw on the floor. He had seen pictures of the stunning museum, but pictures never compared to the real thing. The sunlight played off the sides of glass as people crowed about around the base. "I'm so happy I'm experiencing this with you." Crow pulled Ethan in tighter. They walked in unison toward the museum, admiring the bright green waist-high hedges that bordered the garden. As they got closer, Crow could see a that the floor on either side of the museum was actually a shallow pool, the water reflecting the building and making it seem all the more magical.

"Wow," Crow said. He let go of Ethan's hand for a second as he walked toward the water, mesmerized. He had totally thought it was a floor moment ago. That's how calm the surface was. When he turned around, he expected to see Ethan.

"Huh?" Crow looked around for a split second before his eyes were drawn downward. There, he saw Ethan, his beautiful blue eyes glittering up at him, more impressive than any glass building could ever be.

"Ethan," Crow said, stepping back with a laugh. Ethan was on one knee, in the center of the square, the garden framing him from behind, the Louvre behind Crow. He held out a black box, its lid open, a ring set in the center of a white satin pillow.

"Crow," Ethan said, not taking his eyes off a shocked Crow. "You have changed my life in so many different ways, all for the better. You brought me out of the dark and I've been seeing sunshine ever since. Even during our darkest moments, you gave me strength. Hope. You were there for me, and I want to be there for you." His smiled widened. "Forever. Crow Kensworth, will you marry me?"

"Absolutely," Crow said without missing a beat. He held back a giddy shriek, thinking it would be way too rom-com of him. He swore he had seen that exact scene in a Hillary Duff movie. So, instead of shrieking, he grabbed Ethan and pulled him up for a kiss that sealed the entire deal. Crow held Ethan's head in his hands as their lips collided, their futures cementing. Crow was so into the moment, he didn't even realize that there was a crowd surrounding them, all of them cheering and clapping.

Ethan Winter

ETHAN HAD DIED and gone to heaven. He died when Angela stabbed him in the back and this was just his version of heaven. It had to be. That's how perfect it all felt. He was kissing his fiancé in the middle of Paris, the city known for love, surrounded by a cheering crowd, clapping as two men kissed and promised their lives to each other. It was beyond beautiful. Ethan had joked that Crow was the crier out of the two, but that moment brought tears to the both of them. They separated, wiping each other's cheeks as their smiles stayed cemented on their faces.

"Wow," Crow said, looking down at the ring on his finger. Ethan smiled on, looking proudly at his man. He pulled him back in for another kiss. The crowd was beginning to take photos by then, some realizing who it was that just got engaged.

"I should tell my brother before he finds out through TMZ," Crow said, hearing the shutters of cameras. He kissed Ethan again and grabbed a hold of his hand. He said a huge thanks to the crowd for cheering them on and then broke through the circle, his head down and his eyes focused on his phone as he looked up his brother's number. Some people followed them, but for the most part, everyone respected their privacy by then.

"Holy shit, holy shit." Crow's hands were shaking. He laughed and handed the phone to Ethan, who had a steadier hold. They dialed Shepherds number, asking to connect for a FaceTime call. In a second, Shepherd was on the screen, a wide smile on his face and eyes that immediately asked 'did he do it yet?!'. Crow, being his twin and all, immediately picked up on the expression.

"Wait, you knew?!" he asked, his uncontrollable smile making Ethan's heart almost flutter right out his chest.

"Of course! Ethan told me like a month ago. He asked pops, what, last week?"

"You asked our dad?" Crow turned to Ethan, his eyes wide.

"I wanted to," Ethan said, smiling. "He told me that as long as I promised to be on his team for the next Pictionary Thanksgiving marathon, then it was all good."

"Of course he would," Crow said.

"Dad gave you away for an unbeatable Pictionary team-mate," Shepard said with a laugh.

"I am pretty good," Ethan added.

"Congratulations you guys! This is exactly what I needed to hear today." He looked like he was standing outside of a library. He was wearing his scrubs, so he must have been going into work soon.

"I'm genuinely surprised you were able to hold that secret for a month," Crow said, laughing. "Check out the ring." Crow lifted his hand, showing off the classy and sleek silver band, the thin sapphire blue line running through the center and setting it apart from every other ring.

"He's seen it," Ethan said with a smirk. He was so happy that he got along well with Crow's entire family. It was a big thing for him, especially since his own father had abandoned him at an early age. The Kensworth's opened their arms wide from the start. "He helped me get it fitted."

"Damn," Crow said, "you guys are sneaks."

"Gotta do what you gotta do," Ethan said, kissing Crow's cheek.

"Alright, guys, I've got to go." Shepard threw a nervous glance over his shoulder but quickly adopted the big, wide smile the Kensworth brothers rocked so well.

"Everything ok?" Crow asked, sensing it.

"Yeah, yeah, I'll fill you in when you get back." Shepard was clearly holding something back, but Ethan knew he would open up to them later. For now, he said another heart-felt congrats and hung up the call. Crow turned to Ethan, his eyes glowing, crinkling at the corners.

"You're incredible. How did I get so lucky?"

Ethan answered with another kiss. He couldn't get enough of Crow, and he was excited with the fact that he was going to have him for the rest of his life. The love they shared was strong and proven to be unbeatable. It was the kind of love people wrote songs about. The kind of love happy endings were made from.

This was the kind of love that had him seeing crystal blue oceans.

THE END

THANK YOU

Thank you for reading the *CODE BLUE*. If you enjoyed Crow and Ethan's story, please consider leaving a review. They help immensely in getting these two guys out to more people!

The next book in the Sierra View series will be following Crow's twin, Shepard, as he falls for one of his medical school professors, someone that he's sure hates him.

Things are going to get complicated.

Keep reading for a sneak peak!

And be sure to connect with me on Instagram and Twitter @maxwalkerwrites

Max Walker
MaxWalkerAuthor@outlook.com

ACKNOWLEDGMENTS

Thank you to Donna, who worked her rockstar magic and helped make CODE BLUE the story it is today.

I also want to thank you, the reader who toured the country with Crow and Ethan. Thank you for making my dream to write these stories a reality!

CODE WHITE

SNEAK PEEK

33 SHEPARD KENSWORTH

Shepard was a medical school resident. He should have been at home, studying drug interactions and preparing for his two-week rotation on the surgery floor. He should *not* have been in the on-call room, on all fours, with his ass in the air, an uncomfortable mattress squeaking underneath as one of his attendings slapped his hard dick against Shepard's ass, both of their scrubs discarded in a heap on the floor.

But of course, life isn't always about the "should haves." The "shouldn't haves" are often much more interesting.

Shepard bit down on the flat pillow, preventing a rogue gasp as Dr. Nicholas White pressed the head of his cock against his hole. The doctor's strong hands gripped Shepard's hips and steered his ass for easiest access. Shepard pushed his ass back, asking for more, begging for it. He could feel the doctor's thick cock rub against his crack, already slick with lube. Shepard couldn't help but reach behind and grab Nick's girthy tool, giving a few good tugs, feeling the slick rubber of the condom on his palm mixing with the heat rolling off of Nick in waves. He guided the head of Nick's fat cock to his hole and pushed back. Shepard had been wanting this the minute he laid eyes on the doctor, but he had also believed this would never happen. Nick didn't hold back. He pushed in, drawing a gasp from Shepard and a groan from Nick.

"Did I hurt you?" His tone was immediately caring. It only made Shepard hotter.

"No, no," Shepard reassured, wiggling his ass to take more of the doctor, "just a little fast at first. I'm ok."

Nick went back to gyrating his hips, his cock sinking deeper and deeper as Shepard became more comfortable. It was slow, and passionate and *so fucking hot*. Shepard was seeing stars. He could feel himself accommodating to the size and sensation of being filled as Nick thrust a little deeper, harder, he was going faster. Shepard was biting back the moans. A quick flash of pain morphed into a dose of ecstasy as Nick fucked him deep, burying himself down to his balls before drawing out. Both his hands were holding on tight to Shepard's hips, guiding him as the doctor's thrusts started getting faster. Shepard's ass slapped against Nick's groin. He could hear Nick grunting from behind, low and muffled as he tried to keep it quiet as well. The hospital was still buzzing outside of the locked door with nurses and doctors running past, orders being called over the intercom system, other residents making their rounds. All of them unaware as to what was happening on the other side of the thick wooden door.

Shepard's mind being blown, that was what was happening.

If someone told him a year ago that he would be having sex with the hottest doctor in all of Sierra View, he would have laughed in their face. Not only was Nicholas White an enigma to most, he had also been married to a bubbly brunette named Anna, leading Shepard to believe that he wasn't Dr. White's type anyway.

"You're so sexy," Nick said in his gravelly growl from behind Shepard. He felt the doctor's hands glide up from his hips and rub over his lower back, giving Shepard a sensation of pure bliss. His lower back was one of his favorite spots to be touched, so that, coupled with the intense pleasure he was getting from having Nick's thick cock fill him, and he was already close to coming. Shepard held himself up on one arm, using the other to reach between his legs and tug on his own leaking cock, his balls already tight against him. He looked and saw a string of precome drip down onto the soft white towel they had placed underneath them. Nick continued to pound him, pushing against Shepard's P-spot and subsequently sending shockwaves with every thrust.

Shepard woke up from plenty of dreams where sex with Nicholas White was the feature presentation, but those were just dreams. They would leave him with a throbbing boner in the morning and that was it. An empty bed and a messy stomach. The dreams had started the moment he met Dr. White months ago, when he had started his residency rotations for the first time. Since then, he had been admiring the doctor from afar, wishing he could have a taste but accepting the fact there was a nearly-impossible chance of that happening.

Nearly being the keyword.

"You're so big," Shepard moaned, keeping his voice low as he spoke into the pillow. This seemed to have spurred the doctor on, because he started driving into Shepard. He could feel the doctor's balls slapping against him, his ass filled with the doctor's entire cock with every thrust. It was enough to have Shepard's arms shaking, his toes curling.

"Come here," Nick said, grabbing Shepard's hips again. He stopped thrusting, but stayed inside Shepard. He pulled Shepard toward him, off of the bed, so that Shepard could stand, all the while his ass was still plugged by Nick's cock. It was incredibly hot. Shepard bit his lower lip as Nick started pounding into him as they stood. He was shorter than the doctor was, so Nick had to bend his knees and drop down a bit. Shepard jerked himself off, starting to get scared his legs would give out soon from the intense pleasure he was feeling. His knees were already shaking.

"Fuck, fuck," Shepard moaned. He bit a knuckle, stopping himself from crying out.

"I'm going to come," Nick growled into Shepard's ear. "Oh, fuck," he said, biting Shepard's ear lobe as his thrusts became erratic. Shepard couldn't hold back, either. He didn't even give a warning. He just grabbed his cock at the base and felt it throb in his grip as he erupted, shooting his seed all over the white towel while Nick unloaded inside him. They were both quivering and huffing and completely overwhelmed with the post orgasmic bliss. Nick kissed Shepard's neck as he pulled out, leaving Shepard feeling empty all of a sudden. He was surprised at how ready he was to go again. His cock was usually the first to tap out, going back to soft status pretty soon after sex. But this time around, Shepard was still hard, ready for more.

Unfortunately, the clock on the wall was saying there wasn't time for more. Shepard had ten minutes before he had to be back outside.

That's enough time for a cuddle, at least.

Shepard was getting ahead of himself. This was a one-time thing and that was it. He highly doubted Dr. White would want to cuddle with him, he had to keep things clear in his head. They were both horny and that was it. Sure,

Shepard had dropped subtle hints during office hours, and sure, he may have given Dr. White the eye a couple of times in the hall, but that was it. Just a sexual attraction where the both of them were looking for a release and both of them got one.

Shepard grabbed the towel from the bed and set it on the floor. "That was... fucking incredible," Nick said, breathless as he fell back onto the bed, condom already wrapped up in a paper towel and thrown away.

Well... if he's going to lie down.

Shepard was equally starved for breath. He felt like a bowl of Jell-O. Completely useless, at the whim of whatever breeze blew their way. He collapsed onto the bed next to Nick. "Honestly?" Shepard said, "That was the best sex I think I've ever had."

Nick nodded. His cheeks were a cherry pink, matching the same flush that had spread across his chest, underneath a sexy dusting of hair. "I'm going to have to second that." He looked up at the ceiling, an arm underneath his head. "Guess that's not too bad considering it was my first time with a man."

"Seriously?" Shepard asked. "Because it felt like you've had a good amount of practice."

Nicholas laughed at that. Shepard enjoyed hearing that sound. It felt good. Especially here, while they were still together on the bed, naked and sweaty. The laugh almost made it feel even more intimate.

Shepard, for a moment, let himself be fooled into thinking this wasn't simply a burst of hormones and nothing else. It was then that Nick surprised him by rolling over and throwing a hand over Shepard's chest. For a second, Shepard froze, not expecting this kind of cuddling. But he quickly warmed up to it. It was exactly what Shepard wanted. He rolled over so that he could scoot back and tuck his butt into the curve of Nick's body. His semi-hard cock pressed against Shepard's butt. Shepard couldn't help but give a wiggle. Nick responded by squeezing his arm a little tighter around Shepard. There was something in the way Nick held him that put Shepard into a trance.

"You know," Nick said in a hushed tone. "The second I laid my eyes on you, I wanted this to happen."

Shepard felt an urge to roll back around so he could look into Nick's eyes. "That's weird. I felt the same thing." Shepard didn't roll over. A kernel of fear kept him looking at the bland yellow wall. He wanted to believe that everything the doctor was saying was certifiably true, he didn't want to witness any evidence of the opposite.

"It was just so complicated."

"With your divorce?"

"Yeah, these past few months have been really rough on me. I couldn't go from a divorce and straight into a relationship, especially since I'd never even been with a man before. I just focused on work and getting through the days without bumping into you. Also, I felt like I was a complicated mess myself, and complicated messes don't make for great relationships. Why risk making things harder for you? Medical school is already hard enough."

Relationship...

Shepard scooted his butt back, rubbing it against Nick. "Tell me about it," he said with a chuckle. "I'm cool with it. Sorry about your ex by the way... well, maybe sorry is the wrong word."

"Yeah, I wouldn't use sorry, either. The divorce was what I needed. If I never ended things with her, I never would have acted on feelings I've had for a long damn time."

"What happened?" Shepard asked. He rolled over for

this one. Nick's amber brown eyes were captivating in their depth. Shepard could stare at him for days and be totally fine.

"We weren't a good fit," Nick said. For a moment, Shepard thought the conversation was going to end there, and that would be fine. Even though Shepard found himself wanting to know more and more about the devilishly handsome doctor, he also felt like that would come in time. The last thing Shepard wanted to think was that this would be their only rendezvous.

No, no.

This felt too good for it to be the last time.

"I'm pretty sure she was cheating on me. I just kind of went along with it for a while because I didn't think I had any other choice. I didn't think I'd really be happy again. I felt like I was just kind of floating along." Nick cracked a smile in the dimly lit room. Shepard was still a little flushed, his cheeks slightly pink, his hair messy, a couple of thick dark strands circling down on his forehead. He was the most beautiful thing Nick had ever laid eyes on. Like a work of art created by the most gifted of savants. He wanted to stare at the man for hours. He wanted to memorize every singe freckle on Shepard's face, every small detail, every crinkle next to his eyes. He couldn't believe how attracted he was to this man. "Then you came along." Nick was being way too open, and honestly?

He didn't give a fuck. Not in that moment.

He felt like letting it all out for Shepard. There wasn't a reason in the world he could think of that would prevent him from opening up. It was something in the air. Something in the way Shepard looked at him. With big hazel eyes that expressed captivating depth. "You had such a huge smile, and you're so handsome, and smart. I always see everyone laughing when they're with you. Everyone's always happy when you're around. I was almost jealous. I had to stop myself from being around you because I knew your smile was dangerous, and yet everyone else was around you, enjoying you."

Shepard chewed on his lower lip, a smile on his face. Nick couldn't hold himself back. He went in for a kiss. He thought it would be soft and quick, but that would never happen when Shepard was involved. Their tongues met and danced for what felt like days. Years. Decades. That was how long he felt like he had known Shepard. This was the first actual, deep conversation they had ever shared and yet Nick felt like Shepard had always been a part of his life.

The kiss broke as a pager started going off, vibrating against the floor. "Oh shit," Shepard said, eyes snapping open. He jumped out of bed and hurried to the corner where his scrubs were thrown. He dug through the pocket and silenced the alarm. "I've got to get to work," he said, smiling as he tugged on his underwear, moving to his scrubs next. Nick sat up on the bed, still a little blown away by the fact that he had just made love to a man, and it was beyond his wildest expectations. The pleasure was intense and the sense of intimacy he shared with Shepard was unbeatable. A high he wanted to get hit with again.

"Let's have dinner tomorrow," Nick said as Shepard was working his arms through his shirt.

"Dinner?" Shepard asked again, clearly taken aback. "Sure, yeah, definitely." He smiled at Nick, who was beginning to get dressed as well.

"I'll see you then."

"See you," Nick said, already counting down the minutes left until they met again.

NICK GRABBED two Stellas out of the fridge and popped them open. His best friend, Aaron Diaz, was sitting on a barstool and wasting his time on Tinder, swiping right like it was his job. Nick handed him a beer and walked to the couch, sitting down and taking a sip of the cold beverage, hoping it would be enough to stop his mind from obsessing over Shepard and his naked body.

Fuck.

Just thinking about Shepard made Nick's cock twitch. He squeezed his thighs together and threw his feet up on the glossy white coffee table. Maybe he could redirect blood flow away from his dick. He was definitely going to need more than one beer. Aaron must have matched with someone because he gave a hoot and fist-pumped in the air. "Fuck yeah," he said, hopping off the barstool and making his way over to Nick. He stepped over Nick's legs and sat down on the couch next to him. "Check this one out."

Aaron showed off his phone like he had earned a damn Nobel prize. Nick looked at the screen, seeing a very beautiful girl in a barely-there bright blue bikini, sunning on the deck of a huge boat. She was someone Nick could see Aaron with. His best friend was a lovable douchebag. A frat guy that actually did have a heart and didn't purposefully go out and mess with people. He looked the part, too, in his tan Sperrys, short khaki shorts, and light blue polo with some weird animal logo on the chest.

"Nice, yeah, she's cool."

"Cool?!" Aaron said. He pressed the back of his hand to Nick's forehead. "Dude, are you coming down with something? A weird hospital virus you should be telling me about?"

Nick chuckled. "No, I think I'm already immune to everything out there."

"I dunno, man, I've seen Thirty-Eight Weeks Later."

Nick arched an eyebrow. "You mean Twenty-Eight Weeks Later? The zombie movie? Thirty-eight weeks later sounds like a bad movie about a slightly premature baby."

"Yeah, that one." Aaron laughed before taking a drink of his Stella. His phone vibrated as he matched with someone else on the app. "Oh, oh, ok, look at this girl. She needs way more than a 'cool'."

Aaron flipped his phone, showing Nick a beautiful woman in a bright yellow sundress, her breasts spilling over the top. "Cool."

Aaron dropped the phone on the couch. "Ok, seriously, what's going on?"

"Oh, I don't know, maybe it's the fact that I made my divorce official two months ago?"

And I'm also done with women.

That was something that was going to have to wait to be said. Nick wasn't sure how his best friend was going to take the news. Hell, he wasn't even sure about the news himself. Throughout his entire life, he had always had an inclination for the same sex. That inclination grew as the years passed, evolving into a deep yearning that had been tugging at Nick since he entered medical school. By then, he had met Anna and was perfectly happy dating her, so he never explored the side of him that cried out for a man's touch.

Then, his relationship with Anna began to crack. She became more and more distant, starting fights with Nick over things that previously never even mattered. Things like a pair of socks left by the couch; that would have her close to smashing dishes. She was staying late at work and had surprise meetings on weekends. Things didn't feel right.

Nick also started to suspect something was up when she had left her phone inside the bathroom one night. Nick had stepped in and closed the door, which was almost cracked in half with how fast Anna threw it open, looking for her phone and giving a relieved sigh when she grabbed it from the countertop. A divorce ending their year-long marriage soon followed. In the immediate aftermath, Nick felt lost. He was angry and taking it out on the residents, he could tell. He hated himself for being an asshole, but he was just so damn frustrated. He felt like he had wasted so much time with Anna, in a relationship that was fractured to begin with.

Then he shook Shepard Kensworth's hand, and everything suddenly shifted. The world made a little more sense. It felt like there was a track to get on. Fast forward to the current day, two months later, and Nick had snuck Shepard into the on-call room for the absolute hottest fuck of his entire life. It was more than a spur of the moment thing. Shepard had been making Nick's heart race for weeks, and he knew he wanted to get to know him. Nick wasn't expecting to go all in when he invited Shepard into the room, but both of them instantly discovered that the chemistry between them was stronger than the valium they kept locked up in the cabinets.

Nick couldn't believe how good it had felt. He was getting hard just thinking about it.

"You're right," Aaron said, picking up his phone and beginning to type a message to his potential dates. "Sorry, I'm being stupid. I just thought, maybe getting out there again might get your mind off of her, you know?"

"I think I'll take it easy for now." Nick took another drink of his beer. He couldn't say anything more. He wanted to tell Aaron what had happened, but Nick also knew that religion made up a huge part of Aaron's life and he had never expressed any positive attitudes toward gay people. He never bashed anyone, Nick wouldn't have stood for that, but he also didn't seem thrilled when one of their mutual friends had come out as a lesbian. They had never truly discussed it, but Nick wasn't sure if this was the proper time to bring it up. He wanted to enjoy this feeling. He wanted to ride it as long as possible. Things would get complicated soon enough, but Shepard already proved to be more than worth it. He hadn't been this excited about getting to know someone since... well, since no one. Not even Anna had captured his attention this intensely. Even before their mind-blowing sexual connection, Nick had been captivated by the charming medical school resident with those caring hazel eyes and that sharp wit, all matched with a mastery at the sinful smirk that made Nick's knees weak and his dick swell.

"I dunno, dude," Aaron continued. "Some good pussy is the best kind of medicine. You're the doctor, you should know that."

"Thanks," Nick said. "I must have slept through that lecture in med school."

"Well, you're welcome." Aaron laughed as he took a chug of his beer, finishing it off. He wiped his mouth and placed the empty bottle on the coffee table. Nick offered to grab another one but Aaron mumbled a no, his fingers furiously typing up another message.

"Hey, man," Aaron said, setting his phone aside, "thanks again for letting me crash at your place."

"Of course, Aaron." Nick got up from the couch and went to grab himself another beer. Maybe he'd stop thinking about Shepard when he reached the bottom of this one?

"We've been friends since high school, I'd never turn you away."

"I know, but it's not ideal. I promise, I won't be here longer than another month. I promised a week, and I know it's been a little longer than that, but my fucking philosophy degree is completely useless. I'm getting my real estate license now and should have some property lined up to sell in no time, though. I'll get out of your hair, man, I swear."

Nick stood in his kitchen and waved Aaron off. "I know you'll figure it out soon, Aaron." Nick's home had an open-concept style kitchen with a massive marble island serving as a divider between the kitchen and the living room. It wasn't a huge house, but it was big enough to have Aaron stay over without feeling like he was impeding too much. He mostly kept himself to the guest room on the opposite end of the house, on the first floor. Besides, Aaron was entertaining. It had been a while since they had spent a good amount of time together. Nick had become too busy with his career and Aaron had spent a long time traveling the country on money he had won from a scratcher.

Nick leaned on the kitchen island, drinking the beer and beginning to wonder if the alcohol was actually having the opposite effect of what Nick intended. He wanted his mind cleared of Shepard, but instead, all he found himself wanting to do was grab his phone and call the guy. He didn't even care if they couldn't see each other that night, he just felt a powerful desire to hear his voice.

Wow, Nick thought. *Shepard's dick must be magic.*

That was when his doorbell rang. Aaron had ordered pizza and was getting up from the couch but Nick moved faster, putting his hand out. "I've got it," he said, grabbing his wallet and walking toward the door. He was feeling more than generous. The least he could do was buy his best friend a pizza.

He opened the door and cocked his head in sudden surprise. In the place of a polo shirt-wearing delivery boy holding a box of cheesy goodness was Anna Turron, his ex-wife, and last person he expected to be seeing.

"Anna," Nick said, surprise clear in his voice. She had been crying, Nick could tell by her puffy pink eyes. She was wearing an old red T-shirt from their trip to San Francisco and a pair of baggy white sweats. She held something in her hand. A pen? Why was she holding onto it so tightly? Her fist was balled up at her side, but Nick could see the end of it poking out of her tight fist.

"Nick, we need to talk."

"Come in," Nick said, stepping aside. Anna hurried in, but stopped cold in the entryway when she saw Aaron sitting on the couch.

"Shit," she said. Nick looked from Anna to Aaron, both of them staring at each other like a pair of bank robbers caught in the vault.

"Well... I'm pregnant," Anna said, breaking the thick silence.

Nick took a sharp intake of breath.

"And I'm not sure if it's yours or Aaron's."

Nick momentarily forgot how to breath.

One Year Later

Dr. White was being such a fucking dick.

He was doing this on purpose. He had to be. But why? What had Shepard ever done to the man? Besides give him an incredible fucking orgasm, of course. Both of their bodies had reached heights that neither of them had thought possible. Shepard had felt a surprising and profound connection with Nick that day in the on-call room. He would never be able to explain it, but he damn well knew he had felt it.

That was a year ago, and a lot can change in a year's time.

The exam room was deathly silent as everyone had their eyes turned to Shepard. Even the patient, with her big sad brown eyes and her light blue hospital gown, was looking anxiously at Shepard.

"I, uhm, don't know the answer to that, doctor."

And you fucking knew that I wouldn't know the answer.

Shepard was internally fuming, but he was able to mask it well. He had quickly learned that being a doctor meant he had to be an expert at controlling his emotions. There was a fine line he had to balance whenever he was delivering bad news. Sometimes his base instinct would have been to break down and cry right there with the patient, but he had to always separate himself from the news enough that he wouldn't be affected and yet still avoid being ice cold.

Those were the skills that kicked into high gear as Shepard stood in the center of the circle of four other residents. Nick was standing on the other side of the hospital bed, typing something out on his iPad. His face was etched in an expression Shepard couldn't read.

He assumed it was assholish satisfaction that he had successfully stumped Shepard in front of everyone.

"Right, well," Nick said in his gravelly voice. The same voice Shepard had been salivating over as he pounded him from behind. It momentarily took him back to that day in the on-call room. Where life had felt so fucking good. He was on top of the world. Not only did he have the fuck of his life, he had done it with a man who he had genuinely felt a deep connection with. Nick finished answering his own question and looked to Shepard.

"Got it," Shepard said, "I'll have to study that chapter tonight." His gaze fell down to the floor. He shouldn't have felt like a scolded child, but he did. He reverted back to being in fourth grade and getting shoved into a corner by the teacher. Sure, he may have been acting like a brat and bothering the class while they were taking a test, but that moment still had a pretty profound impact on Shepard. He remembered the awkward glances his classmates would give as he was pressed up against the corner wall, the pastel yellow walls doing nothing to soothe him. He hated that feeling of being called out and put on the spot.

This isn't fourth grade. White is testing me, that's all.

He looked back up from the floor and was surprised to

lock eyes with the doctor. There, Shepard saw the same warmth and intrigue that had captured him so powerfully in the first place. It was a momentary flash, though. Another moment later and Nick was focused in on the patient, asking more questions about the symptoms she was presenting with, his eyes no longer rooting Shepard in place.

Shepard shifted his weight, glancing down at the notes he had for the patient; Sandra O'Leary, who had come in for some intense stomach pains. His mind wanted to swirl around the image of those eyes, Nick's eyes, but he honed in on the notes, working through his mental library of gastrointestinal conditions. She had come to the emergency room for severe stomach pains along with some accompanying joint discomfort. Shepard not only wanted to help Sandra, he also wanted to get something right. He wanted to stand up to Nick and prove that he wasn't just going to sit there and take the abuse. And what better way of showing it to Nick than getting Sandra's diagnosis correct?

That was when it hit him. There was a crucial test missing in the intake chart for someone presenting with her symptoms.

"Dr. White, I'd recommend a blood test for tissue transglutaminase antibodies. I'm thinking this could be celiac disease."

Nick cocked his head, his eyes going back down to his notes and then up to Shepard. The doctor looked at him for a loaded moment, his eyes seeming to examine Shepard on the spot. Shepard felt exposed. He crossed his arms, suddenly feeling a warmth spread up his legs. Nick's face cracked into a smile. That stony jawline was highlighted by a genuine smile that warmed the doctor's face. It felt as if a proud father had just learned his son earned straight As.

"You're right, Dr. Kensworth. I'm going to have to find out who handled your intake, Sandra, because they definitely should have included that in your blood panel. Have you eaten anything with gluten recently? Pizza, pasta, a sandwich?"

"I had pizza earlier, yeah."

"Ok, that's a good thing. We want gluten in your system to provoke those antibodies into coming out. If it tests positive, we'll have to take a biopsy of your small intestine and check for any damage caused by the celiac disease. If it's there, then we'll have a diagnosis. And don't worry, the procedure is painless and outpatient." Nick looked up from Sandra, a smile still on his face. "Good job, doctors. I think we're done with rounds for the day, so just make sure to handle all your paperwork and then I'll see you all tomorrow, bright and early."

Shepard managed a smile and a nod and left the exam room, letting the other three residents walk ahead of him down the busy hospital hallway. He was thrown off by Nick's smile. It was so warm. So welcoming. Shepard had seen Nick smile before, but something in the way he looked at Shepard made this one different. Or maybe it was simply an effect from getting railroaded by a difficult question and then coming back with a proper diagnosis.

Shepard was going to go with the latter. He couldn't let himself fall for a steely doctor with an addictive smile. He knew almost nothing about Nick and had no time to try and figure him out. Between studying for the boards and getting his stress out at the gym, his free time was mostly taken up. Work and sleep took up the rest of his days.

He left the hospital still in a state of confusion. He was also feeling a kernel of frustration take root in his chest. Why couldn't Nick just admit that they had shared something that was worth following? And what had happened that changed the doctor so suddenly? They were supposed to have dinner, but Nicholas never followed up on it. Shepard was sure he wasn't the only one who felt the connection, so why was this so damn complicated? He walked to the parking garage, climbing the stairs to the third floor where his aging Honda was parked. He got in and sat at the wheel, trying to figure out whether he wanted to just head home or if he had enough energy to lift weights.

Nick's smiling face formed in his mind's eye. The frustration grew from a seed into a gigantic redwood. Fuck it, even if he didn't have the energy, he was going to head to the gym and work out this mess.

THE GYM WAS PACKED with people. It was the evening crowd that came in after a hard day's work. Shepard usually worked out during the mornings, before he had to make his way to Sierra View. He wasn't always a morning person but medical school changed that and now he felt weird not waking up early every day, even on the days he had off. The morning crowd at the gym was also a little easier to get around and the wait time for the machines was pretty much nonexistent. Shepard looked around the massive warehouse-turned-gym, taking stock of the situation as he walked toward the locker rooms. It seemed like most of the lower body machines were taken, and since Shepard planned on working out his legs, that made things slightly more complicated.

He turned a corner and walked down a short hallway toward the men's locker room, denoted with a neon pink arrow with 'men' scrawled across the top that seemed spray painted onto the far wall. The women's locker room was a neon blue and directly across from the men's. He followed the pink arrow and walked around a large mirror that separated the actual locker room from the outside hall. Inside, he found an empty locker and dropped his black Nike duffel bag on a silver bench. He started changing out of his scrubs, planning out his workout and doing his best to keep Dr. White out of his head.

Shepard was tying his sneakers when he heard a voice from behind that froze him. He pretended to keep tying his sneakers, meanwhile his mind was racing to try and figure out a way to sneak out of the locker room without being noticed.

What the hell? Since when does he come here?

Nick couldn't shake Shepard Kensworth. He was standing by the nurses' station, looking over some charts and wondering why the hell he was being such a dick, especially toward the man who had captivated him from the start. He hated himself for it.

But he also knew there was no other option, especially not right now. Nick's life had gotten infinitely more complicated a year ago, when he had opened up the floodgates for Shepard and was then told he would soon be a father (depending on the DNA test), all on the same day. His life was completely uprooted and thrashed around a bit. He didn't see himself with a daughter at thirty-two, but life had ways of twisting even the surest of plans.

The birth of his daughter, Emma, was a twist that changed Nick to the very core. He didn't think he was capable of such a sincere, powerful, deep-rooted love, but when he looked into his daughter's eyes for the first time, felt her tiny fingers wrap around his, his entire world shifted and he found an endless depth to the love. The lead-up to her birth wasn't as magical, with Anna fighting and Nick becoming overwhelmed. His frustrations were leaking out into the hospital halls. It was affecting the way he treated nurses, other doctors. He felt like he just wanted to do his job and get home, where he could be alone. He found a solace in the solitude. He wanted nothing to do with people for those nine months.

And then Emma came into his world and suddenly the thick gray clouds were shoved aside by bright beams of light, all held in her smile. He wished he could call it a day and rush home so he could hold her, smell her, feel her breathing against his chest. She was his little miracle and Nick wanted to do nothing else but hold her.

Anna was making that extremely difficult to do, and that was leading Nick back into his shell of frustration. Anna had denied the fifty-fifty custody split and went for an agreement that had Nick seeing Emma only two days a week. She argued that she would be a better fit to raise Emma for the majority of the time because Nick's schedule could get hectic. It was bullshit. As an emergency doctor, Nick knew the times he would need to be in the hospital, with only the rare moments when he would be called in if they were short on hands. That only happened if there was some kind of catastrophic disaster which involved a lot of victims. And if that were to ever happen, he had three sitters he could call at the last minute, and if that didn't work, there was a day care center in Sierra View.

Nick wanted to fight for more time with her. He was tempted to challenge the custody ruling, but it was a risk. Custody came down to the judge and he could have landed with one who just flat out didn't like him. There was even the possibility of a judge removing the two days he had already and granting sole custody to Anna. The court always leaned in the mother's favor to begin with, so he already felt like he was facing an uphill battle. Then there was the fear that Anna would get even crazier and demand that sole custody. He wouldn't put it past her to come up with more lies, or find a way to influence the judge somehow. It would completely wreck Nick. It created a huge well of frustration inside him, one that was constantly overflowing. He felt it in how he lashed out at Shepard for no reason other than that he knew Shepard could handle it. He asked him that question because he was angry he couldn't just go home, with Shepard holding his hand, where Emma would be waiting for them with that big sunshine smile of hers. That was all Nick wanted, and he was getting none of it.

Fuck.

He checked his watch. He was set to finish in ten minutes. Nick couldn't picture himself going home and doing nothing. He felt too amped up for that. He remembered he had brought his gym clothes with him and figured hitting the gym would be the best thing he could do with the feelings that were boiling inside him, creating a pent-up energy that had to be released. He wasn't a gym rat by any stretch of the imagination, but he had signed up recently, inspired by Emma's birth. The first few weeks were rough, but he was getting into it more and more as the days passed. He couldn't find time to go every day, but managed about three times a week. More than enough for now.

"Here you go, Norma." Nick closed the folder and handed it over to the nurse. She reached up and grabbed it, her bright pink scrubs engineered to put a smile on anyone's face. "Thank you, I'm going to head out. If Ms. Wilson's blood pressure drops any lower, give me a call, ok?"

"You got it, Dr. White." She opened the folder and looked over the chart. When Nick saw she didn't have any questions, he wrapped his knuckles on the counter and waved a goodbye to the other nurses. He started down the hallway toward his office. He was on the west wing of the hospital, where the hallway walls were made up of large windows that looked out at the breathtaking mountain range that surrounded Sierra View. It was already getting dark out, the sun moving down past the tall hills that cut across the sky, sending off its dying tendrils of light past the jagged cuts of the hill tops, lighting them an intense orange.

Nick had reached the end of the row of windows, about to turn when he bumped into Dean Harper, another doctor at Sierra View and one of the only ones Nick could say he considered a friend. Not that the other doctors were shit, but something about Dean really clicked with Nick. Maybe it was his crazy good lasagna or his smart humor that always put a smile on Nick's face. He wasn't always close with Dean, but after he had severed his relationship with Aaron and was constantly arguing with Anna, he found that Dean's friendship was badly needed and greatly welcomed. It took him a few weeks to open up and stop being a bit of an asshole, but Dean had managed to crack him open over a game of pool and a couple of beers.

"Hey, Nick, where you headed?" Dean was wearing a gray button-up shirt tucked into slim-fitting khakis, his white coat folded over his left arm. "Off tonight?"

"Yeah, thinking of heading to the gym for a bit. Blow some steam off."

"You look a little stressed, everything ok?"

"It's been a long day."

And week for that matter.

Dean nodded. "I get it. I had back-to-back patients all day today. I feel terrible when the appointments have to be twenty minutes, but what else are we going to do? This system, man, what a mess." Dean shook his head and ran a hand through his tangle of dark hair. It was clear he had a long day, too. "How's little Emma?"

Nick reflexively smiled at Emma's name. "She's doing great. You need to see her. She's got this mop of brunette hair that always smells like strawberries and vanilla for some reason. And that smile of hers, Dean. It's crazy." Nick grit his jaw, realizing he wouldn't be seeing her smile that night. "Anna has her for the next four days and she's not letting me see her."

"Fuck, man," Dean said. He rarely cursed. "I'm so sorry you're going through this." Dean leaned a shoulder on the wall separating two of the wide windows, his arms crossed against his chest.

Dean was one of the only people he found himself opening up to over the past year. They had become very close friends as the days passed, which surprised Nick because he knew he was ready to close himself off and push everyone away. He had suffered a huge betrayal and wasn't sure if he even knew how to trust people since. Finding out his best friend was fucking his then-wife in Nick's own house was enough to have him say he was pretty much done with the human race. He thought he'd go into work, try saving a few lives, then head home and forget about the cruel world.

Nick couldn't do that, though. He loved people too much. It was one of the reasons he had become a physician. He *wanted* to help people. He *wanted* to interact and create connections again. Especially since Emma had been on the way and he needed to make sure he was a relatively func-tional father for her, with friends and everything. He had put a hold on the boyfriend scenario, since that situation was infinitely more complicated, but Nick could allow

Dean in. It absolutely didn't hurt that Dean was one of the kindest, most genuine people Nick had ever come across.

"Damn it, Nick. I really wish there was something I could do for you."

"It's ok." Nick said. He wished the same thing, but understood there wasn't much anyone could do for him. "I'm thinking of taking the custody case back to court. Hoping to get a fifty-fifty split, at least." Nick didn't want to say much else about Anna or his daughter. He already felt the emotions bubbling up his chest, threatening to unload right there in the hospital hallway. He couldn't do that. He had to put on a strong face. He could break down in private, holding a picture of his daughter, desperately wanting more than just a photo.

"Hey, listen, I know this might not be the time, but... it also might be the perfect time for it. Noah and I are having a little get-together tonight and our friend, Sean, is going to be there. You guys seemed to click really well at our last Game of Thrones night, maybe you can share some mulled wine with him tonight?" Dean nudged Nick's ribs playfully with an elbow, winking the entire time.

Nick managed a smile. Dean was also one of the first people Nick had officially come out to. It helped that he knew Dean was gay so there would be absolutely zero negative reactions. He had told him and his husband, Noah, over a dinner they were having before heading to a concert. He didn't know what had pushed him into telling them he was bi at the dinner... *no*, he did know. It was the spitting image of Shepard who had been sitting at a table across from them that had inspired Nick to come out. He had left out the part about him hooking up with a resident, but he told them that there was one man in particular who had captured his attention. He told them it would be too complicated of a situation and that he had to find a way to move on. Since then, Dean had been pretty persistent about setting Nick up with their close friend Sean. He seemed like an overall nice guy and everything about Sean was technically right, but he didn't spark a flame in the same way Shepard had. There was no comparison.

"Thanks, Dean, I really appreciate it, but I think I'm going to hit the gym and call it a night. I'll have to catch up on Westoros tomorrow."

"Alright, just be careful out there." Dean motioned down the hall with one arm arcing wide, like a prophet speaking about the entire world ahead of them. "There are spoilers everywhere."

Nick cracked up at the over dramatics, although Dean was right. "I'll make sure to have a social media blackout and warn any patients that come in. I can't have anyone ruining it."

"Ok, good. As long as you're aware of the perils." Dean reached out and patted Nick's arm. "See you tomorrow, then. And remember: everything is going to work out. You'll have Emma in your arms soon."

"Thanks, Dean, really. Have a great night," Nick said, feeling a little better after his chat. There was still a pain that hit him square in the chest when he remembered he wasn't seeing his daughter as soon as he would have hoped, but he knew he would see her, and he was going to fight for the right to hold on to her whenever he wanted. For now, though, all he could do was try and work out his frustrations at the gym. That way he would avoid working them out on the residents.

On Shepard Kensworth, specifically.

Made in the USA
Coppell, TX
22 December 2020